The Thirteenth

A girl, a Number, a Destiny...

THE FIRST BOOK
IN
THE THIRTEENTH
SERIES

by

G.L. Twynham

ISBN: **978-1-907211-13-3**

www.thethirteenth.co.uk
sales@thethirteenth.co.uk
Tel:01673 849 813 Media Contact.

Dedication

This book is dedicated with love to:
Chyna and Jason for inspiration and patience,
Mum and John for believing,
Paula and Lucy for listening,
Paul and James for making me dream big dreams,
& Chris for the magic.
Thank You

CHAPTER 1

The Tattoo

A young woman stood alone looking up at the night sky, a cool breeze effortlessly caressing her slim frame as darkness closed around her. At long last it would be her turn to be part of something that had been her destiny since birth.

She moved on, passing the pond; she caught her reflection in the water and smiled. The time had arrived; the moon had reached the tops of the trees. On this particular evening, the shadows of the dense woods, mixed with the bruised sky made the adventure that lay ahead seem all the more exciting.

As she left the village behind and made her way into the woodland, her body filled with anticipation. She began to run.

Knowing instinctively where to go, she weaved like a needle in and out of the undergrowth, dodging the trees as if they were merely smoke trails rising in front of her.

She was moving swiftly when an unfamiliar sound suddenly stopped her dead in her tracks. A strange crackling in the air made every hair on the back of her neck stand on end. Something was very wrong. She span around, trying to find where it was coming from, but soon realised it was everywhere. Then, as suddenly as it had started, it stopped.

She had cautiously started to move forward again, when the silence was shattered once more by another wave of sound. In the confusion, her foot caught under a loose tree root, causing her to fall awkwardly into a pile of leaves. Before she had time to stand up, she heard violent screams coming from the distance. These weren't joyful cries; the cries of pleasure and happiness she had been expecting. These turned her blood cold and left her paralysed where she lay on the wet forest floor, her heart pounding.

After a few seconds, she gathered enough courage to slowly lift herself up and move forward again. She was suddenly very frightened, aware of the risk she was taking just by being there. She darted to an old oak tree, hiding for a moment in the shelter of its huge trunk. Cautiously, she edged around it. Everything was quiet again so she leant the top half of her body out, to see if it was safe. In that split second a ball of light came towards her, travelling at amazing speed and growing as it came, until it seemed to be the size of a mountain. When it hit her, its power engulfed her whole body and she was instantly lifted off the ground. She screamed helplessly as it raised her into the treetops.

Her ears filled with a piercing noise, like nothing she had ever heard before. Her whole body felt like it was burning up, yet still she kept rising and rising, until she was high above the trees.

Then the light and noise stopped as quickly and as it had started. Her upward flight came to a violent halt, and she began to fall. As she tumbled through the trees, the thick branches scratched aggressively at her clothes and face. The ground came towards her at terrifying speed. The scream that was struggling to escape her was silenced when she hit the ground with tremendous force. Her body filled with pain, the taste of warm blood filled her mouth, and she slipped into unconsciousness.

Sweat covering her face, Val Saunders snapped upright like one of those cheap Chinese dolls that only bends in the middle, as she woke from yet another crazy nightmare.

"This has got to stop," she thought. She had been suffering from these dreams for a few weeks now, each one growing in intensity. After several repetitions of the same nightmare, Val was trying to deduce who this strange woman was. She could tell by the wooden houses and the lack of hygiene that the images in her dream came from several centuries earlier. What Val couldn't understand was that she seemed to be able to feel, hear and see everything the woman was going through, as if it was actually happening to her.

Val had given herself a checklist to try to rationalise this. In her dreams, the woman had bare feet and was wearing a long sackcloth dress. Her head was covered by a hood attached to a floor length cloak. Val knew she wouldn't be seen dead in a dress, she wouldn't wear a wizard's cloak and open toed sandals weren't allowed within two miles of her very ugly feet, so bare feet would definitely be out of the question.

What she genuinely couldn't understand was why this was happening to her. Although now wasn't the time for a full analysis, she was sure of one thing: it was very real, because this morning, as on all mornings after the dream, she could feel deep pain in her upper left arm.

Making her way to the bathroom, she bumped into her mum.

"Are you excited honey? One day to go. I can't wait for your party tomorrow," Susan said squeezing Val vigorously.

Susan Saunders was a petite woman with a mass of jet-black hair, that now had flashes of grey in it. Val often joked that she looked like the bride of Frankenstein's monster.

"Yes, I can't wait either," Val smiled pulling out of her mother's grip and backing into the bathroom. The smile was wiped off her face when she saw her reflection in the mirror.

These dreams made such a mess of her hair; she looked like a teenage troll. As Val started untangling the unruly dark brown mass that matched her eyes, she thought it needed cutting, but who had time to sit for an hour while some strange woman told you all about her last client's terrible bowel disorder?

She headed back to her room to get dressed. Preferring the casual look, Val jumped into her jeans, sweater and pumps and headed down for breakfast.

As always, Susan had made far too much. Sometimes Val wondered if her mum had wanted fifteen kids not just one. Her dad was sitting chewing on a piece of bacon, a greying mop of brown hair sticking over the top of a book as normal.

Val ruffled his hair. "Hi Dad. Anything good?"

He grunted and she understood this to mean *'Yes, if you get excited about how buildings are put together'*.

Mike Saunders was a reputable builder and although he was a great dad, he was also the most mind-numbingly boring person to get into a conversation with. Watching paint drying would be fun compared to being trapped in an elevator with him. Val filled her plate with bacon and a few slices of toast and sat down to eat.

"Are you looking forward to starting your summer job today?" Mike asked, lowering his book and smiling at Val. "What is it you're doing again?"

"I told you, I'm working in a bookshop, Dad," she answered.

"Any particular reason for that choice?" her father enquired.

"Yes, because I have a deep passion for the classics, and the stunt woman's position was filled," she said cheekily.

He frowned and she quickly became more serious.

"To be honest, Dad, I'm not really sure." She fumbled with her bacon. "I think I'll be able to cope. I'm just glad to have got a job round here."

Val had been fortunate to find a summer job in the nearby town of Arcsdale, just a short bus ride away. Although working in an antique and first edition bookshop didn't scream out, 'I want to meet new and exciting people,' it fitted Val's personality like a glove. She was certainly not attracted to the position by the money, but she had seen the opportunity for a peaceful summer blending into the wallpaper of existence before deciding what to do with her life.

Val had known from a very early age that she didn't want to be popular, she was just happy being Val. Her school reports had always said "hard worker but keeps herself to herself", never "popular, makes friends easily, will be missed".

Finishing her breakfast, she got up and placed a kiss on her dad's forehead.

"Here you go," Susan said, handing Val a huge bag containing the lunch she had made for Val and her fourteen imaginary siblings, then kissing her on the cheek.

Val took the bag, pretending to sag under its weight.

"The day will come, Valerie Saunders, when you will be grateful for the food I prepare for you," Susan laughed, wagging her finger at her daughter.

"Ah, now I know who packed lunch for Jesus the day he fed the five thousand," Val grinned, dancing out of range as Susan made as if to swipe her with the a towel.

Val laughed all the way down the hall, grabbing her jacket as she passed the coat stand. Opening the front door, she called back, "Bye, I love you both." Swinging the door shut with a resounding crash, she set off for what she hoped was the first of many uneventful days.

Stepping off the bus, Val had a short walk to her new job and, as she strolled along the path, she allowed the warmth of the day's sun to embrace her. She stopped and closed her eyes for a few short seconds raising her face towards the sky and breathing in the summer air, attracting an amused glance from a woman who was coming towards her.

As she opened eyes again, Val felt a shooting pain go down her left arm. "Not now," she said aloud. Grabbing her arm she started to rub the patch; as she did, she felt a sharp burning sensation in the right side of her head.

She felt uncontrollably driven to spin around and look in the direction of the pain. That's when it caught her eye. Across the street was a tattoo parlour; your typical dive, or so Val thought. There were several bikes parked outside and men and women loitered on the pavement. It was not a place Val would normally frequent, but today was different. Nothing was going to stop her from crossing the street to investigate.

She moved swiftly towards the window, her eyes transfixed by an image that she couldn't remember having seen before, but something in her gut told her she had a connection with it.

Val's reached a hand out to touch the glass that separated her from the image. Then, all of a sudden, she felt a presence behind her. It threw her and the image in the window into shadow. Her heart banging with fright, she turned, and found herself facing a very broad chest. Slowly Val looked up into the eyes of a very tall man.

"Can I help you?" he grinned.

Val tried talking, but nothing seemed to be coming out of her mouth, other than "ah" and that really wasn't what she wanted to say. She wondered if she could run away, but her legs were firmly rooted to the spot. "I'm Shane and this is my tattoo parlour," he said slowly, as if Val wasn't quite with it. He offered his hand and she shook it, thinking how small hers was in comparison.

"If you ever want to come in please feel free." Shane released her hand and started to walk off just as Val managed to get her voice back.

"What is it?" she blurted.

"Sorry?" Shane said turning back towards her.

"What is that tattoo?"

He pointed to the zodiac and she nodded. "That, my friend, is a zodiac circle." Shane raised an eyebrow. "People say it bestows on the owner the power of the universe, to rule over all mankind and bend minds to your will." Shane nodded at her with a completely serious face.

"Really?" said Val dubiously, searching his eyes for the truth.

"No, it just costs £50 and hurts a lot." Shane laughed and walked off.

Val was blushing; she could feel the heat in her cheeks. How could she have made such a fool of herself?

Val knew that her parents would be devastated if she came home with an atrocity like that on her arm. So why did she feel so drawn to it even now as she walked away?

Although seeing the strange image had allowed her to forget the pain in her arm for a few minutes, it was still there. She tried to push it to the back of her mind and started to walk briskly to work.

On a bronze plaque on the splendid front wall of the bookshop, were etched the words '*Established by Mr Wallace Frederick Gallymore 1945*'. She imagined that the shop, like its owner, had looked the same since the beginning of time.

Val rang the bell and waited patiently while Wallace slowly opened the door's many locks. He seemed like a nice man although definitely elderly. Val wasn't sure how old he was. She had made a bet with her mum that he was at least a hundred.

"Good morning," she wished him in a singsong voice.

"Not on time; not a good start," Wallace grunted.

Val apologised as she moved past him, noticing that he smelt, as well as looked, a hundred. "The bus was delayed; I promise it won't happen again."

Wallace huffed as he walked back past her. She repaid him with her famous *please let me off* smile.

"Don't make a habit of it. Now, I have to go away for an urgent meeting for the next few days so I need to trust you to run my business efficiently and with the same capability as you offered in your interview, Miss Saunders."

"Please, call me Val, Mr Gallymore," she said in the hope that this would break the ice.

"No thank you, Miss Saunders. Work is work and first names are for family only." Wallace smoothed his perfectly groomed white hair with a crooked hand.

"Yes, Mr Gallymore." Val gave up at this point, knowing she was onto a loser.

"You know what is expected of you. I have a very high turnover for an establishment of this calibre so prepare to be busy." Wallace walked around her, eyeing her up and down. She felt like a soldier on parade.

"Ready to go." Val moved behind the high wooden counter pretending to bow. Ignoring her attempt at humour, Wallace passed her the biggest bunch of keys she had ever seen; she would need a new handbag if she was expected to carry these around.

"Lock up at five p.m. exactly. The code for the alarm is sixteen forty-five. Can you remember that?"

Val wondered if this was Wallace's date of birth. "No problem," she responded, unsuccessfully trying to choke back laughter.

"No there won't be," he said in a very firm voice.

Doing her best to compose herself, she wished him a good journey and told him not to worry, she was a very trustworthy person.

Wallace nodded, and then walked out of the shop, looking behind him and giving her a look that said 'set it on fire and I will find you.'

As the bell rang behind him, Val felt the excitement of having her first *paid* summer job. Relieved that Wallace had gone, she let out a little squeal and she started spinning around like a very clumsy ballerina.

Then it dawned on her she had just been dumped on, on her first day, in her first five minutes. She pulled the phone out of her pocket and called her mum.

"Mum, he's left me on my own," Val whined. "Yes I know I will be okay, but what if something goes wrong?" She nodded as Susan gave her the responsibility talk. "Yes, I will call you if I have any problems. Okay, bye."

Feeling a bit better, Val put the phone back into her pocket. Her mum was right. What could possibly go wrong in a bookshop?

As she moved up and down the aisles investigating, she noticed how deceptive the shop was from the outside. It was a true Aladdin's cave and seemed to go on forever. The wooden counter seemed to melt into the shop and every shelf and door seemed to fit together perfectly, almost as if it was all from one tree. Val was sure that there must be ecological repercussions from the amount of wood that surrounded her.

As she walked down the aisles, she passed her fingers gently over the top of the books. Suddenly she felt a sharp stabbing in her hand. When she looked down, she was shocked to see her finger resting on a book with exactly the same symbol as the one she had seen in the window of the tattoo parlour.

She took her finger away, feeling quite unnerved to see the same image twice in one day. She reached forward to pick it off the shelf, but stopped when the silence was broken by a sharp, trilling sound. It was her mobile. She pulled it from her pocket, giggling to herself when she saw the name *Delta* flashing on the front.

"Bonjour," Val chirped, opening the phone.

"Don't be silly!" You don't sound authentic at all. You would just be kicked out of France, no questions asked. Stop, while you still have some dignity left."

Val laughed and started to make her way back to the desk, where she could see if any customers arrived.

"Now then, my British friend, how are you?"

Val had missed Delta and her wonderful American accent so much. Delta Troughton was an exact replica of Barbie and had been Val's best friend since her father had purchased a summer home that Val's dad had built. It was just down the road from Val's home so every summer holiday, Val and Delta spent time together. Slowly they had become inseparable summer pals.

Val always felt a warm glow when she spoke to Delta; it was like being wrapped in your favourite blanket and eating marshmallow. She leaned on the till and asked, "OK, pretty princess, when are you getting your Yankee butt over here?"

"Well, sorry to say I won't be at your party to hit your precious piñata, unlucky for me, *not*," Delta responded sarcastically. "But I will be there soon to come and taunt you in your amazing new job as the sexy librarian."

"Thanks mate. Well, I won't keep you. I'm sure your Chihuahua needs a walk or a credit card is in need of using. By the way, if you want to know what to buy me, a big handbag would be great. I'll explain why when I see you."

The line went dead. Delta was the worst person Val knew for just dropping the line. She never ever said goodbye.

She put her mobile back in her pocket, trying to remember what she had been doing before the call. "Ah yes, the book."

She turned to go back to the shelf, but soon realised that she wasn't even sure which aisle she had been in when she found the book. Val felt slightly annoyed with herself, but she had the whole summer to look for the book; unless someone bought it, it wasn't going anywhere.

Val spent the next few minutes exploring the shop trying to get her bearings, eventually finding her way back to the front of the shop. That was when she noticed the water cooler. It seemed slightly dated and Val wasn't sure how long the water had been there. She made a mental note to stick to her bottle of juice for now.

Making her way around the counter she noticed for the first time how very old it was and how the wood smelt as though years of beeswax had been caringly applied. It was obviously very good quality. Having a builder for a dad made her notice these things. There was a door behind the counter, which she assumed led to Wallace's office. One of the many keys would probably fit the lock, although she wasn't really interested in entering as it had a huge PRIVATE sign on it. She had spotted the toilets near the back of the shop so felt she knew all the places that really mattered.

Grabbing a duster from the cleaning box behind the counter she set about cleaning, and imagining what tomorrow's family-organised, eighteenth birthday disaster would be like. In a lot of ways she was actually looking forward to turning eighteen, not just for the freedom it brought, but because she felt ready, and had a strong feeling that her time was coming.

The hours seemed to drag. Although a few people came in to browse, she achieved very few sales: not exactly what she wanted for her first day. She tried to stay positive and hoped that tomorrow, when she would be a more mature sales woman of eighteen, would be substantially better.

Val locked up at exactly five, as Wallace had instructed; she didn't want to find him hiding behind the street sign waiting for her to come out five seconds early. As she stepped out onto the pavement, she felt the same strange sensation that she had felt that morning, as if she was being watched. She looked around her, but there was only what she assumed was the usual rush hour hubbub of people and traffic.

Then it hit her: pain, so hard and intense that it made her fall to her knees in the doorway of the shop. She wanted to scream but nothing would come out. It was as if God himself had sent a lightning bolt out of the sky and scored a bull's-eye.

While Val crouched, trembling in the doorway, she was very aware that no one was trying to help her; they looked from the corner of their eyes but moved on quickly in the bustle of passers-by. After a few minutes, Val knew that she had to stand up or she was going to miss her bus. Leaning on the door, she pulled herself to her feet, perspiration pouring down her back. What was happening to her?

She began to walk slowly towards her stop. She couldn't miss her bus; it was the last one that went anywhere near her house. As she made her way down the road, people made it even more obvious that she was behaving oddly, and probably looking strange. One woman was kind enough to pull her screaming toddler onto the other side of the path.

Val eventually managed to get to the bus stop where she lowered herself shakily onto a graffiti-covered green plastic bench. An elderly woman sitting at the opposite end stared blatantly at her. Val threw her a smile, at which point the woman *tutted* in disgust, stood up and walked towards an elderly gentleman, obviously looking for protection from the weird, sweaty girl.

Val really didn't care; she was in too much pain. All she knew was that she needed to get home and quickly. So much for growing up! All she wanted to do was fall into her mum's arms and be looked after. She was breathing deeply as she got onto the bus and the conductor frowned at her as she took her ticket, then watched her closely as moved as far back as she could. Val imagined this was more in concern for his upholstery than for her well-being. She fell onto a vacant seat, trying not to attract too much attention to herself, although that was quite hard as she now felt as if she had just climbed out of a swimming pool.

"Come on, come on," she murmured under her breath. Val couldn't remember a time in her life when she had been more desperate to get home. She stepped off the bus, knowing she was nearly home and finding the reserves of strength to increase her pace to a slow trot. She had never felt so elated to see her street. Outside her house, she gave a last burst of energy and charged across the grass towards the front door crying out, "Mum? Dad?"

The overwhelming feelings she had been keeping in during her journey home now came flooding out. She called out again and banged on the door to no avail, then collapsed weeping onto the front step convinced that she couldn't move another inch, but no one was coming to let her in, so she was going to have to.

She managed to stand and pushing her key into the front door, every movement causing another wave of pain. The door swung open. Val stumbled into the hall, then collapsed, and still there was no answer to her cries. "Mum, please, I need you."

Making a huge effort, Val pulled herself up and staggered towards the kitchen. On the table was a note; she was so disorientated that she could hardly make sense of it.

'We have decided to go out; your dinner is in the microwave. See you later honey, love M & D'.

"No!" Val whimpered. She couldn't believe this was happening. What should she do? Call an ambulance? No, that would be ridiculous. She just needed to get to bed, and it would all be OK when Mum got home. She climbed the stairs slowly, then made her way down the landing to her room. She went straight to her bed and fell onto it, facedown, unable to take off her clothes or pull the covers over her. Within minutes she slipped into a restless, troubled sleep.

Her dream was so vivid that she could actually see the fog, feel the damp ground and smell the trees. The scene was the same as before, but this time, instead of being blown back by the powerful light, the woman seemed to move through it. Val could see a circle of men and women holding hands. There was a small break in the circle. The man and woman on either side of the gap seemed to be waiting for her. She reached out to grab their hands, as if she was the missing link.

As she reached for them she heard a wailing bleep coming from behind her. The noise stopped her from grabbing the woman's hand and she felt as if she was being pulled backwards. The din was getting beyond a joke as she turned towards it in anger.

"Oh my God, the pain!" Val shouted, waking up as she fell off the bed and hit the floor. It was unbearable. She felt like her flesh was on fire. Jumping clumsily to her feet Val felt slightly foolish; it was her eighteenth birthday and she had started it by doing something she hadn't done since she was six years old.

The pain was so intense she wasn't sure if she could ignore it any longer. She needed some form of painkiller. She had also decided to tell her mum and dad about her arm, even if it meant a visit to the dreaded doctor's; she simply couldn't go on like this. Val rubbed her arm forcefully in the hope that it would help and headed downstairs.

"Happy Birthday!" Sue and Mike chorused. They were standing with their arms spread wide to welcome their little girl on her very special birthday. When Val failed to respond, Susan's expression changed and she began to lower her arms.

"Dear me, Val, you look terrible. Are those the clothes you were wearing yesterday?"

Val looked down. Her mum was right; she hadn't even changed. "Mum, Dad, I have got loads to tell you. Just let me change, OK? I think I might need to see a doctor."

Val turned and started to go back upstairs. Susan was about to follow when Mike grabbed her arm. "She said she will tell us when she comes down, give her some space. She is eighteen now." Susan nodded in agreement, but wasn't happy.

Val made it back to her room where she grabbed some clothes before heading to the bathroom and turning the shower on. Pulling her top over her head, she peered into the steam-hazed mirror. Was that dirt on her arm? She looked harder, as she walked towards the mirror. As she got closer, she rubbed the steam that had formed and nearly passed out with the shock.

There was a huge black mark on her arm. Val rubbed it vigorously. It was not only massive; it was a tattoo and not just any old tattoo. It was exactly the same as the zodiac circle she had seen in the window of that man Shane's parlour, and on the book in the shop. Then she realised that this one was slightly different: inside the circle was another symbol that wasn't on the others.

It was a sort of a backwards 'y' with a dot in the centre. As Val took in the enormity of what she was looking at, she heard her mum's voice calling up the stairs.

"Everything OK, Val? Do you need any help?" This was the last person she wanted to see her new acquisition.

"No I'm fine. I will be down in a few minutes, Mum," Val answered.

"OK honey, I love you." Susan's voice was shaky. Val knew her mum was worried and if she saw this, she would become hysterical. Val jumped into the shower pumping the soap onto her hands, trying in a vain attempt to scrub it off. This was the worst thing that had ever happened to her. This even beat being kissed, aged ten, by Barry Green a.k.a. Mr Halitosis behind the bike sheds.

This was supposed to be one of the best days of her life, what was going on? Suddenly she was scared and for the first time in her life she knew she would have to deal with this alone. Her parents would never believe her if she told them a tattoo the size of a saucer had miraculously appeared overnight. Maybe this was what being an adult was all about.

Val jumped out of the shower, her arm now sore from the scrubbing. Throwing on her jeans and a long-sleeved Superman top she hurried downstairs.

"OK, what's going on? Why do you need to see a doctor?" Mike demanded, hoping to get an answer before Susan over-reacted.

Val had to think quickly. "I was feeling a little unwell, dodgy kebab, but after that shower I'm feeling a lot better." Please buy it, she thought, smiling from ear to ear. "Come on, where are my presents?"

Mike and Susan looked at each other. "You had us scared, Val. Don't do that again, OK? And why eat a kebab when I had left you dinner?" Susan clearly didn't entirely believe what Val was saying, but it was Val's birthday and at least she seemed OK now, and that was what really mattered.

Within a few minutes, they were all looking at the many presents Val had received and, for now, she knew she was home and dry.

"OK family, got to go, working girl and all." Val kissed her parents as always and made a dash for the door. Mike unexpectedly grabbed Val's arm and her heart almost stopped beating.

"Give me a hug. You are still my little girl, you do know that, don't you?" As he wrapped his arms around Val, the pain in her arm became torturous.

"Don't be late tonight. There is a lot to do before the party, OK?" Susan called, but Val was gone.

She ran down the road with tears burning in her eyes. Wiping them briskly, she managed to compose herself. The last thing she needed was it getting back to her mum that she had been seen blubbering in the street.

By the time Val got onto her bus, her arm had finally stopped hurting so much. She sat down, unable to watch the world go past today as she had other things on her mind. Luckily for her, the local vagrant didn't feel like sitting next to her and moved a seat further down. 'How thoughtful,' she said to herself. 'Now I can only smell him.'

When she arrived at her stop, she leapt confidently from the bus. She knew exactly where she was going next. She ran across the road, then stopped when someone sounded their horn about an inch from her head. The driver of a red ford truck was about five feet away from her and glaring furiously at her. Val smiled and mouthed an apology, but kept moving across the road. "Focus Val," she told herself.

As she got closer to the tattoo parlour, she felt a pang of apprehension. Was she doing the right thing coming here, and what could he do to help her other than recommend a good plastic surgeon? It was already too late; her legs had carried her to the front door and straight into the arms of Shane Walker.

"Hello again. Wow, two days on the trot. I will be thinking you want a tattoo if you keep coming." He smiled but his expression changed when Val started to cry. "Hey, what's wrong? Come inside." For some reason, Val knew that this man, as enormous as he looked on the outside, was gentle on the inside. She walked in with him, crossing a black and white chequered floor, and sat down on the barber-style chair he offered her.

"What's so wrong that you have come to a stranger crying?" Shane asked.

"This appeared on my arm last night." Val lifted her sweater sleeve to reveal the tattoo.

"Wow, that's some seriously good art work, I have to say. I couldn't do better myself. So, apart from being grounded for life, what's the problem?"

"I don't know how it got there." Val's eyes filled up again. "It's my eighteenth birthday today and I woke up with this."

"Well I have to be honest with you, you aren't the first person to wake up with a tattoo on an important birthday." He made drinking motions with his hand.

"No, I wasn't drunk. That's not supposed to happen until tonight. This has just appeared out of nowhere, you have to believe me."

Val was so intense that Shane knew she believed what she was saying.

"OK, let me have a good look."

Val lifted her sleeve once again to reveal her tattoo and Shane put on his gloves and looked at it more closely. "This is strange. Sorry, what's your name?"

"I'm Val. Sorry that was rude of me." Val blushed.

"Don't worry." He smiled reassuringly. "This is a normal zodiac circle, but I don't recognise this symbol in the middle. Do you?"

"No." Val looked blankly at it.

"OK, let me take a transfer then I will find out some more information for you if you want." He waited for some sign of agreement.

"Yes. Thank you..."

Shane placed the clear paper on Val's arm and had just started to copy the image when they heard a clock chime.

"Oh no! What time is it?" Val looked around hunting for a clock.

"It's nine. I've finished. You can go, but come back later. OK? I will see what I can find out and should have something for you by then."

"I'm late again so pray that my boss isn't at work. Thank you, Shane. I will see you later." Val's eyes started to fill up again. Shane touched her arm and smiled, and all of a sudden Val didn't feel quite so alone. She hurried onto the road, looking this time for traffic, and sprinted all the way to work with her fingers tightly crossed.

She arrived to find the shop in darkness. This was excellent; Wallace must still be away. Finally, something was going her way. Hopefully this would have a snowball effect on the rest of the day.

She unlocked the many locks on the front door. This was how she imagined it must have felt trying to break into Alcatraz. She then chuckled to herself as she entered Wallace's date of birth into the alarm, listening as its beeping came to an immediate halt.

She seemed to have packed a lot into the morning, and it was still only just after nine o'clock. She was warm after her frantic rush to the shop so she went to the water cooler and poured herself a cold drink, not caring today how old the water might be. It tasted great.

Just then, her mobile began ringing; it was Delta.

"Hello crazy Yank chic," Val chirped down the phone.

"I'm not singing so don't hold your breath. Happy birthday and all. Get anything good?"

Val looked down at her arm and felt the irony. "Where are you, Delta? We need to talk as soon as possible."

"Italy. Why? What's wrong? You sound odd."

Val didn't want to tell her over the phone; she would never understand. "Don't worry I will call you in a few days, when you get here, and we can catch up on every-thing then. OK?"

"Fine. Did you get my present?" Delta asked.

"No. Did you post it?"

"Oh, was I supposed to do that bit myself? Isn't that Maria's job? Not to worry, we can go shopping when I get there."

"OK, speak to you…" The line went dead before she could say 'soon' and Val was alone again. She put away her phone and stood looking around the shop. What to do now? The book. Yes, she needed to look for the book with the picture of the zodiac circle.

Val walked impatiently up and down the aisles, look-ing for the book. She knew it hadn't been sold as to date, she had made a total of four sales and the book hadn't been one of them. That didn't mean it couldn't have been stolen, although that would just be very bad luck. Once again she looked at her arm, '*Let's not tempt fate,*' she thought.

Val ended up spending most of the morning and early afternoon looking for the book, in between attempting to polish. Just as she was beginning to lose the will to dust one more thing, the doorbell rang and someone entered. Val got her bearings and made her way to the front of the shop.

"Hello," Val said, greeting the young blond woman with a smile.

"Hi. I hope you can help me. I'm looking for a first edition James Joyce 'The Dubliners' for my fiancé. It's his birthday soon and I've heard that if anyone has it, you do." Val tried to give the impression that she knew what the girl wanted, although really she didn't have the foggiest clue.

"Please feel free to browse while I go and see if that book is in stock."

"Thank you." The woman set off across the shop and Val took her sorry self behind the counter trying to work out how she was going to get out of this one.

She vaguely remembered from her interview that Wallace had mentioned a stock list, not computerised, because he'd said he didn't trust computers. It must be here somewhere she thought, eyeing the various drawers and cupboards that lay under the long shelf-like desk that made up the counter, but it refused to give up the secret of the stock list.

Why had she taken this stupid job anyway? Oh yes, because it was the only one she'd got an interview for. Not even the mighty McDonald's had given her a call back.

Val started to look through the books knowing that it would only be a matter of time before the woman realised that she didn't have a clue what she was doing and walked out. Val followed the aisle to the back of the shop, where she stood looking blankly at the 'new religion' section.

Snapping her out of her miserable reverie, Val heard the front door bell ring again. Great! More unhappy customers. Maybe if she stayed here forever she would never have to tell her parents about the huge tattoo on her arm or disappoint Wallace with his slowest week ever.

"Happy Birthday, Val." What a joke! As she stood bathing in self-pity, Val felt a burning pain in her arm, but this was not the same as the previous pains. "Hey a little variety in pain can't hurt," Val said, annoyed that there was more to be added to her disastrous birthday.

When she lifted her sleeve, she saw that one of the symbols looked as if it was on fire. From her limited zodiac knowledge, she presumed that the symbol showing two fish was something to do with water. Why, she wondered, was it that just one symbol seemed to be alight?

Her concentration was once again broken when she heard a noise that sounded like a muffled scream. Her attention was drawn behind her to what looked like a reflection in the window. She could just make out a blurred image of the woman who had come into the shop, and she was being held down by a large man.

He heart thumping with fear, Val moved nearer to the glass to get a better idea of what was going on. As she did so, her pump caught on one of the old wooden floorboards and she tripped, forcing her to use her hand on the windowpane to stop herself from falling face first into the glass.

As her hand touched the pane she felt a strong pulling sensation that went into her very core, and then everything went dark. When she opened her eyes, she found herself standing at the front of the shop feeling quite dizzy and looking down on a man trying to strangle her customer. She wanted to know how she had arrived here, but the gravity of the woman's situation seemed more important. Although the woman was struggling, she was most definitely not winning the fight. Val's instincts kicked in and she leapt onto the man's back like a wild animal. If she had been given time to think, maybe she would have come up with something better, but it was the best she could do.

The man stood up with Val clinging to his back, and she saw the enormity of her problem. The man was at least six and a half feet tall. At that point, he threw her off effortlessly. She felt a deep pain in her back as she collided with the water cooler, her mobile spilling out of her pocket and smashing into pieces against the wall.

"Damn," Val hissed, looking up to see him attacking the woman once more. This was making her really mad, though she was pleased for a second that she had left the new mobile phone her parents had bought her for her birthday safe at home, charging.

Val stood up and went for him again. Surely two women could beat one man. As she hit the water cooler for a second time, she began to doubt that she was right. She tried to quickly suss out the situation; she couldn't beat him and he was covering the counter so calling the police was out.

What transpired next caught Val totally by surprise. The woman had broken free and was running towards her. As she ran past, Val felt an uncontrollable urge to stand between her and the man who was now coming after her. She darted out in front of him, and he stopped dead, then slowly bent down to look straight into her eyes. Val was almost overcome by the smell of his rancid breath.

The woman was now in the corner, curled into the foetal position and crying hysterically.

"Great," Val thought as she braced for imminent impact, closing her eyes and raising her arms in front of her face.

After a few seconds, when the expected blow had still not come, she cautiously opened her eyes. The man was still in front of her, but now he was gazing up at the ceiling. Val instinctively looked up too and to her disbelief, a large mass of water was floating above his head with steam emanating from the edges. It was like a balloon made of boiling water. The man glanced back at Val and she thought he looked scared. For a second Val felt as if the ball was strangely in her court. She was still wondering how that could possibly be when it fell. The whole lot, it seemed like at least a gallon, came down straight onto his head. He fell to the floor screaming in pain as his flesh turned an aggressive mottled red.

Val was left standing over the man, slightly damp, and unsure what to do next. Just when she was getting seriously worried, he sprang to his feet, knocked her out of the way, and ran out, slamming the door shut behind him. The bell rang almost off its hook.

Val managed to get herself up and made her way to the woman who was still cowering in the corner. "Are you OK? Do you know who that man was?" Val asked hoping that she would snap out of it.

"No, I've never seen him before," the woman said. She was still sobbing and now had more than tears running down her face. Val fetched her a tissue from a tatty box she had found around the back.

"What happened? Where did all the water come from?" the woman asked shakily.

Val shook her head because she honestly didn't have a clue. "Here take these." She handed across a wad of tissues and as their fingers touched, a blue spark flashed between them. The woman watched in petrified disbelief as Val faded and then completely disappeared.

CHAPTER 2

Soldier Down

Val opened her eyes and waited for her stomach to return to what she assumed was its normal position. With a shock she realised that she was once again at the back of the bookshop, looking at the window in which she had originally seen the woman being attacked.

What on earth had happened and where was the woman now? Val wondered. She turned away from the window and was heading back towards the front of the shop when she heard the familiar scream of the woman she had just helped to save. This was followed by the ringing of the doorbell, which had once again been hit with such force that Val thought she would be lucky if it was still on the door when she got there.

At the front of the shop, Val jumped over a large pile of books that had been knocked to the floor during the wrestling match. The mangled remains of the water cooler were also on the floor. Surveying her surroundings, she realised just how much of a mess they had all made. Val felt like she was in a dream. How had all this happened? First the tattoo and now this. What was going to happen to her next? She decided to call the police and made her way to the counter to look for a phone. Then she starting thinking about how she would tell her version of the story. "Yes officer, I have a tattoo that appeared from nowhere, and I skipped through time and space to drop two gallons of boiling water onto a giant's head." Wow, that would go down well. Anyway, she realised that there was no phone; somehow she wasn't surprised. This was the shop of the oldest man on the planet; she was surprised it had electricity.

All Val knew for certain was that she had to get the shop cleaned up before she left work. She couldn't possibly let Wallace arrive back to find this mess. It would be hard enough trying to explain away the water cooler without trying to tell him why his precious books were on the floor. Val mopped up the water with a very dishevelled mop she found in the cupboard near the toilets. Wearily she locked the shop and headed for the bus stop.

As she passed the tattoo parlour, she glanced over the road at its open doors. There were still people hanging around outside, all standing around their precious vehicles, laughing and chatting. Val didn't feel she could face the crowd. Plus, she rationalised, snatching a peek at her watch, she didn't really have time to see Shane tonight. He would have to wait until the morning. She had more than enough on her mind already, and she had to get home in time for her party.

She looked at all the people waiting at the bus stop and wondered if any of them had had the same sort of day as she had had. When she boarded the bus, the driver looked at her suspiciously from under his hat, and for a second she thought he might know something. Val felt uncomfortable under his intense gaze.

"Feeling better today are we, luv?" he asked inquisitively, looking her up and down.

He must have been the driver from yesterday. Val couldn't remember much and his unattractive beard and bottle glasses certainly didn't stick out in her blurry memories. "Yes, thank you for asking," she smiled a wry polite smile back at him. She supposed it was nice of him to ask, but he was definitely creeping her out. She found a place to sit next to an elderly lady who proceeded to spend the journey apologising for her gas, rubbing her chest and telling Val all about her many disorders in great graphic detail. What could be worse than ending your day like this? Well, having to wear the thin-strapped dress your mother had bought for your birthday while displaying a raging black tattoo on your arm would be a good attempt at making things worse!

Val's mum was in the hall waiting like a tiger ready to pounce. The stressed look on her face said it all. Before she became part of the Saunders Birthday Circus, Val wondered why people put themselves through so much hassle for a party, when the guests would eventually complain that there wasn't enough food or booze and that the weather was awful etc, etc.

Susan started firing words in Val's direction. "OK, upstairs, get changed, now. You look a mess. Please, just for me, just today, put on some lip gloss." Susan ushered Val towards the stairs flicking her hands in a pushing motion.

"Can I get a drink first?" Val was thirsty and she looked at her mother in the hope that not every glass in the house was taken.

"No. You can drink later. Go and get ready before I faint due to stress. Do it." Susan was now pushing Val with all her strength, which wasn't much, towards the stairs. At this point Val could see she was onto a loser and did as she was told.

As she made her way to her bedroom, Val's father burst out of the bathroom at a trot heading towards her. A loving smile crossed her face. Although he was a very boring man, his sense of adventure shone through in the shirts he wore. His offence for this evening was a sort of surfer slash Salvador Dali attempt and Val felt intimidated just looking at it.

"Hi honey. Best get ready, your mother is having kittens as usual," Mike cheerfully chirped as he hugged her.

"Looking good, Dad." Val gave him a two thumbs up sign and they both smiled. Mike believed Val really meant it.

Val found *the dress* laying on her bed. She sighed. It really was offensive. Not only did she hate wearing dresses, but how on earth was she going to hide the tattoo? The dress was a soft baby pink with thin straps and a layer of what looked like spider's silk over the top, which Val had to admit flowed beautifully when she had it on.

As she searched in her wardrobe for something to wear over the top, she began to get a sinking feeling that this wasn't going to go at all well. Val pulled out the only two cardigans she owned. One was a sort of multi-coloured long old tatty thing that really should have been dumped years ago, but she loved it. The other was a faded grey, waist length thick winter cardigan. She had no choice but to go for the grey. As she pulled it on over her dress, she knew her mum wasn't going to be happy, but she could deal with her.

Val headed to the bathroom to brush her hair and put on some of the dreaded girl paint. She always felt like a doll putting on lipstick. It almost felt like she was trying to glue her mouth shut. Val had very nice lips and when painted they brought her even more attention than usual, but in her eyes that was never good. Her thoughts were abruptly broken by her mother's calling for her to go downstairs as Val's (or her mother's) guests were arriving. She sounded like she was on the edge of a nervous breakdown.

"I'm coming now," Val shouted to reassure her mother so her stress levels could drop just a little. Val smiled to herself as she went down the stairs, wondering which family member was going to get drunk first and make a fool of themselves. She had a few favourites. Her mum had two brothers, Uncle Julian and Uncle Matthew; they were very competitive and it was always a race to the drinks for them.

As she got to the bottom of the stairs, the door bell rang. "Get that will you please, Val?" "Yes Mum," Val called, and walked through the now heavily decorated hall to the front door. She prepped to give her best fake smile and opened the door.

"Hello…" Val stopped almost instantly, catching her breath, and then letting out a scream of joy. "Oh my God! You're here! How did you? When did you?" Val threw her arms around Delta's neck. "I need to talk to you," she gabbled. "So much has happened. There are things going on and I don't know where to start." Val was now almost in tears.

"Well if you let me in, that would be a good first move. Then maybe letting some oxygen go to the rest of my body would be pleasant too," Delta twanged in her very American accent. She had to almost peel Val off her so she could go into the hall.

Val realised she was causing a scene and instantly let go. For a moment, she just stood smiling at Delta who straightened her dress and re-composed herself.

"OK, now we are unattached and a little calmer, first things first." Delta smiled putting out a hand to stop Val from grabbing her again. "I came home early for your party. How could I miss your 18th birthday?"

Delta could sense Val was itching for another hug so she grabbed her hand in an effort to stop her from falling onto her again. "I like your dress, although you need to get rid of the cardigan," she said plucking at Val's grubby grey sleeve. All the events of the past few days came rushing back into Val's head; she was desperate to talk, to share what had been happening with someone who might actually try to understand.

"We need to talk. Now!" Val grabbed Delta's other hand and started to walk backwards towards the kitchen, pulling her along.

The doorbell rang again and Susan came out this time to answer. "Val, why are you wearing that awful cardigan?" she shouted after her, but Val was in too much of a hurry to acknowledge her mum at that moment. She dragged Delta into the kitchen where every surface was now covered in food.

"Wow!" exclaimed Delta. "There's enough here to feed five thousand."

Val had to smile. "Well, you know my mum! Here theory is that you can never have too much food."

Val's dad marched in and grabbed a crate of beer. "Hi Delta, lovely to see you," he enthused. "Tell your dad I'll be round for a game of golf," he said, patting Delta affectionately on the shoulder.

"Will do, Mr Saunders. Love your shirt," Delta shouted after him in her sweetest voice.

"Creep," Val sniggered.

"And your point is?" Delta shrugged her shoulders.

Now they were alone and face to face, Val started to explain in detail the events of the past days.

Delta, for once reduced to silence, listened with her mouth slightly open, wondering whether her friend had taken to drinking alcohol.

When she had finished, Val quickly pulled up the arm of her cardigan, revealing the tattoo in all its glory. "See!"

Delta took a sharp intake of breath and looked at Val's arm. "Right, if I understand this correctly, you are saying that this thing appeared over night, that you don't know where it came from, that you think you teleported today at your new job, and you aren't sure, but maybe you can make water boil in mid-air. Would that be correct?" Delta now looked almost sorry she had come home early.

"Yes, that's it." Val nodded, watching Delta and searching for a response.

Delta seemed transfixed by the tattoo and stood silently shaking her head.

After a few seconds, Val started to feel slightly annoyed that her best friend didn't seem to believe her story. "Delta it's true," she whined, visibly frustrated.

"Yes, I'm sure you believe that, but as an outsider it's just a little far-fetched, and I'm sure your parents will feel the same way," Delta responded. "It's a bit of sorry excuse for getting a tattoo."

"You're supposed to be my best friend, but if you don't believe me then fine, I will have to deal with this on my own." Val was now really fuming with Delta. On top of that, Delta had a stupid, gawky look on her face, as if Val had a massive spot on her forehead. "What are you looking at?" she snapped at Delta aggressively. "The, the, the..." Delta stuttered and pointed her finger over Val's head.

"There is no need to be stupid about this you know," Val said.

Delta was still pointing over Val's head and managed to release the word "Look!"

Val turned around. There, about a foot away from Val's head were five floating balls of what seemed to be Coca Cola, apparently from glasses that Val's mum had poured out for the party.

The shock of what she was witnessing ran through her body, replacing the anger she had been feeling seconds earlier. The balls immediately fell to the ground, splattering all over her mother's precious kitchen floor.

Val and Delta stood in stunned silence and then, breaking the moment like the shattering of a glass, Uncle Julian came bounding into the kitchen looking for the Birthday girl.

"Wow, what happened here, girls?" Julian peered at the growing pool of Coca Cola.

"Sorry, a little accident," Delta responded and moved past him to look for some cloths to clean it up.

"Happy Birthday, special girl."

"Thank you," Val smiled. She had to admit that Uncle Julian was her favourite. As he hugged her, she could smell that the drinking competition was well under way. She hoped he would win.

Julian grabbed a couple of bottles of wine from the side and made his way out again. "Bye girls, have fun," he called back.

Delta was frantically mopping up the sticky liquid before it dried. Val grabbed her hand. "Delta, now do you believe me?" she demanded. She desperately needed Delta on her side.

"I do, Val, but I'm scared. What's happening to you?" Delta said not lifting her eyes from the floor.

Val grabbed Delta and hugged her. "Thank you for believing me. It's all going to be OK," Val said gently.

Delta politely removed herself once again from Val's death grip just as Val's mother came in.

"What's going on here, girls?" Susan sighed. "Slight spillage, Mum, nothing to worry about. We have everything under control," Val said smiling up at her mum and hoping that would be enough of an explanation.

"Val, your father's boring everyone to tears so I want you to come outside and do the cake to shut him up." Susan made signals at the girls to rise. "And take that ridiculous cardigan off."

Val smiled at her mum and they obediently followed her into the garden.

"Are you OK?" Val turned to look at Delta as they stood next to the barbecue soaking up the fumes.

"Give me some time," Delta responded. Their eyes met and Val knew in her heart that Delta was on her side.

"Come over here," Mike called to Val as a crowd started to gather. "I think it's time to cut the cake and get rid of all these unruly relatives before the police come to close this party down." Mike waved towards uncles Julian and Matthew who could hardly stand.

As they all sang to her, Val felt the sweat running down the back of her neck. The heavy cardigan was really meant for the cold of winter, not a summer barbecue.

To add to the embarrassment, everyone had now commented on it.

Val spent time chatting with the relatives she liked and the few token friends her mum had invited to make Val look a little more popular. She was kissed by the oldies who always dribbled on her, and she was truly relieved when everyone started to leave. It had been a long day and she was looking forward to a rest and a little quiet time to herself.

Val was standing outside her front door waving her relatives goodbye when Delta came out. Val grabbed her hand. "Come to the shop tomorrow Delta, we can look for the book together, you know, four eyes better than two and all."

"What book, you haven't told me about a book?"

"It was…." Val started.

Delta waved her hands in front of her face. "Don't bother explaining. I can't cope with any more today. I'll see you in the morning." Delta gave Val one of those strange air kisses that she could never understand and jumped into her shiny new red Mini Cooper S and drove off like someone from *The Italian Job*.

Val chuckled as she watched Aunty Janine and her dad lifting Uncle Julian, who had definitely won all the drinking competitions, into their car. As the guests, young and old, moved into their cars she thought how good it was to have such a close family, how they always pulled together in a difficult situation, and just how lucky she was to be her. Val also felt an ache deep inside her chest, which she recognized as her conscience. She knew that nothing good would ever come from the web of lies she was beginning to weave - although she was also sure that not telling her family was probably the best option, for now.

Maybe being eighteen meant you got to appreciate the grown up things you hadn't noticed before. Perhaps coming of age meant that she finally appreciated such values as protection lies. Her parents had done it - she could think of several examples: just standing there waving everyone goodbye as if they were sad to see them go, Father Christmas – and, her special favourite; the dentist is your friend. She gave an inner laugh as everyone finally left, then hurried to her room to get out of her suffocating cardigan.

Val called goodnight through her bedroom window to her parents who were still in the garden, giggling like teenagers as they danced around to some old people's music.

Val slipped into some pyjamas and lay on her bed for a moment of contemplation after her mad day. Wondering what tomorrow would bring, she slowly slipped off into another restless dream.

A beautiful woman in a dark sack dress moved through a soft, swirling mist towards Val. This dream was new and Val didn't know where exactly she was. However, one thing was the same: the ugly dress. Was there nothing else to wear in these dreams? It seemed that they were inside a rustic house, almost like a round house she had seen once on a school trip. A fire was burning in the middle of the room and over it was a large black pot with some sort of fragrant steam coming out of it. As the woman moved closer to Val, she started to speak. Val had to strain to catch the words.

"What?" Val asked disturbed that she felt she knew this woman without knowing how.

"It's time," the woman said. "You have come of age. The others are waiting. Remember, don't be late." She smiled as she moved past her.

Val instinctively knew what she had to do. She left the hut and found herself once again in the village square where her other dreams had started. She turned on the spot, surveying the whole village. It was amazing how vivid it all was. It felt like home, a safe place; as if she had been there forever. Before she could make it to the pond, which seemed to mark the centre of the village, the sharp trilling sound of her alarm forced her into consciousness.

Val jumped out of bed in one of those instant *right side of the bed* good moods. One look at her arm instantly wiped the smile from her face. The tattoo was still there in all its sharp black glory. *No,* Val thought to herself forcefully, this wasn't going to take over her life, and she had a cushy job to get to so she'd better get moving. Covering her arm, she ran to the bathroom and showered, then dressed in double speed.

She made her way downstairs and was greeted by a weary looking mother with very dodgy hair, and a hungover father. They were still cleaning up after the party.

"Morning. I won't stop for breakfast, Mum. I need to get to work on time for a change OK?" Val shouted as she ran towards the hall, knowing that her mother was the old-fashioned type who believed an army marches on their stomachs and breakfast like a king, etc. She actually made it to the end of the path before she was caught in the snare of guilt by a sorry looking wild-haired woman who came to the front door holding out a slice of toast and a packed lunch. In her heart, Val knew that later she would be grateful for her mother's thoughtfulness. She returned to her mother, head down, and took the parcel and the toast. "Thanks Mum," she muttered.

"I'm very proud of you, Val; you do know that, don't you?" Susan put her finger under Val's chin and lifted her head up.

"Yes and you always will be. I love you to the stars, Mum."

"I love you to the moon and back," Susan said, making them both smile, then released Val to run for her bus.

This was something they had said to each other as far back as Val could remember, and it always seemed to make her feel warm inside. Today it made her feel terrible because for the first time in her life she was keeping something really important from her parents.

Once in town, she headed straight to Shane's tattoo parlour to find out if he had any more information on the symbol in the centre of her tattoo. Shane was just opening up and welcomed Val with his wonderful smile.

"Morning Val, how's the world domination going?" Shane smiled.

"It's going very well, thank you." Val reciprocated the smile. She was pleased to see Shane, but didn't feel safe enough just yet to tell him about the other things that had happened to her.

"I was expecting you yesterday. I don't usually get stood up on a first date," he teased, signalling for her to follow him. "Show me your arm."

As they walked into the shop, Val tentatively raised her sleeve.

Shane laughed kindly. "Don't worry, Val, most people who come here have one of those or want one."

Val went red, feeling a little silly now.

Shane looked closely at Val, frowning slightly, one eyebrow raised as if in question.

"What are you looking at me like that for?" Val asked, feeling uneasy.

"Have you got anything you want to tell me?"

"No," Val replied, almost breaking under the pressure, but managing somehow to keep it together.

"Val, one of the symbols on your tattoo is missing."

"What?" Startled, Val looked down and counted. There were twelve in total. "Er…Maybe there were only twelve yesterday?" she said, though even to her own ears she sounded unconvincing.

Shane pulled the tracing he had taken the previous day from his pocket and showed it to Val. As she counted around the zodiac, she quickly saw that he was right: one symbol had disappeared. It was the fishes, the one that had become inflamed the previous day.

"Is there anything I need to know, Val?" he persisted.

At that moment, Val's mobile started to ring. It was Delta and Val realised she was once again late for work.

"Shane, I have to go. I'll come back later and we can talk then." She pulled down her sleeve and turned to leave the shop.

Shane just managed to catch her arm. "Here's my card. Call me if you need me." He gave Val a look that reassured her he could be trusted, but for now she had to keep her job.

"Thanks," Val called back, shoving the card into her pocket and running across the road.

Val sprinted the half mile to the shop in what felt like a world Olympic record. Delta was already standing outside in her perfect clothes with her perfect hair, face and accessories, putting Posh Spice and Paris Hilton to shame "Good morning, nice of you to show up at last." Delta was sarcastic but truthful at the same time.

"Sorry, I was getting my tattoo looked at. Shane spotted that one of the symbols had disappeared." Val pulled her sleeve up and showed Delta where the fish sign had previously been.

"Why do you think that has happened? And you can put it away." Delta pushed Val's sleeve down again with the tips of her manicured nails as they walked up the steps to the bookshop together.

"I'm not sure, but it's the same sign that felt hot yesterday." Val opened the door's many locks. "If it's going to keep on disappearing then maybe this will all be over soon. What do you think?"

"Who's to say? Does this Shane guy know about yesterday?" Delta said, following Val into the shop. Just inside she stopped suddenly and sniffed loudly. "Nice smell. I think maybe a little scent of old man, and a splash of public libraries." Delta waved her arms around like a chef spraying some highly expensive perfume around their heads. She smiled at Val, trying to lift the atmosphere a little.

"Don't be so rude." Val coughed. "No, Shane doesn't know about yesterday, but he suspects that there is something wrong. I think I'm going to tell him everything, just not today," Val replied as she switched off the alarm.

"Is this water cooler a victim of your escapades?" Delta asked.

"Don't go there. My back is still killing me. Do you think I should call the police?"

Delta shook her head from side to side. "And tell them what? If you even attempt to tell them all of this, you will be laughed at and maybe locked up. Don't bother," Delta said.

Val nodded. At least Delta had backed up how she felt.

"So, do you think you have any other powers, Val?" Delta asked, jokingly rubbing her hands together like a crazed scientist. "Can you fly, or turn lead into gold, or turn horrible people into toads?

"Delta! This is serious!" Val felt irritated, but looking at Delta's infectious grin soon found she was laughing too. "I don't know. What do you think I might be able to do apart from float fluids."

"Perhaps you *can* fly. Have you tried?" Delta opened her arms like a bird and started to flap. "Run up and down, see what happens." Delta pointed towards the main aisle of the shop.

"OK, but if you laugh I won't save your life when you need me," Val warned in a stern voice.

"I will take that risk. Have a go." Delta now moved out of the way to give Val room for a good run up.

"OK, here goes." Val put her arms out to the sides and started to run. Nothing happened apart from Delta nearly having a major aneurism from laughing.

"On the way back, try it with your arms in front, like Superman," Delta tried to shout but could hardly speak through her laughter. Val allowed herself to have fun, running back with her arms stretched out in front of her shouting "Up, up and away" in a silly deep tone of voice. She decided flying wasn't going to be her thing and joined Delta who was sitting on the floor, laughing uncontrollably. She was so pleased Delta was here; they would get through this together.

"Right, less playing super-hero and more looking for the book," Val ordered, knowing she had to find it. She had seen it and no one had purchased it, so it still had to be here somewhere.

"What does it look like?" Delta cambered to her feet.

"It's dark tan leather and has a zodiac circle on the spine like the one on my arm." Val showed Delta the tattoo again.

"Thank you, you can put that thing away, I can remember what it looks like." Delta walked off faking a full body shudder in disgust at Val's tattoo.

"OK, you start on the left side of the shop from the water cooler, or what's left of it and I'll go from the right hand side near the counter." Val pointed at the aisles with arms outstretched like an airhostess, and they both started to laugh again.

Setting off, Val waved goodbye to Delta as she headed towards the back of the shop. The shelves went from floor to ceiling so there was no way of seeing each other. The only way of communicating was by shouting, and that felt so wrong in a bookshop.

After about ten minutes, Val was heading up aisle number three. She hadn't heard a single noise from Delta in the past few minutes so she decided to head back towards the front and wait for her. Plus, it was lunch time and Val was hungry. She was sure there would be enough food for both of them in her packed lunch.

As Val headed towards the counter, she felt a strange sensation in her arm. For a few seconds it was just an uncomfortable tingling feeling, and then sharp pain hit her. Within an instant, she was in serious pain and needed Delta's help. Val felt her knees buckling. Unable to call out, she grabbed the nearest shelf for a support. After a few moments and several heavy breaths, Val stood shakily and pulled up her sleeve to glimpse at her tattoo. Once again, only one of the symbols was inflamed. It seemed to be like a flower or some sort of curly horns. Val had a very poor knowledge of the zodiac, so there was no chance that she would know what symbol it was, but maybe Delta would.

As she slowly made her way to the counter, she heard a car. It was quite loud and sounded as if it was closing in on the shop, getting nearer and nearer, the way you would hear a lone car on a quiet street at night.

Something felt different. Val was suddenly confused, no longer knowing where she was, let alone where the noise was coming from. She needed to find Delta and the time for silence was now over.

"Delta!" Val shouted. In that instant she spotted Delta busily re-applying her lip-gloss in the mirror next to the toilet door. She moved in, shaking her head like a dog with an itch. The noise from the car got louder and more irritating, and as she reached Delta, who hadn't even noticed her coming, she couldn't even hear her own thoughts. As she moved towards the mirror that Delta was gazing into, Val saw the flash of an image in the reflection. She grabbed Delta's arm and Delta almost jumped out of her skin.

"Val, you scared me! What's wrong? You look awful." Delta said almost supporting the whole of Val's weight. Val was shaking her head from side to side in pain although her eyes were still fixed on the mirror. She needed to see exactly what was in there. As she pulled herself up on Delta's arms she saw cars. First was a red Ford. It was racing along, and was being followed by a black BMW. As Val attempted to move closer to the mirror, Delta could no longer hold her weight.

"Val, stop!" Delta called, stumbling backwards onto the wall as Val grabbed at the reflection.

Val's stomach seemed to be pulling into her back, but all she could think was how good it was that at last the noise had stopped. She opened her eyes and as they adjusted to the new light, she saw Delta crouched next to her on what seemed to be grass. Then Delta proceeded to vomit violently before toppling sideways. Val tried to grab her.

"What the hell just happened?" Delta spluttered as she wiped her mouth on Val's sleeve.

"Hey!" Val pulled her arm away, "How in God's name am I supposed to know?" Then it happened, just as Val had seen it in the mirror.

The red Ford came around the corner at full speed, with the black BMW in hot pursuit. Val and Delta watched as the BMW clipped the back end of the Ford, causing it to spin uncontrollably off the road. It collided with a lamppost, which fell on top of the car amongst a firework display of sparks. The BMW hadn't even changed gear and had now disappeared from view. Delta looked at Val in disbelief.

"Why are we here? And what are we going to do?" Delta looked to Val for answers that she couldn't supply.

"Don't worry about that for now, let's go and help the driver." Val started to cross the road and Delta followed slowly, almost begrudgingly. As they got to the centre of the road Val could see the driver waking up and she waved at him to reassure him that someone was coming to the rescue, even if it was just two teenage girls who had no idea how they had arrived here or how they were going to save him.

"Come on Delta," Val urged. "I don't like the look of those sparks."

She had barely spoken the words when the car exploded into what seemed like a million fireflies rising into the air, and was completely engulfed in flames.

Val was thrown back by the explosion and for a moment she stared around in confusion. When she looked back at the car, she could see that the man was now frantically trying to get out, pulling desperately at the handle of the door. Val jumped back onto her feet and went to check that Delta was OK.

"I'm on the floor in my new Dior skirt," Delta whimpered. Val knew that Delta was fine and although she was sitting on her bottom in the middle of the road, she would survive. Val lifted her by the arm and dragged her quickly onto the grass verge. Now she needed to help the man in the car.

Val crossed the road again and moved closer, expecting the heat to be intense. However, she had already made up her mind that she was going to get as close as possible, though she wasn't sure exactly how this was going to help the man. She was going to have to do this in stages. The closer she inched towards the fiery car, the more she expected to get burnt.

'Why aren't these flames even hot?' Val thought. Then she felt the irresistible urge to reach out through the flames that were licking all around the car. Her hand passed straight through them and she felt nothing; it wasn't even warm. How could this be? Val felt scared but exhilarated at the same time.

The intense heat emanating from the flames didn't seem to be harming her. The flames seemed to dance over her like feathers brushing her skin.

"Val, no!" screamed Delta looking up from her skirt and becoming aware of her friend's fiery journey.

"I'm OK," Val waved back at her.

Val looked through the window of the car and saw the panic in the man's face as she called to him, "It's OK. I'm going to save you." She smiled through the flames as he proceeded to passed out. The side of his face hit the window and instantly started to blister under the intense heat. Val looked back for a moment at Delta who was sitting on the floor with her mouth wide open, obviously unable to comprehend the fact that she was watching her best friend in flames.

"Great, now no one will remember my moment of glory," Val muttered. She pushed forward and as she reached the door, the flames engulfed her whole body. She pulled at the handle, readying herself to grab the man. After several forceful attempts, she managed to pull the door open. The man's limp body fell out. Val grabbed him under his arms and pulled with all her strength, trying to drag him away from the blazing car. The edges of his hair were beginning to singe from the intense heat. She had to get him out of this, and fast.

Val was surprised at how quickly she managed to move away from the car. Although the man didn't seem too heavy she was beginning to feel fatigued. She called over to Delta for assistance. Delta had realised that Val might need her and had managed to compose herself and go to her friend's aid. Together they grabbed an arm each and dragged him to the side of the road where he lay limp on the grass.

Delta grabbed his wrist. "He has a pulse," she said with a huge sigh of relief, leaping over the unconscious body and grabbed Val, hugging her tightly. This display of public affection from Delta was most unusual and Val was quite shocked.

"He is going to be OK, but he needs an ambulance. Call the police, Delta. That's if they haven't already seen the smoke. Oh, and find out where we are as well," Val said, feeling a little silly with Delta still holding onto her. Val took a moment to feel good about the fact that she was completely in control of the situation. It was as if she knew inside that she was supposed to be doing this.

Delta released Val and grabbed her pretty pink handbag off the ground. Pulling out her pink mobile phone, she started to dial. "So, do you have a name?" Val asked the unconscious man. "Let's see." She cautiously pulled his jacket lapel open and fumbled around in a feeble attempt to find his wallet.

She would have never made a good thief; she had more thumbs than fingers. Val assumed that if his wallet wasn't there then it was in his trouser pocket and that wasn't a place she was prepared to visit.

Delta came running back over. "I've called the police. They are already aware of the accident and are on their way." She smiled like a child who had just received ten out of ten for a test.

"Great, so where are we then?" Val asked.

"Er...Didn't ask that one, sorry."

Val smiled at her. It was hard enough, without worrying about minor details she could deal with later.

"Let's see if we can wake him up," Val said as Delta knelt down on the other side of the man, tapping his hand in a very limp attempt to wake him. Val looked at her and wondered how she had made it to the age of eighteen with so little physical contact with the rest of the world.

Val looked at the man for a second, then raising her hand she brought it down on his face with a thundering crash. Val had hoped the shock factor would work, but what happened next she really hadn't expected. A blue flash sparked and crackled between them, and everything went black. Her insides went in, then out, and she found herself crashing face first into the mirror at the bookshop. With no time to put her arms out to cushion the impact, her head hit it with full force and she fell to the ground unconscious.

When Val opened her eyes, she was instantly aware of a banging pain in her head. She was too dizzy to stand so for a moment she just lay there, wondering how long she had been knocked-out.

Looking at the light coming in the window she could tell it was still daylight, but that wasn't much help; she could have been out cold for hours or minutes. She pulled herself up on one of the shelves and called out Delta's name. There wasn't any answer.

"Delta, where are you?" Val stood very still but there was still no noise at all. Val span around, in the hope that Delta was behind her. At last, the reality hit her: she was alone and Delta had been left behind.

Val rushed over to the mirror and peered into it, but apart from her own reflection, there was nothing to see. She didn't even notice that there were chunks of dried blood on one side of her face. Val felt sick. Where was Delta and how was she going to get her back? Val whimpered under her breath, "I will find you."

Delta stood at the side of the road next to the unconscious driver's body, not sure she could cope with what she had just witnessed. She was alone, her friend had just faded into thin air and she had no idea where she was. She lifted her head towards the sky and cried out, "Val," but there was no answer.

Chapter 3

Mistaken Identity

Within seconds of Val's magic show Delta was surrounded by police cars and ambulances, lights flashing, sirens wailing.

The oppressive black smoke billowing from the burning car had almost obscured their position. Delta beckoned to the emergency services, holding her pink handbag aloft, almost like a siren, calling them onto the rocks.

"Typically British," Delta thought to herself as she waved. "Like you guys say, they are like buses: nothing, then they all arrive at once," she told the injured man who, thanks to Val's electric slap, was now conscious. All Delta was genuinely concerned with was finding her friend, getting out of this smoky situation and returning to civilisation and a hot skinny latte.

Delta leaned over the man, keeping far enough away from him not to get herself any dirtier than she already was. "Do you know where you are?" she asked.

The man lifted his head slightly. "I was on my way to Lanron. It's two miles from here," he responded weakly, then his head fell back onto the grass. Delta didn't have the slightest clue where that was. Why didn't they have more descriptive names in this country? If the man had said they were two miles from the nearest designer shopping outlet or Starbucks, she would have known where they were. Not that she was seriously worried. She was absolutely sure that she could get home eventually. Having Daddy's plastic in her purse was a first class ticket to anywhere. What Delta didn't know, was where exactly her best friend had popped off to. Val could be on Mars for all she knew!

Val stood for a moment trying to get one clear thought into her head. "Come on," she banged her forehead with the palm of her hand, "sort yourself out." She looked around wildly for any visible clue to give her some sort of direction. She started to pace the shop floor. Pushing her hands into her jeans pockets she felt the sharp stab of cardboard under her nail making her wince in pain and pull out her hand. After inspecting her finger for damage, she cautiously reached back into her pocket and pulled out a business card. On the front, in what looked like gothic text, were the words; *'The House of Art'* Proprietor: Shane Walker, tattoo artist, Address: 10 the High Street, Arcsdale, AE2 4JR Tel 01675 849666. Val pulled her phone out. "Great, no signal!" she spat at the screen, flipping it shut and shoving it back into her pocket.

She needed to get to Shane's. At least she could tell him and he (possibly) wouldn't think she was as barking mad as the police would. "Don't worry Delta, I'll find you," she said into the mirror before swiftly turning to leave the bookshop.

Back at the crash, site Delta was surrounded by several hunky police officers and a few attractive paramedics. She smiled and for a few moments soaked up every second of attention, hoping that firemen were coming as well. She directed them all to the man on the floor, telling them quite bravely that she was fine. At that point, a young and very attractive policeman introduced himself as P C Flinch and asked Delta to move to one side of the road with him.

"So tell me, madam, what exactly happened?" The young man leaned towards Delta, obviously drawn in by her American bombshell magnetism.

"I have to be honest and say I don't know. When I arrived he was on the floor and unconscious," Delta replied sweetly, flicking back her blond hair and moving closer. Becoming visibly nervous he realised he was way out of his depth and staggered backwards, clumsily making room between himself and Delta.

"Don't go anywhere," he stuttered. "I still need to ask you some more questions. I'm just going to get some advice from my Sergeant; we need to know what to do with you now." He stumbled backwards almost falling into the ditch in his haste to get away from her.

Delta watched as he made his escape towards what looked like the man in charge.

"I think it's time to leave; I need to find my friend," she said under her breath. Looking around, Delta spotted a road sign. Making her way through the gathering crowd of uniforms she pulled out her phone. The sign read 'Lanron 2'. Well better Lanron than nowhere. As she started walking, she flipped her phone open and began dialling.

Out on the street Val ran as fast as her legs would carry her. Luckily Shane's was only a fifteen minute stroll from the bookstore and, at speed, a five minute sprint.

All Val could think about was where Delta was. She was so distracted that she almost missed the shop completely. Coming to a halt just past the doors, she paused for a split second, questioning whether Shane could be trusted. Well, it's time to find out, she thought to herself, bursting through the double doors, which were heavily decorated with art.

As Val stepped inside, she began to feel the effects of her sprint. Flopping over completely breathlessly, her hands firmly placed on her hips for support, she took deep gasps of air. Her intense focus on her mission had made her oblivious to the poor man who was face down in front of Shane having Marilyn Monroe's face tattooed across his back.

"What day is it?" Val gasped.

"Wednesday, and hello to you too, Val," Shane responded.

"Good, I haven't lost a day then." Val strutted up and down. "Shane, we need to talk, now!" Val stopped to look at Shane.

He knew that she was genuinely in need of immediate attention, but it wasn't that simple. "Val, I'm just with a client at the moment." Shane's looked down at the man's back and for the first time, as if by magic, Val became aware of him.

"I'm sorry, but this is an emergency. I need you *now.*" Val made a crazy-eyed expression whilst patting her arm, in the hope that Shane would interpret this as very important.

Shane tapped the guy on the back and, what had looked like a table top, now sat up. Even in the seated position he was nearly as tall as Val.

She stepped back, troubled that she had actually got that close to him in the first place.

"Val would you mind going out back to the office while I finish with this customer?" Shane smiled at her with exaggerated politeness.

"But…" Val started to speak but Shane had placed his glove-covered index finger to his lips.

Val knew instinctively to do as she was told. Walking past them quickly, she moved through a swing door and found herself in a corridor with three more doors. The one to the left was obviously the toilets as it had the girl/boy sign on it. The one in the middle said *Private* and the one to the right had no sign at all. Well, that was just great. She had to go somewhere. She decided most offices where private so she would go straight ahead, but when Val pushed the door, something instinctively told her that this was wrong. Nonetheless, she just had to keep going.

She peeped around the door and her eyes were met with the most glorious sight. Nothing could ever have prepared her for this. There were paintings from floor to ceiling. Not tattoos, as you would imagine, but *art*. Val stepped inside mesmerised by the beauty that was spread out before her like an extravagant canvas rainbow. Most of the paintings were of women, although there was one woman in particular who stood out because of her extraordinary beauty. She looked almost like a bird with jet-black hair that flowed down her back, a somewhat pointed nose the deepest green eyes that Val had ever seen. She was standing transfixed by the beauty of the paintings when a heavy hand grabbed her from behind. Val let out a scream and spun around to see who had collared her.

"This isn't my office," Shane said with a stern tone in his voice.

"I'm so sorry, I got lost." Val was honestly sorry and she really didn't care about anything but getting her friend back. "I really didn't know which one was your office."

"Come with me." Shane pulled Val gently back out of the room and led her to the door with no name.

In the small and cluttered office, Shane sat on the edge of a large white desk and Val stood in front of him, like a patient at the doctor's. "What seems to be the problem? Is it your tattoo?" Before she could answer, Shane pulled Val's shirtsleeve up and began inspecting her tattoo.

"I need to tell you so much and I don't know where to start." Val took a deep mouthful of air as if she was going to get it all out in one breath. She started with more or less the same story she had told her friend, Delta, except now she had a slightly longer version with the addition of the car crash incident. As Val talked, she slowly gathered steam and then realised that the pressure Shane had on her arm was getting more restrictive, as if with each word, he was holding onto reality a little tighter.

"Are you OK, Shane? I understand that what I'm saying must sound crazy, but I don't know where my friend is and you are the only person I can trust." Tears started to form in Val's eyes and she looked like a five-year-old who had just lost a favourite toy.

"Val, this is the craziest story I have ever heard, and believe me, you hear them in this job. If it wasn't for the fact that you are now also missing the Aries symbol from your tattoo, and you are the most honest-looking person

I have ever met, I would have kicked you out about ten minutes ago."

Shane stood still, holding onto Val's arms with slightly less vigour. "Tell me, where do you think your friend, Delta, could be? Did you see any distinctive signs at the place of the accident?" Releasing Val, he turned and walked towards a grubby black radio on top of a filing cabinet that looked almost ready to burst. He switched it on and music started to blare out.

"Do you really think that this is an appropriate time for music?" Val felt quite puzzled by Shane's actions.

"I want to see if anything will come on the news about an accident. It might give is a clue" Shane now sat down again on the corner of his very untidy desk.

"How well does your friend Delta know the Arcsdale area? You said she comes here on holiday every year."

"I think she knows where the shops and cafés are, but she uses a satellite navigation system to get her from her bedroom to the toilet." Val gave a feeble grin and then started to cry. "This is my fault. She's lost because of me. How am I going to tell her parents?" Val put her hands over her eyes.

Shane leaned over and put his hand on her arm. "It's going to be OK. She'll be fine and I'm sure she'll find you soon enough." As the words came out of Shane's mouth, Val's pocket started to vibrate then sprang into life with the soundtrack from 'Star Wars'.

"Aren't you going to answer it?" Shane asked.

"Yes, just a second." Val leaned around almost like a dog chasing its tail as the phone was in her back pocket. If it hadn't been such a sombre moment, Shane thought he might have laughed at her. As she pulled it out the expression on her face seemed to melt. She flicked the phone open and gasped, "Where are you? Are you OK? Is the man OK?" Val stopped talking for a second, fixed on listening. A different type of tear now seemed to be running down her cheeks. She looked up for a second at Shane as he mouthed the words "Is it her?" She smiled back nodding.

Val continued talking to Delta, explaining what had happened to her, and how she had ended up back at the bookshop, knocking herself out on the mirror. As Val talked, she worked her way out of the office. She explained how she had come to see Shane. Shane, now intrigued by the fact she was on the move, followed her as she headed out of the swing door and across the black and white tiled shop floor. When she reached the front doors, she turned around pushing them open with her back. Out on the street she stopped so suddenly that Shane almost bumped into her.

Val closed the phone and turned to Shane. "I can't thank you enough for helping me today." She grabbed his hand tightly and, as she turned back towards the road, a taxi pulled up. A beautiful blond girl jumped out and ran towards them. Val released Shane and opened her arms but, just before Delta reached her, she stopped dead.

"I'm not touching you ever again! I don't know where you'll send me, and thanks for leaving without saying adios," Delta huffed. "I could have been on Mars for all you knew." Delta turned her back on them. Val wasn't offended as she knew that this was the best hello Delta could give.

"Was the man really OK?" Val enquired as she lowered her arms.

Delta turned back, grinning broadly. "Of course! He had me to look after him." She flicked her long and amazingly immaculate blond mane behind her in a sign of total confidence. "So, introduce me to your new friend." Delta offered her perfectly manicured hand to Shane. "I'm Delta Troughton. And you are?" She looked Shane up and down.

Shane was intrigued by this young girl's confidence. If she hadn't had such a strong American accent, he would have thought her British aristocracy. "I, madam, am Shane Walker." Shane smiled as she shook his hand. It was almost like meeting the Queen.

"So this is your shop. I love shops. However, I feel you have nothing for me." Delta walked past Shane and made her way into the tattoo parlour.

"Come in please. Make yourself at home." Shane opened his arms in welcoming gesture.

"Does he know everything?" Delta asked Val in a stage whisper.

"Yes, we can trust Shane." Val nodded.

"Hello ladies, I'm still here you know." Shane made his way towards the swing door. "I suppose, if we're all going to be honest, I should do my part as well." He headed towards the door with the private sign on it. "Come into my Bat Cave," He invited with a grin. "I have always wanted to say that to someone; shame it's two teenage girls who probably won't appreciate it, or even know who I'm talking about."

Val grabbed his hand just before he could finish opening the door. "You don't have to do this, Shane. I'm happy with the trust you have already given me, and yes I do know who has a Bat Cave, its Bruce Wayne, but I'm more of a Marvel Comics fan than a DC."

Delta looked at them both in disgust. "If you are going to talk in Nerd, I'm leaving," she said, digging a finger into

Val's back. "I thought we had a deal; no more comic talk, hey Val." She pushed Val who in turn pushed Shane through the door. As they crossed the threshold, Val was once again taken aback by the sheer beauty of the pictures.

"This place is amazing, Shane. Who paints these pictures?" Val made her way closer to the nearest painting and bent to read the signature *Elizabeth Reed*. "Who is Elizabeth? Is she a friend? You have so many of her paintings." Val looked at Shane and saw the pain in his eyes. "I'm sorry. I'm asking too many questions."

Shane lifted his head with a softened expression. "Elizabeth was my wife. She passed away 10 years ago. She loved my paintings, although the art world didn't love me. A tattooist isn't their idea of a real artist. So, I sell my pictures through a gallery under my wife's maiden name. It pays the rent." Shane glanced at Val and she understood that he had just shared a secret as personal as her own; she knew exactly how he felt.

Delta had already left them and had made her way past the pictures through what she presumed was a gym, and was now on the other side trying to get the coffee percolator to work.

"Hello? Assistance required over here please." Delta wasn't very good with electrical appliances. Shane walked up behind her and flicked the switch to ON. "I swear these things are so easy that my inner genius can't cope." She turned and walked to a square glass table with four chairs round it.

Val watched as Delta made sure that the chairs met her standard. Luckily for everyone they did, and so did the coffee.

"Now what do we do?" Delta asked as Val and Shane joined her at the table.

"Well, I have some news for you, Val. I would have told you before but we've been slightly distracted up until now," said Shane, pulling what looked like a computer printout from his pocket. "A friend of mine managed to find this out about your symbol." Shane unfolded the paper and placed it before Val.

"A friend? Who? Why did you tell anyone?" Val looked slightly concerned.

"Until a few hours ago, Val, all I knew was that you had a strange tattoo. I had no idea it was going to lead to this. Anyway, this guy is one of my very closest friends. You can trust him."

Val had to agree that up until now Shane hadn't known all the facts. So, the damage was minimal. Nevertheless, this was as far as this so-called friend was going to be involved.

"Whatever. Just look at it, Val." Delta's patience was wearing a little thin.

Val looked down at the paper nervously, almost scared of what she might see. It was a copy of what seemed to be a pencil drawing of a woman. She was in her late thirties, early forties and was dressed almost identically to the woman in her dreams. The woman's arms were exposed and on the top of her right arm was the tattoo symbol that was in the centre of Val's Zodiac. She seemed to have a soft friendly face and looked almost angelic in the picture. Val knew that this image was important and she needed to know more.

"Wow, she looks like you, don't you think?" Delta looked at Val.

"No, not at all." Val glanced up, seemingly agitated that she had even compared them. "So where did this come from and how did he find it so quickly?" Val looked across at Shane.

"My friend found it in some museum archives from the sixteen forty-five witch trials." Shane looked Val straight in the eyes. "The person who found this picture has access to documents that neither you nor I could ever dream of seeing. I met him while I was in the army and he has the ability to place his hands on secrets that most people only dream about."

Val felt even more insecure about this new friend. "Was there any information with this about who she was? Or what the symbol actually means?

The look on Shane's face said it all. "There was nothing with the picture; he just matched the symbols by chance. It was one of several images of village people who I can only presume died. She was the only one with the tattoo that matched yours. Val, these were all innocent people who were persecuted for no reason in a time of madness."

Val gazed thoughtfully at the image.

Delta, unable to cope with the uncomfortable silence that seemed to have fallen over them, chirped up, "OK, so who is going to take us home? I don't do walking."

She stood up and walked towards the sink to drop off her cup.

"Tell your friend thanks and to please keep looking. If he is as good a friend as you think he is, then tell him about me." Val looked seriously at Shane as if she was making a life changing decision.

"If that's what you want, then I will." Delta, who was ready to leave, shuffled impatiently. Shane shook his head and laughed, taking the hint. "I'll call you girls a taxi. I need to close up and get home."

"And there was me thinking this was your home." Delta looked Shane up and down like an icicle with a tan.

Val glanced up at the old train station clock that was on the wall. "Oh my goodness it's nearly six o'clock! My parents will be waiting for me."

Within minutes the taxi was outside. Val gave Shane a friendly hug. Whatever the future might bring, she had made a new friend, someone she could trust and had shown that he cared about her.

"I'll call in tomorrow to see if there's any news," she said to Shane as she got into the taxi.

Feeling a tap on his shoulder Shane turned to face Delta who had come up behind him. She signalled with her index finger for him to bend down to her height. With a very stern face Delta spoke in an almost Al Capone tone of voice.

"Firstly *do not* try to hug me; I don't do touchy feely. Secondly, if you betray my friend there'll be no stone left unturned until I hunt you down and make sure you wish you had never been born." Shane tried to look serious, acting as if he was intimidated by Delta just so he didn't hurt her feelings. It was nice to see that they cared so much about each other.

"I promise," Shane mimicked a cross on his heart while nodding profusely. Delta flicked her hair back over her shoulder and strutted off to the taxi. Shane turned towards the shop, feeling the inclination to go and call a good friend for some serious help. What had he gotten himself into?

Delta parked her bottom next to Val in the taxi. As it pulled away from Shane's shop, they moved in as close as was comfortable for them both.

As Val looked at Delta who was gazing out of the window, she felt something she hadn't realised before. It was love for her best friend. Their relationship had just moved to a new level, something that Val thought very few people would experience: a friend who would risk everything to keep you safe.

The streets seemed to rush past and they quickly reached Delta's house. As Delta got out of the taxi she turned to look at Val. To Val's surprise there were tears in Delta's eyes. In the seven years they had been friends Val had never seen Delta shed a tear, not even when she had fallen from the tree in Val's garden and broken her leg.

"I'm sorry, Delta, I don't know what's happening to me." Val moved into Delta's spot in the taxi almost leaning out. "If you want me to go tonight and never darken your doorstep again I will completely understand." Val looked up at Delta waiting for what seemed like an endless time for an answer.

"Val, don't ever leave me again, do you understand?" Val nodded. This was a good sign. Delta bent down now, leaning back into the taxi so their faces almost touching. "Because if you do I'll have to spend the rest of my life looking for you and I have much better things to do, OK?"

"I didn't mean to leave you, but, yes, I promise. That's fine with me." Delta stood back up, slamming the door shut and signalling the driver to pull away.

Val watched as Delta turned and straightened her skirt before walking up her drive. "I promise," Val said under her breath as Delta moved out of sight.

When the taxi pulled up outside Val's house, she found herself paying the driver almost as much as she had earned to date. She didn't care; she was just glad to be home. She could already see her mum standing in the window of the living room, looking for her.

Val knew she was in trouble. Wednesday was family night. Her mum went out of her way to keep up traditions. As a child, Val had never been allowed to attend any after school clubs or go to play at friends' houses on sacred Wednesdays.

Seeing her mum come out of the house, Val really wanted to tell her everything. Nonetheless, she knew what had to be done.

"Where have you been? You know what night it is!" Susan was shaking in anger, then she noticed the bloody lump on Val's head and her face melted. "Oh dear me, what happened to you?" Realising what her mum was looking at, Val lifted her hand to her forehead.

"A book fell on my head at the shop. I was nearly knocked unconscious. I'm sorry I'm late," Val said convincingly.

"Why didn't you come home on the bus? And why didn't you call us?" Susan was now picking at Val's head as if she was a mother gorilla checking for fleas.

Val pushed her mum away. "I didn't call because I knew you would worry, and I'm fine. I came home in the taxi because I didn't want people on the bus staring at me, OK?" Val had now managed to break free from her mother's vice-like grip and was speedily walking into the house with Susan in hot pursuit.

"Your dad is really disappointed that you didn't make it home in time for dinner. He has an amazing new job he wanted to tell you about. You'd better speak to him about it." Susan pushed Val towards the lounge where her father was busy watching golf.

Val had to shout to be heard over the TV. "Hi Dad. Have a good day?" There had been questions in the past about Mike's hearing although they had eventually agreed it was selective rather than damaged.

"Huh," and a back-handed wave was the total of Mike's reaction.

"OK Mum, now can I get something to eat?" Val moved into the kitchen with Susan still hot on her heals.

"There's food still left from the party in the fridge." Susan started sniffing around Val. "Can you smell smoke?"

"Do you think Dad has been smoking again? Val asked searching Susan's face for a reaction; she got exactly what she was looking for. Val felt guilty for lying but she couldn't take another minute of questions.

"Do you think? If he is, I'll kill him." Susan picked up the cordless phone and headed towards the French doors that led out onto the patio. "I'll check out here for evidence while I call your aunty Janine." Susan was now dialling and Val knew she was scot-free. Her mum would be on the phone for the next sixty minutes with only a break for the odd breath.

"See you in the morning, Mum." Val filled a plate, grabbed a bottle of water and was off. Her mother didn't even bother trying to answer. Val made her way past the lounge, popping her head in to wish her Dad good night and received the same meaningful grunt as before. Well, at least she could rely on them for consistency.

Val dropped her plate of food onto the bed and took a long and much needed drink of water. Putting the bottle down, she checked that the door was shut and slipped off her clothes. Putting on a pair of long sleeved pyjamas, she made her way down the landing to the bathroom. The mirror there revealed horribly matted hair and various bumps bruises and bumps. She wondered how many more she was going to get before this was all over.

Val made her way back into her room to devour the plate of food she had thrown together. Being a strange teleporting, water floating and fire-resistant creature sure gave you an appetite. She finished up and grabbed another sip of water before climbing into bed. What would she dream of tonight Val wondered as she started to drift off into a sound and restful sleep. That was until she woke to the sound of a woman's screams.

Val sat bolt upright. She was covered in cold sweat. The scream had been so loud! Turning to look at her clock, she realised that it was only three in the morning. Then she heard the scream again. It was here, real, and she instantly thought it must be her mum. She leapt out of bed, quickly moving in the dark towards her bedroom door. The screams seemed to be coming from the landing. She touched the door handle, then had to release it quickly as sharp pains shot up her arm. Taking a deep breath, she grasped the handle again and pushed it down. She needed to find out who was in trouble and where. Coming out of her room, Val was surprised it was so dark given the volume of the screaming, which must have surely woken everyone. Nor was there any light coming from under her parents' door.

Where was the noise coming from? She stopped and listened, and then it became clear: it was coming from the bathroom. Val opened the door placing her hand hesitantly around the wall to turn on the light. Everything looked normal. Moving cautiously she crossed the room towards the window, still hearing the pounding screams in her head, and feeling the pain in her arm that didn't seem to be lessening. Opening the frosty window, she leaned out to see if anyone on the street was in need of assistance. The street was empty apart from a couple of stray cats, visible only by the glow of the dim street-lights. No one screaming for help out here, she thought.

Closing the window, she made her way back to the door and locked it. Once she knew for certain that she was alone, she lifted her pyjama sleeve to find out which symbol was causing her so much pain. It looked like the pi sign Val had seen in maths: two straight columns with a flat line on the top. Not only did she not know what it was, she didn't really care as the noise was getting out of control, just like the cars had on the previous day. Real-ising that the screams weren't going anywhere, Val started to search the bathroom to find where they were coming from and spotted a flicker in her dad's shaving mirror. She pulled it on its flexible bar, drawing it closer to her. Now she could see where the screams were coming from. An old lady was being tied up by a young woman. "That's terrible," Val mumbled under her breath, barely able to think straight under the double assault of the pain in her arm and the terrible screams.

For the first time, Val knew she had a choice of sorts. She could touch the mirror and possibly be transported into a very dangerous situation, or she could go back to bed and suffer with the excruciating pain in her arm and the old lady's wails resounding in her head. Fantastic! Well, at least there were options for a change.

Val took a deep breath. "OK lady, here I come," she said, touching the mirror. The pain in her arm faded, along with any control over the rest of her body. It almost felt this time as if she had been put through a blender and spat out the other side. Val landed on the curb of the road with quite a jolt; the fact that she only had her pyjamas on didn't help.

Standing up and brushing herself down, Val checked herself out: arms - two; legs - two; head - one; It all seemed to be there. Val turned around, absorbing the panorama. Where was the old woman? In her vision, she was being tied up to a chair and there were definitely no chairs in the middle of the street.

The place she had landed in definitely didn't look familiar. She wasn't even sure what country she was in. As she started to walk down the street, the only light to aid her journey was that coming from the streetlamps, which, at three in the morning, were still lit. What now, she wondered? She didn't know what step to take next. She had been expecting to fall directly into the situation with the old lady, and now she was completely lost. How was she supposed to find the woman? She looked around carefully. Surely there would be a clue somewhere. Ah! Could that be it? About four houses down and set back from the road, was an open front door. A tree partially obscured it, making it impossible to see in, but as Val cautiously made her way towards it, she could already hear faint cries. She reached the path in front of the house and started to make her way up the gravel drive. "Ow!" Val yelped as a stone cut deep into her foot. She didn't have time to look at it, but it really hurt. *Note to self, always wear slippers or possibly heavy-duty military boots in bed from now on.* There was a red Ford KA parked in the driveway so Val used it as cover, and quietly made her way around it in the hope that no one would spot her. She reached the open door safely.

"Please don't hurt me. I will do whatever you say." The pleading voice reached her quite clearly. It was definitely an old woman's voice; it could have been Val's grandma. She didn't know how she was going to do it, but she was going to help this woman. As Val stepped into the doorway she spotted what looked like a rounders bat leaning on a sports bag against an inside wall.

Odd thing, Val thought, for an old lady to have. Maybe it belonged to one of her children or grandchildren. It didn't really matter; it would make a perfect weapon. Picking it up, she slowly made her way down the hall.

Her nerves were beginning to get the better of her and it sounded almost like her heart was beating in her head. She was surprised that she could still hear the cries through the drumming. The old woman's moans had become a whimper; Val guessed she had been gagged.

The closer Val got to the room the old woman was in, the more her fear grew. She stopped when she heard what she thought was a younger woman's voice. This was good news. Val knew she would stand a better chance against a woman than a man, unless of course she had a mute accomplice. Val was now outside the door, which was open just enough for her to see into the room. As she peeked in, she saw the old woman's thin frame. She wasn't in a chair, but on the floor, face down. A younger woman was pushing down onto her back with her whole weight while she bound her hands with what looked like a very colourful silk scarf. That done, the girl started to speak into the old woman's ear.

"What did you think you were going to achieve? Are you crazy?" The woman was completely irate and prodded the older woman angrily.

Val knew she had to move quickly, while the younger woman was busy. She lifted the bat above her head and she moved into the room.

The younger woman was just about to raise the old woman up; Val knew it was now or never. Swinging with all her force, Val swung the bat at her head. With one massive blow, she knocked the girl to the ground.

The young woman's slumped over the old woman who was trying to speak, although her face was being forced into a very thick pile carpet. "It's going to be OK, don't worry. I'm here to save you," said Val, rolling the young woman aside. It felt like a silly thing to say, but she wanted the old woman to feel safe.

Astonishingly the old woman started to laugh. This wasn't quite the reaction Val had been hoping for. Something else was bothering her too. The room looked too young in style for an old woman. The furniture was very contemporary. Looking for more clues, Val took in the pictures on the walls. There was one of several girls on what looked like a crazy holiday. Leaving the old woman on the floor, Val picked up the picture. Moving it into the light she saw something that made her stomach churn even more than teleporting: it was a picture of the young woman she had just merrily knocked out. Looking around the room again she saw the laptop, the games console, the fashionable high-heels lying by the settee, shoes that certainly would not fit the old woman who was wearing practical flats. This was the younger woman's house, Val was suddenly sure of it! That meant that the young woman was the one Val was supposed to be helping. What a huge mistake. How could she get out of this one? Val didn't even know if she had killed her with the blow from the bat. As she turned towards the young woman's body to check her pulse, the old woman pushed herself up onto her knees.

"So you are the chosen one; all this time, and you're it," she cackled, hugely amused by something that Val didn't understand.

Val moved swiftly towards the old woman, not bothered any more that she resembled her grandma, or any grandma.

"What do you mean, the chosen one, you stupid old cow?" This was completely out of character for Val, although what was normal about any of this?

"Well that's just rude. You should have more respect for your elders, even if you are nearly four hundred years their senior." Val stood for a moment looking at the annoying old woman on the floor, wondering whether she was trying to confuse her or just get on her nerves.

"I don't care what you say, you're a crazy old woman and I'm calling the police. They will come and take you away."

The old woman was now howling with laughter. "What will you tell them? That you teleported here? That you have a special tattoo? That you don't understand any of this? You stupid little girl! You don't even know where you are, do you Val?"

CHAPTER 4

And you are?

Val's whole body tensed with the old woman's words. How could she know all these things about her? She needed to find out *now*. Crouching down, she leaned in close to the old woman's face.

"Who told you my name?" Val's voice was slow and venomous. The force of her hot breath blew the old woman's grey fringe up over her forehead. Val moved forward another inch, until their noses were almost touching. "How do you know about the tattoo?" she seethed.

"Does it matter?" spat the old woman. "I'm just disappointed that you are the best they could offer." Turning her face away from Val in disgust, the old woman began to squirm, slowly altering the way she was propping up her body.

Suddenly her head snapped unnaturally back towards Val. Looking at her with an apple-pie baking, sweet old lady face, she started to speak. "If you untie me, dearest I could tell you everything." Her voice was almost as thick as treacle. Val thought she was going to be physically sick.

"Shut up. No better, I'll shut you up." Val stood up, grabbing the old woman by the arm and lifted her off the ground. Pushing her onto a wooden chair in the corner, she forced her arms backwards over the top of the chair and looked around for something to shut her up.

Val grabbed a discarded yellow duster from a small side table. As she tied it around the old woman's head, she snapped and snarled at her like a rabid dog. Val had to be careful not to lose a finger, but she needed peace to think clearly if only for a second. After a struggle, she managed to tie the duster over the wrinkly old lips, then gave her a victory slap on her creased forehead.

"That's for trying to trick me you bitter old hag."

Val now saw that the young woman on the floor was beginning to stir. Leaving the old woman secured to the chair, Val crouched down by the other woman's side.

Slowly she opened her eyes. Pain streaked across her face as she looked up At Val. "Who are you?" The woman winced; the pain of speaking was obviously intense.

"Don't speak for a second." Val rubbed her arm reassuringly. "My name is Val. I heard screams coming from the street and came to investigate. That's when I found you on the floor and that old woman going crazy. She seems to be one sail short of the wind, so I have put her over there for her own safety. What happened?" Val felt guilty for lying but it was in her best interest.

The woman carefully placed her hands behind her as she started to sit up. "I came home from my night shift at the hospital, and this crazy old woman, who by the way you *do not* want to untie, must have been waiting for me. Can you believe it, she jumped me from behind." The woman flinched, drawing a sharp breath, and then carried on telling Val her story. "She was ranting on about how I was special and that the bait was set." The young woman raised her hand, drawing circles with her index finger on her temple as if to sign that the woman was mad. Val smiled.

"By the way, my name is Jenny." She offered her hand to Val who gently shook it.

Val took hold of Jenny's arm to help her to her feet and admitted, "I suspected something was odd. It's not every day you find an eighty-year-old woman tied up face down on the carpet laughing her head off." Val noticed the matted bloodstained hair on the back of Jenny's head. "Do you have a first aid kit handy?"

Jenny nodded and pointed towards the kitchen. "Then let's go and get you cleaned up." Val took her arm as Jenny began moving at a snail's pace towards the kitchen.

All of a sudden Jenny froze. "There's someone else here." Val tightened her grip on Jenny's arm to support her trembling body.

"Who? Was there someone else with the old lady?" Val was beginning to get nervous as well; she didn't need to meet anyone else tonight.

"Well someone hit me over the head," Jenny pointed to the lump, "so they must still be in the house." How embarrassing. Val felt her cheeks getting warm; she was now going to have to look for *herself*.

She patted Jenny on the arm to reassure her. "Let's have a look around, but first let's get the bat for protection."

Val could sense Jenny pulling away. "Just a minute, how did you know I have a bat? Who's to say you aren't the old woman's accomplice?" Val knew she needed to do something to convince Jenny she was not the enemy and fast.

"I saw the bat near you when I walked in, believe me I'm not the person who hit you over the head." Val looked Jenny straight in the eyes and slowly reached out for her hand. "Do you think I would still be here if I was guilty?" Val said sincerely. Jenny smiled weakly at her; she looked too tired to fight, even if Val had been the attacker.

They cautiously moved back around the room together. The crazy old woman was still reeling like a wild animal in her chair. Releasing Jenny, Val reached out and hastily grabbed the bloodstained bat, and they cautiously moved out of the living room.

As they headed towards the kitchen, Jenny's voice broke the silence. "I'm going to call the police. They can come and look for the other one," she said breaking free from Val and heading back to the hall.

Val felt desperate. How could she explain herself to the police, who would quickly realise that she was guilty of attacking Jenny. She still wasn't sure how the teleporting thing worked, she had touched Jenny several times and nothing had happened. So maybe she hadn't yet done whatever it was she was suppose to do. Val's head was starting to hurt with all the unanswered questions spinning in and out. The one thing she was sure of was that she didn't want the police involved.

She needed to stall Jenny and fast. Val had no better plan in that instant than to started coughing; it had worked on her mum once when she had burnt a hole in one of her tops. She started with a convincing wheeze and then quickly moved to full blown gasping.

"Are you OK?" Jenny asked, moving closer to Val, losing interest for a moment in the phone call. Val instantly took advantage of this opportunity to go into overdrive; it was almost as if she was having a mini convulsion of some sort. Dropping the bat, Val gasped for breath like a pro; she could feel an Oscar coming to her.

"Val, do you want a drink?" Jenny had now changed direction and was leading her by the arm towards the kitchen.

"Yes," Val spluttered, "please," coughing a little more and nodding her head. This was going better than expected.

Jenny pulled a glass from a shaker style cupboard above the sink and filled it with water. "Here take this."

"Thank you. I don't know what happened. Could we sit down please?" Before Jenny had time to answer, Val was sitting down at a pine table, facing the kitchen door.

Jenny looked concerned. "OK, but only for a second; we really must call the police." Val nodded and started to gulp the water down. "Can I ask you a question, Val?"

Val nodded she was up for anything that would stop Jenny picking up a phone. "Yeah, sure, fire-away," she said between gulps.

"Why are you out in the middle of the night in your pyjamas?" As the last word escaped her lips, Val saw the old woman appear behind Jenny, leaping through the air. Val was amazed at her agility. How on earth had she got free? Val was so busy distracting Jenny she hadn't thought to check on psycho Gran.

Everything seemed to happen in slow motion. Val put her hand down, instinctively reaching for a bat that wasn't there. Where was it? *Damn*, she had left it in the hall earlier. She realised the seriousness of that mistake when the old woman raised her arm, preparing to smash the bat into the back of Jenny's head again.

"No!" Val shouted, a surge of anger filling her body, knocking what was left of her water across the table and smashing it into the wall. Val raised her arms, stretching her hands out in front of her, feeling the sensation of lifting an invisible blanket of air. As it rose, Jenny was violently thrown backwards off her chair landing with a heavy thump on the floor.

The old woman was also lifted, twirling into the air like a rag doll in a hurricane, hitting the ceiling with such force that she cracked her silhouette into the plaster. Shards of the ceiling light exploded, flying down onto the floor almost as if it were raining diamonds. Then she landed lifelessly on the wooden floor.

Val stood for a second, her breathing shallow and deliberate, taking in the full extent of what she had just done. It felt like a tornado had been released from each of her hands. She didn't know how it worked or why, she was just glad it had.

After a few seconds, Jenny appeared over the rim of the table, her hair just slightly dishevelled. "What on earth was that?" She was looking at Val not with fear, but almost in wonder, as if she was intrigued rather than scared by what she had just witnessed.

Val slowly let her eyes focus on Jenny. "I don't know, but whatever it was I'm sure of one fact, that old woman is not getting up in a hurry." Val moved over to Jenny's side of the table to help her to her feet.

Looking at the old woman on the floor surrounded by glittering specks of glass and covered in white plaster, Val contemplated the fact that she actually looked quite angelic.

"Call the police, Jenny, and an ambulance as well." Val offered her hand to pull her up. As Jenny accepted it, a blue spark went off between them, and Val was gone.

Her insides fizzed and she knew what was coming; as always, the journey back was so much sweeter. At least she knew what was on the other side, even though the trip did resemble a bad fairground ride.

Val landed with a thud, a white toilet seat about three inches from her nose.

She lifted her face slowly. "Just lovely! You try to help people and all you get is a loo in your face. I bet Superman never had to face a deadly toilet." Val managed to raise a smile as she sat slumped between the toilet and the bidet. All of a sudden, the enormity of what she had done began to sink in. The crazy risk she had taken and the fact that her life was spiralling out of control were deeply disturbing. She curled up in a ball, her arms wrapped around her legs, and began to sob quietly.

After a few minutes, Val realised that the sun was rising on a new day, not just for her, but thanks to her actions, for Jenny as well. Maybe, through all the chaos, something good was eventually going to come from this. Wiping the tears from her cheeks, she looked at the rippled sun through the etched bathroom window and was just thankful she had made it home again. Whatever the reason for this thing happening to her, she now knew that if she didn't follow where it took her, someone would probably get hurt.

Val suddenly realised that she needed to get back to bed before her dad got up. Mike went to work at the crack of dawn and she didn't want to get caught out of bed and raise any suspicions. She pulled herself up, acknowledging her aches and pains and made her way out of the bathroom. Sneaking down the landing, she slipped into her room and climbed under the bed covers. Her whole body seemed to let out a sigh. It was like slowly releasing air from a tyre. When the whooshing sound had finally stopped coming from between her lips, Val closed her eyes and fell instantly and peacefully asleep.

The morning came far too quickly. Val woke to find her mother was gently shaking her into consciousness and knew that she had managed to sleep through her alarm.

"Come on Val, you will be late for work." Susan stroked her hair.

"OK Mum," Val responded sleepily.

Susan stood up and went towards the door. "I will do you an extra food pack since you don't have time for breakfast."

Val gave a tired grin in her mother's direction. "Thanks," she muttered, starting to get out of bed and letting her feet slowly hit the soft carpet. As she fished around for her slippers, she realised that her feet were absolutely filthy and the bottom of her pyjamas looked like they had been caressed by her dad's lawn mower.

Val lifted her sheets and saw that her bedding was not only muddy, but bloody as well. The stone she had stepped on the previous night had obviously cut her deeper than she had thought. Val stood up stripping her bed and shoving her pyjamas into the centre of the bundle in the hope that they would come clean.

After a quick wash, she threw on her clothes and headed down to the laundry room. "What are you doing, Val? Come on," Susan called impatiently.

"I'm on my way, Mum." Val ran into the kitchen. The pain in her foot was uncomfortable, but bearable. She found her mother with something that looked like a rucksack.

"Please say that's not all food?" Val laughed, grabbing it from her mum.

"Shut-up and go." Susan kissed Val on the head. "Tonight I want you home early; your dad wants to see you."

"OK, I will be back at about six," Val shouted back and headed for the bus.

As she walked her mobile phone rang. Pulling it out she saw it was Delta and she automatically slowed her pace to answer it.

"Morning. Have I got a story for you," Val gushed down the phone.

"Hi. Before you fill me in, do you have time for lunch today? I feel that retail therapy is the only thing that will help me cope with the situation we are in, and to help me recover from what you are about to tell me," said Delta vivaciously.

Val laughed. "OK, I get from twelve till one. Come to the shop and pick me up." The idea of a trip out sounded good, a little normality was tempting. "So are you ready for my story?"

"Yes, I'm having a manicure, so I suppose it can't hurt." This was exactly what Val needed, Delta made everything that wasn't to do with her personal care sound insignificant.

Val arrived outside the bookshop to find the front door ajar. She checked her watch; it was still a good ten minutes to opening time. She cautiously made her way up the stairs to the front door. So much had happened she couldn't take any risks. Pushing the door, she stepped in. There seemed to be no sign of life. She made her way around the counter and checked that the till was OK. Everything seemed to be as she had left it the previous day.

She headed down one of the aisles. "Hello," she called. "Anyone here?" A stern masculine voice rang through the shop. "Yes, there is someone here and I am pleased to see you are on time." Val nearly jumped out of her skin. She realised instantly that it was Wallace 'call me Mr Gallymore'.

"Morning Mr Gallymore, I'm so pleased to see you." Val called out.

"Well Miss Saunders, unless you can see through walls, you haven't actually seen me yet," answered Wallace. Val mouthed several words whilst pulling child-like faces as she walked back up the aisle. As she came out into the reception area, Wallace was just locking the private door behind him.

"I wasn't sure when I was going to see you. How did your trip go?" Val made her way around the counter dropping her rucksack of food and grabbing the feather duster. She thought that looking productive would please the old man, who actually looked really well. Maybe his trips abroad were for those Botox injections. Val smiled to herself.

"I see you have made adequate sales Miss Saunders and I will be leaving this afternoon to go to a classics convention. I trust I can leave you to carry on in charge?" Wallace stared at Val through his piercing brown eyes.

"Yes of course. I'm so pleased you are happy with my work. I have been thinking, maybe an alphabetical system would work better for us and what about a computer?" Val was filled with excitement. She had lots of ideas for the shop and thought that maybe she might actually end up liking her boss.

"I don't pay you to think, I pay you to dust and serve. Do you have a problem with that?" Wallace shot bitterly at her. Val felt a sharp arrow pierce her heart; there was no hope for them now.

"No, Mr Gallymore." Val lowered her head. She had never met such a mean old man in her life. She imagined for a moment that the old hag from last night was Mrs Gallymore, which lifted her morale a little.

"Another question, can you please explain exactly what happened to the water cooler?" asked Wallace. Val had forgotten about that. She was going to have to make up a good excuse to get past him.

Val walked around the counter towards the water cooler. Placing her hands on what was left, she spoke in a hushed tone. "I fell on it while I was switching off the code for the door. I'm so sorry." Val didn't even bother lifting up her head as she was sure his reaction was going to be harsh.

"Are you alright? That must have hurt," he asked sounding concerned.

Val couldn't believe her ears. "Yes it did. I have several bruises down my back if you want to look." She started to lift her top.

"No!" Wallace retorted swiftly. "No, that won't be necessary, thank you. Just take more care. I don't want to be the one to call your parents telling them that you have had an accident, now do I?" Wallace turned and before Val could respond, he was heading towards the door, talking to her as he went. "I'll order you another one. There are several boxes being delivered tomorrow. Unpack them with care and put them out in the shop. I'll return in a few days." Without turning, Wallace left the shop.

Once he was out of sight Val grinned to herself, "He loves me really," she muttered, turning and heading off down the aisle, dusting as she went.

Before she knew it, there was a toot outside and Delta was sitting there in her sparkling red mini, ready to go shopping. Val grabbed her things and headed out, locking the door behind her.

"Hello Yankee," Val greeted her.

"Hello Alien," retorted Delta, as Val jumped into the car.

Val gasped. That was a bit risky in public. "Don't say that. People might hear you, and I'm not."

"Like people here give a damn. Have you not noticed that you can be dying in the street in this country and no one even bothers to help you? Consequently, I will call you Alien as much as I like, Alien." Delta held her head high.

Val had to agree that she had lain, in pain, on those very steps only a few days earlier and not one person had tried to help.

"So, where are we going?" Val turned to Delta with a quizzical look on her face as she fastened her seatbelt.

"The place I call paradise. The shopping centre." Delta grinned, checked her rear view mirror and sped off.

Two shops and a coffee later, Val checked her watch. "We're going to have to leave soon. I need to get back to work," she said.

Delta winked as she walked into Topshop. "Did you know, Val, that super model Kimmi Nero is the Topshop it-girl this season? I don't care what she does to her insides, her outer packaging is perfect."

Val looked at a huge pin-up of a stick like woman hanging in the middle of the shop and felt slightly nauseous. She couldn't imagine how little you had to eat to be that thin and smiled as she imagined that woman at Val's dinner table trying to fight off her mum.

As she scanned the clothes, Val wondered if there was something wrong with her. There were at least thirty women flapping around the aisles, picking things up, pressing them up to their bodies and looking at themselves in mirrors. She knew that Delta always looked fabulous, Val didn't want any of it. Such a high maintenance look it wasn't her thing at all. She glanced again at her watch; they were going to be pushing it even with Delta's crazy driving.

"Come on, *now*," Val snapped.

Delta nodded and ran to the till to pay for a tiny piece of cloth. Val couldn't distinguish if it was a top or bottom part.

As soon as it was paid for, Val grabbed Delta's arm and dragged her from the shop. "As fast as you drive, Delta, you walk so slowly." Delta obligingly started to trot.

They turned a corner so fast that Val almost toppled.

She was still off-balance when she was struck in the centre of her back by something solid. Val was completely winded and was saved from a nasty fall by a large set of hands that grabbed her around the waist.

"I'm sorry, I was in a hurry," she spluttered as she was carefully set back on her feet again. She looked up, and up. As she reached the summit, she found herself gazing into the eyes of a very tall young man. Her first thought was 'Wow, he has perfect hair.' It was mousey brown and he had deep green eyes, the sort you see looking back at you from the front of magazine covers.

"It's OK. It's not every day you get run into with such force by a pretty young woman in a Spiderman t-shirt, cool." Val looked down acknowledging her top. She wasn't quite sure if she had taken a breath since the clashing of bodies and was starting to feel a little faint.

"I... I... have to go." She grabbed Delta's hand and started to run.

"Slow down...high heels...not made for running," Delta gasped. "You are going to ruin my tips," blurted Delta between breaths.

Val came to an almost mule like halt and looked around in a panic. "Has he gone?"

"Yes, about half a mile ago, Val." Delta pulled her hand out of Val's grip. "You nearly made me perspire. Do *not* do that again," she said tensely. Looking at Val it dawned on Delta what was going on. Delta was now moving in closer and pointing her finger at Val. "You liked him," she poked Val's arm, one strike for each word, "Val-I've-never-had-a-boyfriend-Saunders."

"No, I did not. He was invading my personal space, that's all."

Delta laughed, it was painfully obvious that she did. Nonetheless Delta didn't know what to do; this wasn't a situation she had ever encountered with Val. Val pushed Delta affectionately to stop her from poking her arm.

Their banter was interrupted when Val heard a voice calling her name.

"Val! Val, hello."

Val looked around. Where was it coming from? Then, appearing from inside a group of girls, Val spotted Wendy Whitmore.

Panic filled Val's eyes as she grabbed Delta's arm. "Delta, it's Wendy." Val was once again running. Wendy was a girl who had been in Val's class at school and had always wanted to be Val's friend. Val hated her. She was whiney, skeletal and smelt funny; it was as if she would break if you looked at her too hard. They usually managed to escape her unwanted attention, but today it seemed that they weren't going to have such luck. Wendy was already on top of them blocking their exit.

"Wendy, how are you?" said Val, greeting Wendy with a fake smile.

"I'm fine. What are you two up to then?" Wendy looked at Delta, devouring every inch of her body with her eyes. Extraordinarily Delta was visibly uncomfortable.

Val tugged at Delta's top as she started to work her way around Wendy. "I'm just going back to work, so you will have to excuse me as I'm late already, but it's been lovely seeing you, again," she said as they started to run towards the car park lift. "See you around then," said Wendy wryly, waving a thin wimpy arm at them as they disappeared into the lift.

"Does she scare you?" asked Delta in a very concerned tone.

"I'm not sure. I'll have to think about it." Val looked at Delta with both eyebrows visibly raised.

"No, don't bother. You want to be thinking about tall, dark and handsome." Delta threw Val a glance as the lift stopped.

"Don't be silly. I will never see him again, and I didn't think he was handsome at all." Val stepped out and moved quickly back to the mini, avoiding eye contact with Delta.

They drove back to the shop at speed and in silence, coming to an abrupt halt outside the bookshop.

"Do you want to stop for a while or do you have any other beauty treatments today?" said Val as she ran up the stairs and started to open the door to the shop.

"Claws away, I'm not the one in love," said Delta who was already out of the car and making her way to the steps. "What did you have planned for us?" Delta passed Val as she made her way in.

"Well, there is dusting, dusting and if you are lucky, a little more dusting," said Val switching the alarm off as Delta moved behind the counter.

Delta caressed the private sign with her manicured nails. "What do you think is behind the locked door?" She jangled the handle.

"Don't do that. It says private for a reason," said Val firmly moving around the counter to remove Delta. "Staff only." Val circled an invisible barrier with her finger behind the counter.

"Oh, how can I be more like you?" Delta lifted her hand to her forehead pretending to swoon.

"Well you can start by getting a job." Val came around and handed Delta a duster. It looked so ridiculous in her hands. She was never going to have to do the dirty work. It was almost written in the stars that *Delta Troughton should never break a nail*.

"Should we look for that book thingy or have you found it already?" asked Delta.

Val looked up, she had forgotten all about the book. "Great idea. You see, you aren't just a pretty face." Delta did a curtsy and wandered off. "Keep meeting me back at the counter, just in case I do the old Houdini act," Val shouted at the aisle down which Delta had just disappeared.

"Will do," Delta called back.

Val started to look. She decided to do the same as the other day and ran her finger down the books in the hope that they would speak to her. She was trying her hardest, but all Val could see was the face of the young man she had bumped into. She wouldn't admit it, but he had made her feel something she had never felt before. It could only be described as a warm, fuzzy feeling in her stomach. She imagined them holding hands, chatting, laughing, walking down the road and sitting having a coffee together. "He liked my t-shirt," Val blushed to herself.

A voice in her ear abruptly broke into her daydream. "Hello Alien, I'm bored. What time do you punch out from this place?"

Val snapped back to reality. She looked at her watch, but Delta couldn't wait for a response.

"Can we go now? I haven't found anything."

Delta had her pleading face on and Val had to admit she was tired. It was a quarter to five and she knew Mr Gallymore would not be back today, so she agreed to close.

"We need to stop off at Shane's on the way home. I want him to check out my tattoo and tell him about last night."

Delta nodded, making her way out.

As they arrived at Shane's, Val felt a pang of apprehension. Would he have any more news for her today? Would his secret friend have any more facts to make some sense of Val's life? They went towards the double doors through a group of rough looking men. Delta grabbed Val's hand.

"Hello, ladies." Shane appeared before they could get in. "Lads, these young girls are my friends. If they ever need anything, you help them out, alright!" The large men all nodded.

"Oh, I do feel better now," said Delta ironically, looking at Shane with a weak smile. "Many tattoos today?"

she asked. Val had to take her hat off to Delta; she was trying to be nice.

"Not a bad day at all." Shane grinned at Delta. "I'm just about to close up, so would you girls like to stop for a coffee or a cold drink?"

Val nodded.

"Let me see your arm," Shane said, waiting for her to roll her sleeve up. "Ah! I see you have lost another symbol, Gemini, this time. Have you had another adventure?"

Val pulled down her shirtsleeve, nodding. "Yes, last night. Short version: crazy lady knew all about me. I'm freaked that she knew so much. It was as if she was waiting for me to arrive."

Shane was obviously concerned. "Are you OK? Did you get hurt?" he asked.

Val sat on one of his chairs pulling off her shoe to show him the gash in the bottom of her foot.

"Doesn't look too bad, but let's get it cleaned up. Wait here while I get my first aid kit." Shane walked out through the swing door leaving the girls alone.

"Why didn't you tell me about your foot, Val?" Delta looked hurt.

"Because it's nothing, and I know how much you hate blood." Val looked regretfully at Delta.

"Don't do it again. We could have come here in your lunch break to get this sorted instead of prancing around town." Val knew Delta cared, though, if they hadn't been in town, she never would have seen her mystery man.

"Delta, Shane is taking a long time. Maybe you should go and have a look for him." Delta huffed as she walked off through the swinging door. Within seconds, Shane was back.

"Where's Delta?" he asked.

"She's looking for you. Haven't you seen her?"

Shane shook his head. "Let's sort this foot out. She's probably out the back, getting a drink. We can go and find her in a second." He lifted Val's foot and gently started to clean the wound. Val spent the next few minutes giving Shane the full run down of the previous night's events and by the time she had finished so had he.

"Have you spoken to your friend again?" she asked. I don't want you to think I'm badgering you, so please tell me to give it a rest if I am."

"I spoke to him this morning. He's going to investigate deeper. He was very interested in what's happening to you and very disturbed that an eighteen-year-old is disappearing into thin air and falling into situations way over her head. I'm sorry to say I have to agree." Shane patted Val's leg for her to put it down. "We need to find a way to protect you, as we don't seem to be able to stop you, and I think I have the answer right here." Shane grabbed Val's hand and pulled her up. "Come with me."

Val followed Shane through the swing door and out towards the gallery.

"Delta must be comfortable, she hasn't come back," Val said, but even as she said the words, Delta came flying towards her.

"We need to talk."

Val was surprised at the strange look on Delta's face. "Just let me sit down and have a drink first, Delta." Delta was now grabbing urgently at Val's hand. What's the matter, Delta? You can talk in front of Shane; he's our friend." By now they had moved into the gym area and Val was surrounded by the equipment.

"Don't worry, it's too late," Delta said walking over to the table and sitting down. Val watched her, wondering why she was acting so strangely. Maybe the teleporting had scrambled her brain.

"I'll put the coffee on," Val said. "Do you want a cup?"

"No thanks, I've already had one." Delta responded.

Val looked at her in shock; Delta never drank alone if she had to make it.

"OK. You want one, Shane?" Val shouted. Shane called back his request for one and then there was another voice.

"I'll have one too. White two sugars if you are making." Val looked up. Who was there and had they heard her talking to Shane? As she surveyed the area, she spotted the punch bag moving, and a pair of feet at the bottom. Could this be Shane's special friend?

"Hello, coffee coming right up." She turned towards the percolator, not wanting to stare. This was great; she would get to meet him in person.

Delta sat staring over at Val with a smug expression on her face.

"What's your problem?" Val asked.

"Nothing," said Delta still looking at Val.

Val made the coffee whilst she mulled all the questions she was going to ask Shane's friend when he came over.

"Coffee's ready." Val made her way to the table with a tray and placed it down. Shane came up behind her and, reaching round, grabbed his.

"You can stay if you look after us like this," said Shane, his smile filling his whole face. Reaching out for the stranger's coffee, she murmured to herself, "Take your time Val, don't scare him off." She could feel heavy breathing behind her.

She spun around to greet him. "Hello…" The coffee cup slipped, dangling dangerously from her hand with her jaw hanging almost as low as the cup. Val just stared at the young man standing in front of her.

Delta got up and made her way around the table to Val's side. "Val, please let me introduce you to Shane's son, Jason." Delta seemed to be revelling in Val's silence. "He is here on holiday." Delta made her way around the back of Jason and stopped on the other side of Val. "So next time, when I say I need to speak to you, maybe you will listen." Delta laughed a small wicked laugh, flicked her hair and made her way back to the table.

Val was still fixed to the spot. It was him, the young man from the shopping centre. What was the chance of it being him?

"Are you OK? Nice to see you again. I couldn't forget that t-shirt." Jason broke the moment by grabbing the hanging coffee cup, luckily still containing most of its contents.

"Yes." Val was blushing a painful red. She noticed that even sweaty, he smelt great.

Shane walked past her. "This is my son. He is going to teach you to box and fence."

"Sorry, what?" Terror streaked across Val's face.

"Jason can teach you both boxing and fencing if you want. They will at least give you a better chance of defending yourself." Shane sat down with Delta. Jason, who now had his drink under control, also moved past Val, who seemed stuck to the spot. Her brain was throbbing with the thoughts shooting through it. She needed to calm down and make her way to the table.

"Yes, that sounds good to me." Val turned and grabbed the first available chair. Looking into her coffee cup, she questioned Shane. "Does Jason know everything about me?" She wasn't ready to look up yet.

"Jason knows you need help, that you are at risk of getting hurt, and he can help you." Shane moved his hand over the table and gently placed it over Val's hand. "All the people at this table want to help you. Last night you could have been in serious trouble. I know you have powers that you can't control, but that's not enough."

Val could feel a burning behind her eyes. Although it wasn't as bad as the pain in her arm, she knew it signalled danger. Out of nowhere she heard moving water. She concentrated. No, it was more like waves crashing on a beach. She looked around the table; her friends obviously weren't hearing the same as her.

"Shane, I think I'm going." Val pulled her hand from under Shane's.

"Val, don't go. We want to help you. Please stay. Tell us what you need?" Shane said, misunderstanding.

"*NO* Shane. I'm really going." Val leaned forward. The sound of waves was even louder. Then she spotted it, an image in the coffee jug in the middle of the table. It was a man drowning. As her eyes focused on him, Val was completely oblivious to Delta who was trying to get her attention.

"Time to go, *now*." Val reached out and touched the coffee jug.

Shane, Jason and Delta watched as Val disappeared.

The arrival was soft. Val was quite impressed. Maybe, just maybe, she was getting used to this teleporting thing. As she opened her eyes, all the colours of the rainbow seemed to be flapping in her face. Looking down she noticed that her feet were sinking into sand and then, out of the blue, a child's face popped over the top of what Val realised was a wind breaker.

"Hello," he said.

"Goodbye," said Val to the boy as she stood up and hurried off.

She looked around her. She was definitely on the beach she had seen in the coffee jug. It had soft white sand and its crystal blue waves were caressing the shore. Val realised this was definitely not Skegness. The beach seemed quite busy. Arriving inside the temporary changing area was a stroke of luck, and consequently no one seemed to be paying her any attention.

"Where is she?" Shane looked at Delta.

"How am I supposed to know?" Delta raised both her hands.

"What should we do, Dad?" Jason looked at Shane for an answer.

"Wait, that's all we can do. What's the time?" asked Shane. Delta looked up at the clock.

"Five-forty-five. Her mum is expecting her home in fifteen and she is already in trouble." Delta voiced her concern for her friend.

"Is this her mobile on the table?" Jason picked up a phone.

"Yes it is, you can tell by the drab black exterior." Delta took it from Jason. "I'll send her mum a text message saying she'll be late," she said.

"OK, you do that. Val said that she returns to the same place she left from" Shane pointed to Val's chair. Delta nodded in agreement.

"Jason, let's move the table and prepare for her coming back then." They both stood and started to move things out of the way.

Val wondered *where* in the world she was. Under different circumstances she and Delta would have loved being here. However, her previous experiences had taught her that something, possibly nasty, was about to happen.

Val looked across the beach and out to sea for a sign. Within seconds she spotted an arm waving frantically above the water. Then the arm became a man rising in the waves, then sinking again. Val wasn't prepared to rush in like last time. While she was still considering the best course of action, Val was practically knocked down by a masculine figure in red shorts, holding a float under his arm, running towards the water.

Well, this was going to be easy. Lifeguard saves man; Val pulls man out of water and 'pow' we touch hands and that sparkly thing happens and back to Shane's I go. Val felt quite pleased with herself. She watched as the lifeguard made his way purposefully through the waves towards the man, who was at least consistently drowning. As he reached him, he threw out his float. Val felt quite nervous. She had never seen someone drowning before. The man came above the water again and as he grabbed the float, Val felt a deep sense of relief. However, this was fleeting. With a violent jerk, the lifeguard disappeared.

"No! Not again." Val kicked the sand and she stood on her toes, praying that they were just out of sight. Within a few seconds, she knew what she was going to have to do; the only problem was that she was a seriously poor swimmer. Val bent down, pulling at her laces like an angry six-year-old. She wasn't taking anything else off; she didn't care how many women on the beach had three inches of cloth on their bodies. As she straightened up, she was still hoping that they were going to suddenly reappear above the waves, but nothing happened. Val headed towards the water at a snail's pace, the waves starting to lap over her toes and the impending *save* now looming heavily over her head.

Unexpectedly and out of nowhere, she felt two large hands slamming into her back, and then she was tumbling uncontrollably to the ground. Looking around to see who the perpetrator was, she was shocked to see the man who only moments ago had been drowning.

"Why are you here? Where's the lifeguard?" Val was getting to her feet, shouting at the man who was now running away backwards in a mocking fashion.

"Go, fetch, chosen one," he shouted, blowing her a sarcastic kiss, leaving Val standing in the sand.

CHAPTER 5

Under the Sea

"I will, don't you worry," Val shouted indignantly. If she was going to be pushed around by these strange people, it didn't mean she couldn't answer them back. Brushing the sand off her clothes, she began making her way back into the water.

"*Chosen one* was what the old lady had said and now him. Did they know each other? There's obviously some connection between them." Val realised she was muttering and looked around to see if anyone else had spotted her. No, it was all clear, so she started to stride into the waves with a newfound determination.

"I may be the *chosen one*, but chosen for what?" This was frustrating. Val had been an average girl all her life and had tried her hardest to stay in the shadows of the attention tree, but now there was someone who needed her, and she wasn't going to let them down.

Val's was now waist high in cool seawater and there was still no sign of the lifeguard surfacing. Glancing back towards the shore, she couldn't make out anyone else coming to the rescue. She was on her own. The water was now up to her armpits and she knew that she was going to have to swim. With a grunt of frustration, Val lifted her feet off the seabed and started a form of doggy paddle, aiming for the point where she thought the lifeguard had gone down.

Through the crystal water, Val observed far too much sea life swimming near her. She didn't much like fish unless it came in batter with a portion of chips in white paper.

Then, between two waves, about ten feet in front of her, she spotted the lifeguard's float, doing exactly what it was suppose to do - *floating*. He must be close. Val knew that time was of the essence and it was running out. She paddled over to the float and grabbed it, taking a few seconds to catch her breath. "Where are you?" Val put her face in the water. Opening her eyes and blinking away the salty sting, she spotted him. He was resting on the bottom, his blond hair swaying softly in the current, about fifteen feet below her. He looked lifeless and Val knew she had to act fast. Taking a large breath, she released the float and let her body relax. With a little help from her very heavy jeans, she began her descent, like a deep-sea diver. Lower and lower she went and within a few moments she was standing on the bottom next to the body of the lifeguard.

Val knew she was rapidly losing her air supply and panic was setting in. She reached down to grab his arm, but he was far too heavy to lift that way. As she let out her last stream of air, her lungs began to burn intensely and Val knew that this attempt would have to be it or she was going to lose him for good. Her brain now in a spin with the lack of oxygen she pushed her hands under his arms and gave it every last bit of strength she had in her body. Nothing happened, the lifeguard barely stirred. Val kept trying, knowing that if she didn't rise soon there would be two dead bodies to collect.

Her lungs were bursting; her head was going to explode and still the lifeguard wasn't moving. She knew she couldn't last more than another second or two down here.

Then, just as she let go of him, preparing to fight her way to the surface, something happened. A tingling feeling prickled in her hands and tiny bubbles rose in a stream from her fingertips. Her lungs no longer hurt; her head cleared. With renewed strength, she took hold of the lifeguard and he immediately began to rise. Her hands seemed to be transporting him on a bed of bubbles. The more effort she made, the larger and more aggressive the bubbles became. As they rose together to the surface, Val felt a force pushing them upwards. They seemed to explode onto the surface on a fountain of water. Finally, after what had felt like a lifetime, Val took a deep breath. Never has H^2O been so sweet, she thought, trying to pull the hair out of her eyes. "*Note to self: next time put your hair up.*"

The lifeguard's body was now moving on what looked like an air driven conveyor belt with Val pushing him along. It didn't take long for people on the beach to notice them. When the water was only waist deep, the power of the bubbles diminished and Val was left with a very heavy lifeguard on her hands. People on the beach were watching in amazement and, to her horror, there now seemed to be an abundance of on-lookers moving in their direction. There were also five lifeguards running at speed towards her. 'Where were you twenty minutes ago?' Val thought. Within seconds, the heavy body was being pulled from her and a lifeguard was helping her to the stability of the solid sand.

Delta walked anxiously around the gallery, her best friend was once again missing in action and no one on this planet knew where she was, when she would return or even if she would return. She had received several agitated texts from Val's mother and knew that Val was going to get a good telling off from her mum.

"Shane, how long has it been now?" Shane, who hadn't moved from the spot he had prepared to catch Val on, looked up at the clock.

"Six fifteen. So about half an hour. I'm sure she will be back soon," he said, hoping he was right.

Jason hadn't spoken since Val had gone. He was sitting in silence, staring at the spot in front of him, awed by what he had witnessed. He didn't know Val and didn't understand what was happening to her. Nonetheless, he wanted her back safely, and preferably now.

A young muscular lifeguard pulled a blanket around Val's shoulders. "Are you OK?" Val recognised the accent instantly. She must be on a beach somewhere in America. The irony was that Val hated flying. After seven years of invites, Delta's parents had given up asking, and here she was on a beach in the sunny United States.

"I'm fine. Can I see the man please?" Val pushed the lifeguard off. She needed to get home and from her recent experiences she knew she had to touch the lifeguard.

"In a minute. First I need to know how you did that." The lifeguard blocked Val's path.

"What?" said Val aggressively. She was now getting agitated and scared; she wanted to go home.

The lifeguard grabbed her arm. "He's going to be fine. Don't walk away from me. I still have some questions."

He sounded like a police officer and his hostile suspicious tone scared her even more.

Val was panicking and she could feel herself losing control. This man was stopping her and she didn't know what to do. "Get off me," she said frantically. As she turned to push him off her arm, there was an explosion of air and sand. The lifeguard was thrown several feet through the air, landing with a thud at the feet of a small child holding an ice cream. Val was filled with horror. What had she done? She was shaking, but knew there was a man she needed to touch. So, staying on track, she grabbed her shoes from the sand and ran towards the rescued lifeguard who was still on the ground. As she moved in closer, the man who was administering mouth to mouth pulled back. The lifeguard jerked and coughed out a mass of dirty water. He was taking the first breath of a new life and Val knew this was going to be her only chance. A mob was starting to form behind her, led by a very agitated and sandy lifeguard. Val leapt forward, reaching out to grab his hand. To her delight, the blue spark passed between them and she was gone.

Jason and Shane were still sitting in the same spot when they heard a distant crackling. It was as if they could hear the electricity running through the cables surrounding them. They exchanged looks, each knowing what this meant, and tensed. A second later, a neon spark of light filled the area above their heads. As they looked at it in wonder, the light spread until it was almost three feet wide and suddenly, Val fell out of the gap, her shoes in tow.

Val opened her eyes and once more she found herself in Jason's arms staring into his green eyes.

"We seem to be making a habit of this," said Jason softly. The tender moment was destroyed by Delta who, screaming loudly, piled on top of them, hugging and touching Val. Val, in danger of suffocation for the second time in fifteen minutes gathered her strength. Then, like a rugby player break from a scrum with the ball, she burst from the middle.

"Stand back," she shouted at them, wobbling backwards. Jason, completely dumbfounded by this weird but wonderful creature, obediently stepped back, leaving Delta hanging on Val's leg.

"Well, don't I look silly," said Delta standing up and brushing herself down. "Yuck! You're wet. And covered in sand," she said accusingly. "Look at what you've done to my clothes."

"Oh please..." said Val dropping to the floor again.

Shane, who had been observing in silence, asked, "Are you hurt?"

Val looked up, tears in her eye. "No, not in the way you think." She started to sob.

"Val, I'm going to get you a coffee, don't move," Shane said. "Jason, get her a blanket."

Jason didn't move.

"NOW!" Shane shouted at him and he snapped out of the strange world he was in and ran over to the gym to fetch a blanket.

Delta gently stroked Val's wet hair. "We need to get you home. Your mum is worried."

Val looked up with panic in her eyes. "How does my mum know? Who told her?"

Delta pulled out Val's mobile. "It's OK. I have been texting her all night pretending I was you, but I won't promise you aren't in the doghouse. You'll have some explaining to do when you get in." Delta flashed Val a loving smile and for the first time Val smiled back.

Within seconds there was a blanket around her shoulders and Shane had given her a very hot, very sugary cup of black coffee.

"I'm OK. It's just the shock of teleporting. Don't worry, I will be fine. Anyway, what choice do I have?" Val shrugged her shoulders.

"Where were you?" Jason sat down on the floor next to Val. Val was still embarrassed by Jason's presence and found herself looking at the ground as she told her tale.

"America! Amazing!" Shane sat down next to Jason and they looked like two extremely large reception kids at story time.

"You went to America without me! I just get zapped down the road to a car crash and you get to swim in sunny California." Delta was walking around waving her arms, complaining.

"I scared myself. This guy tried to restrain me and I threw him miles away without even touching him." Val looked almost ashamed of herself.

Shane perked up. "Are you kidding? This is great. Maybe you can protect yourself with your powers. This is good news."

"What powers do you have, Val?" Jason had risen onto his knees eager to hear what Val could do.

"She can't fly," Delta laughed.

"Thank you." Val pulled a face at Delta. "I think that I sort of have the power to control stuff like air, water and fire. I wasn't burnt by the car and I didn't drown today, and that old lady and the lifeguard certainly learnt how to fly. I guess that's about it for now."

"Cool," said Jason nodding at Val.

"Today was the first time I have used them on someone innocent though. It scared me. I need to learn to control myself more." Val was looking at the floor again like a naughty child.

"No, the lifeguard was OK, Val, don't feel guilty. He was trying to make you do something that wouldn't have been safe for you. You did the right thing. You must protect yourself with everything you have, *always*. You are the one with the disadvantage here. Until we can work out how to help you, you need as much power as you can get." Shane lifted Val to her feet. "If you don't get home your mother will do more damage than any of us can repair." He smiled and Val hugged him.

"You are truly special Shane Walker. Come on, Delta," Val pushed her shoes on, "get that mini revved up. We have to get me home before I turn into a pumpkin." She grabbed Delta's hand and they headed out, waving goodbye to the two men who were now officially their partners in crime.

The red mini screeched to a halt outside Val's house, arriving in record time. As Val pulled her fingers out of the handrail and got out of the car, she considered her stomach was more messed up now than when she shifted uncontrollably through time.

"Thanks for texting my mum, Delta. Once again you have come through for me." Val leant into the car and went to hug Delta.

"There is far too much of this going on at the moment, so let's just call it a day for the full contact sports. I will call you in the morning." Delta waved at Val who jumped back just in time to escape being maimed by the mini's door as it slammed shut.

Val looked at her front door. "Well, as Elvis said, 'it's now or never'."

As Val passed the threshold she heard her mother calling her from the lounge.

"Val, quick! Come here. You have to see this." This wasn't quite what she had been expecting, although anything below a scream was good. She entered the lounge nervously. The TV was on and, instead of demanding to know where she'd been, her mother signalled her to watch.

The red flag on the screen said *Breaking News*. A slim, redheaded female was talking. "This afternoon, on a Californian beach, tourists were witness to a miracle." Val watched in awe as she appeared on screen. Although blurry, Val knew it was her, walking on water.

"I have seen this twice now, Val and if I hadn't known you were working till late for that slave driver, Gallymore, I would have sworn that was you," said Susan.

Val let out a thin laugh. Her parents both looked at her.

"You look a mess!" Susan exclaimed.

Val smiled pulling her hair behind her ear realising she was still slightly wet.

"You OK, Val?" asked Mike looking concerned.

"I'm fine, just tired. Is there any food?" Stupid question really. Tescos called them if they had a shortage.

"There is a plated dinner in the microwave, honey." Susan smiled at Val. "Three minutes should be enough. Go and eat. You do look tired. And have a bath, your hair looks a mess." Susan turned back to the TV. "See if you can find it on another channel, Mike. I want to watch her again."

Mike started to flick and Val took the opportunity to leave them to it.

Making her way into the kitchen, Val moved to the microwave and turned the knob to nuke her dinner. Once it was done she sat down at the table to eat, but it was hard work. She was so tired that she could hardly keep her eyes open while she chewed each mouthful. However, Val knew that if Jason was going to train her in the arts of boxing and fencing, she was going to need every bit of energy she could muster.

After a few minutes, she left her empty plate in the sink and headed up to the bathroom. Catching her reflection in the mirror, she grimaced. "Wow, that's grim." She took off one her shoes and a thin stream of golden sand started to fall to the floor. "Fantastic!" Val shrugged. The other shoe was full of sand too; she tipped the rest down the toilet. Throwing her washing in the basket, she checked that her mum and dad weren't about, then sneaked back to her room with a towel around her.

Walking in, she let out a grunt of annoyance. Her mum had obviously not been in to her room and so she still had no bedding after stripping her bed that morning. She slipped into her pyjamas and, for about ten seconds, contemplated going out to the airing cupboard for some clean sheets before falling onto the bed and into a deep and restless sleep.

Val opened her eyes to the darkest ebony night she had ever seen. Raising her head to the sky, she could see a million shiny stars. Looking down she realised she was in her adorable black dress and cloak. The material they were made of felt like the bags her mum bought bulk potatoes in. "Quality," she mumbled to herself.

In the distance, someone was calling her name. They weren't calling 'Val', but something else. Nonetheless, it felt right. They called again and, as her eyes grew accustomed to the dark, she noticed a group of people, all dressed in cloaks like her, standing around a fire, in the middle of some trees.

One turned to face Val, and she recognised the woman from her previous dream. She was beckoned to Val to join them. As Val made her way over, she became aware of the damp earth beneath her feet. "Fabulous no shoes again."

Val joined the circle. There were six of them in total, although she didn't recognise any of them.

The woman who had beckoned Val lowered her hood. "We will make our move soon. Too many of our brothers and sisters have been murdered." The group made noises of agreement and Val joined in.

"The chosen-one is nearly ready." The group began a chorus of cheers.

"He will not win; we need to take action at the rising of the full moon. It's our only chance." Once again, everyone chorused their agreement. Then silence rested upon them and one-by-one they started to disperse. Val stood, not sure what to do. Then a figure from the other side of the fire made its way towards her. Val could see it was a young man. Maybe he was one of Val's friends.

"Hello," she said, thinking that maybe exchanging a few words with him would help open the chains of communication. It didn't work and, as he stopped in front of her, she realised that only the bottom half of his face was visible.

"So... nice evening." She tried again, hoping he would speak.

The man put his finger under Val's chin, lifted her face and moved in closer, placing a passionate, knee-buckling kiss on her lips.

Val woke with a jerk. Her cheeks felt warm. She felt embarrassed about a kiss, in a dream. How crazy was that? She knew for certain it was a dream, but it had felt so real. Slowly pushing herself up, she thought about what the cloaked figures had been saying. Many innocent people had apparently died, but, she wondered, were they dead? Strangely, that was also what Shane had said. Did his friend know more than he was letting on? After all, he had found those pictures really quickly. More importantly, what could she do about any of it? They were just dreams and a picture from four hundred years ago. It made no sense, but she felt an underlying sense of danger. Hadn't she nearly died under the sea? Wouldn't that old lady have killed her if she'd had the chance? As she lay back down, trying to make sense of it all, her head began to pound. She would need to find some answers to these questions, but the only thing that loomed ahead was another day at work.

After a slow start, Val's morning was going to plan. Delta had called early to organise a picnic lunch at the bookshop. Although Val was sure that Delta was doing this so that she could keep an eye on her, she didn't mind. Delta's picnics were amazing (obviously Delta didn't make them; that's why they were so fantastic) and it would break up her day.

As she moved around the shop, she realised she was starting to get the hang of things. Most of her customers knew where to find the books they wanted, and so they came and went easily, and sales were improving.

She was serving a young woman in the Classic Romance section when she heard her mobile going off behind the counter.

"Please excuse me. I will be back in two seconds." The woman nodded and continued to browse the books. Val made her way to the counter and grabbed her phone. The screen flashed: number withheld. Val flipped it open. "Hello."

"Hi Val. It's me, Jason." It was great to hear his voice, although Val didn't remember giving him her number.

"Before you ask, Delta gave me your number yesterday. You have a boxing lesson at twelve fifteen today." Val's mouth dropped open. "Oh, and before you try to get out of it with the excuse you are having lunch with Delta, I have already spoken to her and she is bringing the picnic here." Val still had her mouth wide open. She really wasn't happy now. Sharing one of Delta's picnics wasn't part of the deal.

"Hello, are you still there? You aren't saying much." Jason asked.

"Yes, I'll be there, but only because you have hijacked my lunch." Val flipped the phone shut and went back to the woman who was still looking as confused as she had when Val left her.

"OK, romance is what you want, then romance is what we will give you." The woman smiled as they both started to look at books together.

Val helped the woman choose a suitable book. As Val was taking her money at the counter, the front door flew open and a large wooden crate came flying in. Val stared at the doorway wondering what was happening. She smiled in relief as a delivery man followed, kicking the crate the last few feet into the shop.

"Thank you once again for visiting us and please come back again." Val handed the woman her bag and watched as she negotiated her way around the box and out of the shop. "Wallace Fredrick Gallymore here, luv?" asked the delivery man who Val could not only see but smell.

"No, I will sign for it, thanks." Val signed the clipboard he thrust at her then, manoeuvring around the counter, she ushered him out before she passed out from his pungent fumes.

Looking at the box, Val decided that it was too close to lunchtime to begin unpacking the books now so, with a large amount of effort, she pushed it out of the way, next to the mangled water cooler. 'How does he expect me to put more books on the shelves, the shop is close to bursting as it is?' Val wondered before she turned back to help another customer.

By twelve, Val was seriously in need of food, so she locked up promptly and made her way to Shane's. As she crossed the road, she was met by Delta and two rather large men. She was showing off her mini and they seemed genuinely engrossed in what she had to say.

"Hi Val, please meet my new friends." Delta opened her arm towards one of the men. "This is Butch and the other gentlemen is Sunny"

"Hello," Val said, giving a small wave in their direction. "So, have you all come to watch me get beaten within an inch of my life?" Butch perked up. "Do you need any help?"

"Well Butch, if you want to have a go at Jason, Shane's son, before he gets to me then yes please."

Butch grinned an almost tooth-free smile. "No thanks. I've seen what he can do. I think he might even be better than his dad, but don't tell him I said that."

Val held a hand up for Butch to stop talking and walked past them into the shop. As she entered, she saw Shane was working, decorating a woman's arm with a huge tattoo of a tiger. He smiled up at her and signalled for her to go out back. "I'll wait for you, Shane." Val started to move towards a chair.

"GO!" said Shane sharply, staring at her.

"I'm going," Val retorted insolently kicking at the floor as she mooched out of the parlour and into the gallery.

In the gym, Jason was already working out. He was wearing tracksuit bottoms and a very flattering sleeveless top. Val couldn't help taking in the moment and adding it to her mental photo album of Jason.

"Hi Xena." Jason jogged towards her, wiping his sweat away with a neck towel. Val wasn't sure where to look until a familiar voice came up from behind her.

"Personally I call her Alien; I think it suits her better," called Delta. Luckily for her she had the picnic in her hands and Val didn't want to damage it, otherwise she would have started her boxing practise on her.

"Grab these, Val." Jason threw a pair of black boxing gloves at her. They had white spots at the ends and lightning bolts down the sides with the word Zeus across the wrists. Val had to admit she quite liked the way they looked.

"Have you ever done any boxing before?" asked Jason.

Delta burst out laughing. "She couldn't do a round with mother Teresa," she sniggered.

"No, to be honest I've never even been in a scuffle at school." Val blushed and Jason smiled back.

"Then let's get you started. Pop on your gloves." Val put one on, closing the Velcro with ease. The second one wasn't as simple and after a few seconds Jason came to her rescue.

"I can't even get the gloves on. Don't you think that maybe this is a bad omen and we should stop now?"

Jason shook his head. "Come on, I know you are going to love this."

Val followed him over to the gym area.

"This is how I want you to stand." Jason positioned his left leg in front of his right, bending his knees slightly. He was softly bouncing and Val followed his movements. "That's great! You are a natural."

Val tried not to show her embarrassment at Jason's comments, but she was secretly quite pleased.

"Let's try a basic jab. I'll give you the moves in numbers to make it easier, OK?"

Val nodded.

"Don't go over nine. She isn't good with double figures," Delta teased, dipping celery into some dip that looked mouth-watering.

"That's OK, we're only going to eight," Jason shouted back.

"Well, I'm so pleased you two are getting on so well," said Val.

Jason pushed Val with his elbow to get her attention back on track. "I'm going to stand in front of you with this pad. I want you to punch forward, through from your foot into your hips and hit the spot. Make sure your wrist is flat."

Val nodded.

"Do it slowly until you get it right. This is number one."

Val slowly swung her hips and landed a punch on Jason's pad. She grinned. It actually felt good; maybe she was going to like this.

"OK Val, now I want you to really go for it." Jason nodded at her as if ready for her punch.

"Kill him tiger," shouted Delta who was now onto some chocolate thing that looked out of this world.

Val aimed and let go. It wasn't quite as hard as she would have liked, but it seemed fine to her.

"OK, good. Now this time I want you really go for it. Think of someone you don't like and release the inner anger."

Who didn't she like? She couldn't think of anyone. Then the images started to rush in. She saw the man knocking her to the ground in the shop, the old lady ranting at her and, to top it off, remembered the man pushing her over on the beach. The anger was giving her pains in her stomach and she let it go full force.

She planted her glove on the spot in the centre of the pad, letting out a massive grunt. The pad started to move away from her. And so did Jason.

"Oh my God, Jason!" Delta yelled.

Jason was about ten feet away sitting on his bottom.

Val was mortified. "I'm so sorry! I was just so angry, remembering all that stuff…" She ran over to him and knelt down.

He was grinning from ear to ear. "That was fantastic! You're amazing," he enthused, visibly exhilarated. "This is going to be so much fun," he laughed.

Delta poked Val's arm. "If you ever hit me, Saunders, I will tell your mum, do you understand?" Val turned and showed her glove to Delta, puckering up her lips.

Jason stood stand up, rubbing his back. "I think that will do for now. Lunch looks like it's ready."

The gym door opened and in walked Shane. "How is it going, guys?" he asked, pushing against Val's gloves. Val pushed back playfully.

"Well Dad, she hit me once and knocked me clean across the room. That's about it," answered Jason while Delta nodded in agreement.

"Are you being serious?" Shane looked between Jason and Val. Jason patted Val on the back.

"Yep. All we need to do is teach her the other punches without making her mad," said Jason gleefully pulling a silly face.

Shane was checking Jason out for damage.

"Dad, I'm fine, get off," Jason laughed as his dad obviously hit a sensitive part.

"All this chatting is making my Pak Choy wilt. Will you please come and get something to eat. Maria spent hours preparing this." Delta was waving a piece of lettuce at them. Shane, Jason and Val all started to laugh as Delta walked away.

"Now we are all seated, I need to tell you guys about my dream." Everyone looked eagerly at Val as if she was about to blurt out that Harry Potter was coming back for another book. She explained about the gathering and the woman, and what she had said, and that there had been something about a full moon. She left out the fact she had had a passionate kiss with a stranger.

Shane's brow was wrinkled in thought. "So what did she mean by *chosen one*. Have you heard anything like this before?"

"Well, the man who pushed me over on the beach called me the chosen one and the old woman did as well."

"OK, so you are chosen, but what for?" Delta looked at the others and the blank expressions that came back making it quite clear that no one had a clue.

"I get confused. She said I was nearly four hundred years her senior." Val shrugged and gave a feeble grin. "It doesn't make much sense, does it?"

"Well I have always told you to moisturise before bed but you just won't listen," Delta mocked, successfully lightening the mood.

"This could be really important, girls. We need to know everything they said to you. It will help us build a picture." Shane looked sternly at Val and Delta.

"I need to tell my friend about this, it could help him. Jason, remind me to call him later on."

Jason agreed and they all started to eat again.

Val glanced down at her watch. "Got to go, guys." Standing up she grabbed yet another chocolate brownie. "Tell Maria she can do this again any day."

Shane escorted Val out. He had closed the shop for lunch, and outside a queue of people was waiting for his attention.

"Will we see you tomorrow for another lesson?" asked Shane turning the key and pausing before opening the door.

"Yes OK, as long as Mr Gallymore isn't there, I'll come over. Thanks for everything and I'm sorry if I hurt Jason."

Shane grinned. "Don't worry, he can look after himself." As he pulled the door open and Val pushed her way out, a very hairy man pushed his way in.

Val waved as she walked away. "See you tomorrow."

Sauntering her way back to the shop, she took in the glory of the afternoon sun. Cars passed and people carried on as normal. The world was still turning, despite the phenomenon that Val was living through.

When she got back, she was pleased to find a few people loitering outside the shop, waiting for it to re-open.

"Good afternoon," Val greeted them cheerfully, letting them in.

Val hustled behind the counter; she had books to put back on shelves and various jobs to keep her going. She really couldn't be bothered with the crate that was staring at her from the other side of the shop. She was sure that it could wait until her quiet time tomorrow morning.

Val was cleaning the front window when she spotted Delta's mini pulling up outside.

"What are you doing here?" Val shouted out of the shop door.

"I tried ringing you. Why aren't you answering your mobile?" asked Delta raising her hands.

"I haven't heard it ring." Val put her hand in her pocket, no phone.

"Are you looking for this?" Delta waved Val's mobile in the air.

"Oh, what would I do without you, Yankee?" Val climbed down from her ladder. "Want a coffee?"

Delta nodded. "Well I might as well stay for a while. The boys and I were worried." She handed Val her phone. "Try to keep your head screwed on, Val," Delta said, smiling at a geeky looking man with thick glasses who was reading a book in the entrance, then turning to pull a face at Val behind his back.

"Are you going to be helping me this afternoon or just insulting my clientele?" asked Val. Delta picked up the duster and waved it at Val as she walked off. Val was shocked but decided for once to leave the sarcasm on the table and accept a helping hand.

It was such a lovely day that Val decided to open the shop doors wide in the hope of attracting more passing trade. She really wanted to show Mr Gallymore she could do well. There was quite a large number of people on the street and as Val said goodbye to a client she spotted Wendy out of the corner of her eye making a beeline for the bookstore. Val turned away, quickly beginning to close the doors.

"Are we closing early?" Delta came up behind Val.

"No! It's Wendy. If she knows I work here we will never get rid of her."

"Too late" Delta muttered. Wendy was already in the door and browsing. "Bite the bullet, Val. Yes she is skeletal, but she hasn't done anything wrong." Val had to agree. Although she didn't much like the girl, Delta was right, she hadn't done anything wrong.

"Hi Wendy." Val swallowed hard and walked over.

"Val! So, you buy your books here as well. We have so much in common."

Val walked behind the counter to give Wendy a clue.

"Oh, you work here! Wow! What a great job. I come here all the time." Then she spotted Delta. "I see your friend is here too. Does she work here?" Wendy's smile had visibly dropped.

"No, she doesn't," Delta responded, from behind Wendy.

"So, how can I help you on this fine day?" enquired Val, needing to get Wendy and Delta apart before there were claws at dawn.

"I was just looking for some summer reading material. Don't worry, I know my way around." Wendy walked off and Val let out a sigh of relief.

"She is such a freak. Why did you let her in?" asked Delta.

Val couldn't believe her ears. "You told me to!"

Delta looked shocked. "Next time I do that, punch me HARD."

Val nodded in agreement and left to make them a drink.

Val and Delta were chatting at the counter as they drank their coffees when Wendy returned with her chosen purchases. As Val looked at Wendy's books she began feeling a little disturbed, but it wasn't her business what Wendy chose to read and she of all people shouldn't be judgmental. She bagged them quickly.

"That will be twenty-three pounds please."

Wendy opened her purse to pay Val. "Well, now I know you are here, I'll try and get back in soon. Maybe we could have coffee one day?" Wendy smiled at her.

"That would be lovely," replied Val while Delta pretended to be sick in the background.

Wendy, suddenly suspicious, turned to find Delta standing statuesquely still behind her.

Picking up her bag she made her way past Delta. "You take care now, Selta."

"It's Delta," Delta fumed.

"Oh sorry, I always get those weird names wrong," responded Wendy as she left the shop.

Val dashed around the counter grabbing Delta by the arm. "Oh my... That girl has more problems than you could imagine. You should have seen the books she was buying."

"What do you mean?" Delta was intrigued.

Val checked to make sure Wendy was out of sight. "She bought five books about witchcraft," Val whispered.

Delta's eyes widened. "Do you think she is a witch?"

"Well, she isn't training to be a mechanic now is she?" Val joked. "Anyway look at the time," said Val pointing to her watch. Delta looked at the watch; it was five minutes to five. "Great. Let's get this place locked up and you home in time for dinner today."

Val couldn't have agreed more.

As they pulled up outside Val's, Susan was weeding the front lawn.

"Hello Delta. Well at least one person can get Val home on time, thank you honey. Do you want to stop for tea?" she asked, placing her gloves in the bucket in front of her.

"Will you have enough?" enquired Delta sweetly.

Val nearly choked.

"I'm sure I can put a bit more on if necessary," Susan smiled.

"That would be lovely, Mrs Saunders."

Val pinched Delta.

"What?" said Delta shrugging her shoulders.

"You are such a creep." Val mimicked Delta, "If you have enough, Mrs Saunders." Val curtsied.

"You are just jealous because you have the personal skills of an adult slug." Delta flicked her hair and followed Susan indoors.

"Whatever." Val followed them both.

Mike was already at the kitchen table. As usual, his head was buried in a book. "Hello girls," he said, keeping his eyes on his page.

"Good afternoon Mr Saunders. How's the swing?"

Mike instantly looked up. Delta was so good at picking up your favourite thing and asking you just the right question. Val's dad was an avid golfer, and had played many rounds with Delta's dad when he was in the country. "Well, thank you for asking, Delta. I'm having a very good season."

Delta turned and grinned at Val like a Cheshire cat.

They ate dinner together, laughing and joking. Val looked at them, enjoying the fact that she still had normal times in her life. She felt that as long as she did, she could deal with the crazy parts. Delta also had Mike and Susan wrapped around her little finger, which gave Val a break from being the only child and centre of attention.

"Do you girls want some ice-cream?" Susan asked.

"Yes please. We'll take it upstairs." Val grabbed two bowls brimming with various flavours of her favourite Ben & Jerry's. "Come on Delta." Val walked out of the room, leaving Delta to give her compliments to the chef before following Val upstairs.

"Do you know how lucky you are to have your parents at home, Val?" Delta said affectionately. Val knew that Delta missed her parents who travelled abroad on a regular basis.

"Well you can have mine anytime you want. I'm sure they prefer you to me."

As they entered Val's room, she felt a twitch in her arm, not as bad as it had been in the past, but it was getting hot. She placed her ice cream on the bedside table and lifted her shirtsleeve.

"What's wrong, Val?" Delta asked, putting her ice cream down as well.

"I don't know. It hurts, but not as badly as it has been in the past."

They both inspected Val's arm. A symbol that resembled a swirl was red and inflamed.

"That's Leo," said Delta looking quite pleased with herself.

"It's what?" All of a sudden, Val couldn't hear Delta for the TV that was now blaring out in her room.

"I said it's Leo. Are you deaf?" Delta stood directly in front of Val, practically shouting into her face.

"Let me turn the TV down. I can't hear a thing," Val shouted waving her hands by her ears.

As she turned towards the TV, the screen showed a young woman hanging off a building's roof. She seemed to be crying hysterically. "Mum must be watching CSI downstairs. She loves those police crime programmes." She reached out to turn the TV down. As she touched the switch, she disappeared.

CHAPTER 6

All that Burns Isn't Fire

Delta was left alone in Val's room. "Fantastic," she exhaled. "Another evening in by myself." Then she grabbed her mobile and started to dial. "Hi. She's gone again. I don't know. She was saying something about the TV being loud, but it wasn't even on." Delta sighed. "No I can't come over I'm stuck in her room with her mum and dad downstairs. I need to stay put. I'll give you a call when she gets back." Delta popped the phone back in her pocket, picked up her ice-cream bowl and sat on the bed, beginning to dig in. "No point in waiting for you," she said to the TV, raising her ice cream bowl towards where her friend had just disappeared, as if raising a glass of champagne.

Landing on the hard pitch of the flat roof, Val fell clumsily into one of those forward-rolls you learnt at school. Skidding to a halt, her face scraping along the wall, she dropped backwards onto her bottom and let out a wheeze of air.

Trying to absorb her surroundings, she sat still for a second. Touching the tender spot on her grazed cheek she wondered what she would tell her mum this time.

"Sorry Mum, I got intense paper cuts from a book trying to sand my face." That's when she heard the whimpers.

"Help! – Help!" a faint, tearful voice called out. Val leapt to her feet and ran across the roof in the direction of the cries.

"I'm coming. Hold on," Val called, spotting the white curled fingertips on the opposite side of the roof. As she approached, Val threw herself full force against the wall. Placing her knees as anchors against the red bricks, she looked over the top. The building looked at least seven floors high and, taking a quick glance at her surroundings, she seemed to be enclosed by several buildings of the same style.

Glancing down, she came face to face with a very petrified, very plump young woman. "Take my hand." Val reached out and the woman instantly grabbed it. "Now the other one. It's going to be OK." Val smiled at her, although it became a mixture of smile and grimace as she felt the strain on her arms. Val struggled with the woman's weight. Val guessed by the strain on her back that she must be at least sixteen stone. That was six stones heavier than Val.

"Don't let me go!" cried the woman.

Val nodded mechanically; too busy contemplating how much her arms were going to hurt once she had stopped trying to stretch them. Under normal circumstances she was sure she couldn't do what she was doing now; her strength seemed to be intensified when she teleported.

"Nearly there, come on." Val gave a final heave and a split second later, they were both falling back onto the roof. Lying together looking up at the first evening stars, they gasped for breath. The woman was still clutching

Val's hands, as if she afraid she might fall again. "Thank you," said the woman, finally letting go of one hand and pushing at a clump of black hair that had fallen onto her. "My name's Sarah. Who are you?"

"You're welcome, and I'm Val," she replied, still out of breath.

After a few more moments of recovery, Val asked, "Do you mind telling me why you were hanging off the top of a very large building?"

The woman looked at Val with a deeply embarrassed expression. Val had the feeling that she wasn't going to like the answer.

"You'll think I'm crazy and to be honest so do I at this very moment in time." Sarah started to sit up, nervously straightening her clothes with her free hand. "I was meeting someone I met on a friendship-website on the internet."

Val sat up. "Do you mean a date?"

"Yes. He was a man called John. I had been talking to him for several weeks and he seemed so nice. I thought this was going to be our romantic first meeting." Sarah looked at the floor with a far away expression.

"Why here?"

"He said he worked here and I had no reason to doubt him," Sarah said.

"What went wrong? It's slightly extreme to throw someone off a building just because you don't like the way they looked," Val said.

"I didn't even get to see him." Sarah's expression became one of anger as she spoke. "I arrived to find a single red rose resting on the wall. I was so blinded by excitement that I rushed over to grab it. That was when something hit me from behind. The rest is history."

Sarah was now beginning to stand and she released Val's other hand as she moved back towards the edge that moments earlier had nearly been her demise.

Rearing out of the silence, Val heard a phone ringing. She looked around and spotted an emergency phone on the wall near the exit from the roof. Unable to ignore a ringing phone and hoping that it might be someone who had witnessed what had happened and wanted to help them, Val lifted the receiver.

"Hello," Val said hesitantly.

"Hi Val," a smooth female voice responded. "Did you think that was easy?" Val felt a sharp pain in her chest.

"I've had harder," she replied dryly, realising that this was one of those lovely people who just wanted to enhance her existence. "Who are you? What do you want with me?" Val yelled down the receiver. There was a moment's silence and Val wondered if the woman had gone. Then she heard her voice again.

"Here is what I want, chosen one - five, four, three…"

Val looked at Sarah, who was standing at the edge of the building, her body filling with fear.

"…two, one."

Val screamed "Sarah" and threw herself onto the ground, covering her head with her arms.

Sarah turned, luckily understanding, and instantly followed suit as a massive explosion shook the foundations of the building.

Alarms began ringing and, below them, people started screaming and running in all directions. Val lifted her head searching for Sarah through a thick cloud of dust. "Are you OK?" Val spotted her and crawled in her direction.

Sarah nodded.

"We need to get out of here and now!" Val said urgently, grabbing Sarah's hand, and standing up making their way towards the roof top door.

As Val reached out to grab the handle, Sarah pulled Val's hand back sharply. "Look, there's smoke coming under the door. It's not safe. We can't go that way." Sarah dropped down to the floor pushing her head between her knees and beginning to sob.

"Now is not the time to give up," Val said firmly, grabbing Sarah's arm and hauling her to her feet. "So you had a bad date; at least you got one." "You just get back on up and start again, that's what my mum says."

Val was trying to find a way to get them out of this. She talked to Sarah, trying to keep her distracted, as she pulled her along the edge of the building. "So, what do you do for a job?" she asked.

"I'm a volunteer Samaritan and a part time drugs councillor," Sarah replied.

Val smiled, nodding as if she was interested. Suddenly she spotted the way out.

"Sarah look! There are some emergency steps on this side of the building. We need to drop about five feet onto the first one as they have moved with the explosion, but then we are home free. Coming?" Val held a beckoning hand out to Sarah.

"You're crazy, has anyone told you that?" Sarah said as she grabbed Val's hand and lifted herself onto the wall again.

"I tell myself that all the time. Now let's go." Val climbed up next to Sarah. "Let's do it." Their hands clasped tightly together, they jumped onto the metal staircase, landing with a thud that made the whole thing shake violently. Sarah grabbed onto Val until the stairs steadied themselves.

Looking down Val saw a redheaded woman watching them.

"Hey you! Call the police. We need help," Val called out.

The woman looked up at Val and gave her an officer's salute before turning to run.

"Did that woman just salute you, Val?" quizzed Sarah.

"Yes, I do believe she did." Val hated these people. What was their problem? However, now wasn't the time to start analysing, there were far more pressing issues at hand, like life. "Let's go Sarah." Val pushed Sarah towards the first set of steps. As they began to climb down Val heard the sirens closing in. At least assistance would soon be at hand. They climbed down the next two flights with speed and Val began to think that they would be off this towering inferno soon enough.

Then something changed; they were in danger; she could feel it. Val instinctively came to a halt, grabbing Sarah's arm.

"What's wrong?" Sarah asked.

"Shh…" Val put her finger to her lips.

They stood silent and motionless. Val heard a rumbling sound, almost like a train as it draws closer. Looking through a window into the building, Val saw empty desks and upturned chairs where people had run for their lives only moments earlier. At the back of the room, a small but rapidly growing ball of flame was moving towards them at speed.

Val grabbed Sarah, pushing her onto the metal stairs, pressing her own body on top of Sarah's as the ball of flame exploded through the closed window. The flames stroked Val's back as the glass shattered all around her. Several thoughts were rushing through her head at that moment. One was how pleased she was that the incident with the burning car several days earlier hadn't been a one-off and she was officially flame proof.

Once the flames had retracted, Val and Sarah stood up. Val could see that not only had their level exploded, but so had another three levels below them, taking out the lower level stairs. Thick black smoke was now bellowing out of the window. They were stuck, like Robinson Crusoe, on a building that was struggling to stand.

"We need to go into the building," Val shouted to Sarah.

"Are you mad? It's on fire if you hadn't noticed, and why the hell aren't you on fire!" Sarah screamed hysterically at Val.

"Don't ask questions, there isn't time. Just do as I say. I know I can keep you safe." Val climbed through the glassless window.

"I can't believe I'm doing this. When I get home my computer is going in the bin," Sarah chuntered to herself, shaking her head in disbelief.

They were walking into the belly of the fire. Val knew that she would be OK, but how was she going to keep Sarah safe?

"Get down low, the air is cleaner there," she ordered, pushing Sarah down. She needed to find a way out that wouldn't strip Sarah not only of her clothes, but her flesh as well. On the other side of the office there was an exit. Val need to see what was on the other side of the door.

"Stay here, I'll be back in a second," said Val.

"I wasn't going to do anything else," Sarah replied coughing as she lay down.

Val walked across the room oblivious to the heat coming from the walls. She placed her hand on a slightly melted handle and opened the door. In that instant, a ball of fire engulfed her entire body. Behind her, she heard Sarah's screams of horror. After a few seconds, the power of the initial flames died down and Val was once again visible. Sarah now fell into complete silence. Val looked about her. She could see the stairs. She needed to get Sarah down there.

"Sarah I need you to move quickly, can you do that?" There was no response. Val turned, worried that Sarah had been overtaken by fumes, but she was just beyond words. "Sarah! Come to me, *now*!" Val shouted, holding out her hand to Sarah.

Although still in shock, Sarah crawled her way obediently to Val's side. Val pulled her up.

"Are you an angel?" Sarah asked, looking into Val's eyes.

"No, just lucky I suppose. Now let's get out of here." Val pulled her body around Sarah's as much as humanly possible, shielding her through the flames. They just needed to make it down the three flights of stairs to freedom.

Sarah cried out in pain. Her arms and legs were beginning to blister with the intense heat. Val could feel her body shaking, but she had no other plan and was sure that if they hadn't come this way they certainly would have died.

When they reached the final floor, Val heard banging from the other side of what looked like the main door. Sarah was passing out with the pain and Val was struggling to keep her upright. Then, with a final bang, the door burst open and there, just visible through the smoke, stood a fireman, fully hooded and with a large axe in hand. Val knew she had done what was needed. She laid Sarah down and held her hand. "Goodbye Sarah." Within a second of the blue spark passing between them, the fireman found Sarah lying alone at the bottom of the stairs, babbling deliriously about how an angel had saved her.

Val felt herself slipping towards her destination with a feeling of completion. She arrived on her knees in front of her TV, with quite a large thump. Her best friend was engrossed in a glossy magazine. Delta's reaction was slightly different from her earlier one. There was no jumping with excitement and no hugs this time, but the look of relief in her eyes said it all.

"You OK? Face looks a mess," Delta said, trying for the casual effect, as she looked up from her magazine.

"Yes thanks, explosions, burning buildings, large women. Yup, that just about explains it." Val put her head down on the bed for support.

"Everything OK up there, girls? I heard a bang." called Susan.

"Yes its fine thanks, Mum," Val answered.

Delta moved over and patted Val's shoulder. "Any more of those strange people this time?"

"Yes, she was a bad red-head. I'm sick of this, Delta. I swear that I'm going to find out what they want, and then I'm going to deal with these people," Val said with a very determined look on her face. Rising up and starting to pull off her clothes, Val reached into a drawer and pulled out a pair of pyjamas. She explained all the details of her expedition as she changed and Delta listened attentively to her story. When Val had finished Delta stood up.

"It's late, I should leave. You're being honest when you say everything's OK?" Delta looked at Val with a schoolteacher's expression.

"Yes. I may not have a choice in this, but don't forget there are only eight more symbols on my arm now." Val lifted her pyjama sleeve to show Delta. "If this keeps up, I will have none in less than two weeks," said Val.

"That's great news, I think. Now, put it away," Delta replied.

They walked down the stairs in silence. Val's parents were still in the kitchen chatting. They often stayed up until the early hours putting the world to rights.

"You leaving, Delta?" Susan called.

"Yes, Mrs Saunders. Thank you for my dinner," Delta replied from the hall.

"You're welcome, honey. Come over whenever you want," Susan said.

"OK Val, I'll come and see you in the morning. Try to get some sleep and don't pop off if you can avoid it." Delta turned and trotted off to her mini.

Val closed the door behind her and headed back upstairs before her mum had a chance to see the state of her cheek.

As she walked back into her room she spotted the two empty ice cream bowls on the side and smiled to herself as she thought of Delta stuffing her face with Ben & Jerry's. She opened her wardrobe to look in the mirror at her cheek. It wasn't as bad as it felt and a medium sized plaster would cover the worst. She closed the door and fell into bed and a deep sleep.

Val could feel her heart was beating fast as, once again, she found herself running through the forest towards her friends. She heard the familiar crackling noise that came before the ball of light, but then it stopped as suddenly as it had started, and so did everything else. A leaf that was falling in front of her seemed to be hanging in mid-air. Val looked up and a blackbird was suspended with both wings extended, held in the middle of a wing's beat. So if everything had stopped, why hadn't she? Val moved cautiously forward.

That's when she felt it. A slow breath, as cold as ice, blew down the left side of her neck. She froze to the spot as another icy breath followed. A white cloud of frozen air slowly appeared around the edge of Val's face. Every hair on her body stood on end.

What was this? She didn't get time to find out. An icy hand came around her elbow and took hold of her arm. "Don't turn around," a deep male voice commanded, speaking directly into her ear. She shuddered as if some-one had just walked over her grave.

"You can't win, chosen one. Time and space can sepa-rate us, but I will destroy you." The breath seemed to be getting colder with every word, if that was possible.

Val felt she had the right to respond although that was possibly not the cleverest option. "I think I can beat you fr... fr... freaks, so maybe we have a battle on our hands," she said. Her lips were so cold that she was struggling to make the words come out.

"You insolent child," the creature bellowed. "You are much deeper than you should be and there is no way out. I will kill them all." The hand released her arm and time started again. Val spun on the spot. He had gone, but she was most definitely still in her dream.

She looked around for something to lean against and heard heavy breathing coming towards her. "Not more," she muttered as a young woman dressed the same way as Val came running towards her with something in her hand. Val was intrigued until she realised that the girl wasn't stopping. It all happened so fast that Val couldn't do anything. The last thing she saw was the book from the shop, then the girl cannoned into her, knocking Val back into consciousness.

Val's eyes opened to daylight streaming in from the window. She's forgotten to close the curtains the previous night. As she got out of bed, she knew exactly what she had to do. She picked up her mobile phone and started to send text messages. She got dressed and within minutes she was ready to go. Making her way downstairs, she prepared to face the music about the state of her face but there was no one there. A note on the counter explained the silence:

Val your dad has gone to work and I have an appointment first thing. Your packed lunch is in the fridge. Love Mum.

PS. I will know if you haven't eaten breakfast.

Val let out a laugh. Val opened the fridge grabbed her lunch and made her way to work.

As she drew nearer the shop, she saw Delta and Jason standing outside on the steps chatting.

"Morning, thanks for coming over so early." Val patted Delta on the arm to make room for her to open the door. "Last night I think I met the thing responsible for the crazy people that are making my life so exciting." Val looked at Jason and Delta, seeing their interested eyes gleaming back.

"What do you mean you met the thing? When I left you were going to bed. Where did you go?" asked Delta.

"He came to me in a dream. It was very similar to the others I've had, but I know this was real. He actually stopped time."

"What did he look like? Did he hurt you? What did he say?" asked Jason.

"Wow, slow down cowboy, one question at a time." Val managed a smile in Jason's direction. "I didn't get to see him. He grabbed me from behind, and no, he didn't hurt me, but he was extremely cold. I don't know if this has any significance, but he told me he was, in so many words, coming to get me." Val's face became sombre. "He was serious and I think he can do it, although I don't know what has stopped him up until now. I don't know how long we will have before he comes, so let's get moving."

Val stepped behind the counter, grabbed three pieces of paper and drew some squares as the others waited in silence.

"There was also a girl in my dream. She was running towards me with the book in her hand." Val hadn't even finished when Delta threw her hand up into the air as if in school.

"Oh, ask me, ask me. I know the answer to this one." Delta grinned at Jason, who found himself wondering exactly what was wrong with these girls. "Was it the Zodiac book?" Delta stuck her tongue out at Jason as if he had lost the quiz.

"Yes, it was and if we have to stay here all day and all night we are going to find it. Here is a rough map of the shop for you both. Mark off any shelves you look at and work down one side and back up the other.

Understood?" Val handed Delta and Jason their sheets with a pen. "OK, let's do it." Val came around the counter and headed off down the first aisle, starting with the first book at the top of the first shelf. Delta and Jason followed suit and headed off down their allocated aisles.

After about an hour, Delta's head popped around Val's aisle. "I need a chocolate fix. Am I allowed to escape for a few minutes?" she asked.

"OK, but don't be long," Val said severely. She had been frightened by her dream. This thing meant business and she knew the book would have the answers.

As Val started to scan yet another section of shelf, she heard the doorbell ring. Someone came into the shop and then she heard her name being called.

"Val, Jason, come here, you need to see this," shouted Delta who had returned from her shopping trip. Val marked off on her paper showing the point she was at, and made her way quickly to the front of the shop.

"Everything OK? You sound excited." Val asked.

Delta stood by the counter with the largest bar of Cadbury's Val had ever seen and a newspaper in the other hand. "Look at the front page, Val." Delta placed the paper on the counter as they all gathered around.

The headlines read: *Doctor saved in car crash becomes hero himself.* As Val read the article, it became clear that the man she and Delta had saved only a few days ago had the very next day saved a young girl from being hit by a car. Val was pleased; it was a bit like a knock-on effect.

"So what do you think?" asked Delta, obviously a lot more excited by the news than Val.

"Well, it's great news." Val shrugged, picking up her paper and pen and then turning to go back to looking for the book.

"Don't you notice any connection? You have saved a doctor, a nurse, a lifeguard and a Samaritan." Delta was waving a large piece of chocolate at her as she spoke.

"Wow, that's true. Look at these people...they all seem to come from some sort of caring profession," said Jason now getting involved.

"Yeah, all this is happening so you can save people who then help others, it's like a mission," said Delta.

"So, I'm on a mission now, am I?" Val smiled. "It's good news, but it isn't the answer to my problems, the book is." Val turned to walk away as Delta grabbed her arm.

"You could be *the disappearing avenger.*" Delta broke off a large piece of chocolate with her free hand. "Whatever you are, you saved someone who then saved a little girl, so ease up on yourself a little, Val." Delta shoved the chocolate into her mouth and handed Val a chunk as she let her arm go. Grabbing her bookshop map, she made her way back down her aisle. Jason nodded in agreement and headed back down his aisle. Val watched them disappear then looked back at the paper. Could Delta be right, was she helping people who were then meant to carry on helping others? Well whichever it was, for a fleeting moment it made her feel good inside. Val popped the chocolate Delta had given her into her mouth.

"Ahh..." there was a scream from Delta's aisle. Val dropped her paper and almost knocked Jason out as they both ran at speed in Delta's direction.

"Go Delta. Go Delta." Val came to a halt in front of her friend who was doing corny circular movements with her arms whilst holding the book.

"You found it! Cool," said Jason.

"Give it to me now!" Val snapped.

Delta stopped in her tracks. "Manners cost nothing, Saunders," Delta retaliated, stopping her dance and holding out the book for Val.

"Sorry Delta, but this book holds all the answers." Val held the book in her hands. "Look at the spine? It only has eight symbols on it, the same as my tattoo." They all looked slightly more in awe of the book now. It was identical to Val's arm, except for the missing symbol in the centre.

"Well, open it," Jason said seeming visibly nervous.

"Yes, this is worse than watching the finals of American Idol." Delta's eyes were now bulging in Val's direction.

Val slowly caressed the cover. "I'm scared." She looked at her friends and smiled. Slowly passing her finger over the lip, she started to lift the cover.

"Should we stand back?" asked Delta.

"Yes, maybe." Val let the lip drop in agreement with Delta.

"Get on with it before I die of old age." Jason waved his hands at Val in a pushing gesture. Val flipped the top and as it lay open in her hand no one could speak for a few moments, they just stared at the book, not sure what to expect.

"There is writing and pictures," Val said stating the obvious nervously.

"Wow Val, it's a book. What did you expect, Einstein?" Delta retorted in a nervous yet sarcastic tone.

"Well clever, the bad news is it isn't in English." Val started turning the pages, annoyed that it was in this strange language and forgetting the fact that only a moment earlier they had all thought that this could be a book from the pits of hell, bringing damnation to all mankind.

"Do you know what it says?" Val handed the book to Jason.

"Why didn't you offer it to me first, I've known you the longest?" Delta walked away from them towards the counter. "I'm hurt. I need more chocolate." She leaned on the counter and began to devour another half pound of Cadbury's. Jason looked at the pages, but shook his head almost instantly.

"I don't have a clue, but I bet Sam could help us."

Val's eyes seemed to double in size almost instantly. "Sam. Who's Sam?"

Jason knew instantly he had messed up and started stuttering and making his way towards Delta.

"Jason, don't make me lose my temper." Val was following Jason towards the shop front.

"Please promise you won't tell my dad what I just said. He will kill me, very slowly," pleaded Jason.

"Tell your dad what?" asked Delta who had been busy comfort eating.

"Sam is the name of our secret friend, but don't tell Shane we know, OK Delta?" Val said, Delta nodded. "OK. We can take it to him later, but for now we can look at the pictures."

Val placed the book on the counter and they started to flick through the pages. Then doorbell rang and to Val and Delta's dismay, in walked Wendy.

"Hello girls." Wendy waved a flimsy hand and Delta waved a piece of chocolate back. "Well, who is your new friend?" Wendy made a beeline for Jason who was trying to move behind Delta.

"She scares me, should I be scared?" Jason whispered into Delta's ear. Delta nodded and Jason stood very still, hoping for the best.

"How can I help you Wendy? Have you read all those books you took yesterday?"

"No, but I can never have enough books." Wendy smiled at Val, walking around her, eyeing her up and down. Then she stood still, both hands resting on the counter. Val realised that the book was lying open in front of her. She felt tense hoping Wendy wouldn't notice it.

"Wow, look at this book!" exclaimed Wendy.

'Well, there goes the not noticing theory,' Val thought. "Yes it's mine." Val hunched her shoulders looking at the others for support.

"I didn't know you could read Theban," said Wendy.

"Theban?" responded Val, falling over herself to get to Wendy's side.

"Yes, Theban, but you must already know that if this is your book?" Wendy turned, surprised to see Val in such close proximity to her.

"Yes I did know, I was just surprised you did," Val said smiling over Wendy's shoulder as she picked up the book. Wendy seemed embarrassed that Val was so close.

"I read a lot, sorry for interrupting your get-together." Wendy turned. "I will go and get the book I forgot yesterday." Wendy shuffled away and left the three of them closely huddled together around the book.

"OK. I'll be here if you need me." Val gave Wendy a small wave. Then she turned towards the others unable to contain her excitement. "Call your Dad, Jason. Tell him to ask Sam if he can help us out with the word *Theban*."

Jason nodded in agreement.

"Val, can you trust Wendy?" questioned Delta.

"Well, it's better than no leads at all." Val closed the book, pulling it behind the counter and putting it in her bag.

It didn't take Wendy long to locate the book she wanted and she paid and left.

"I need to get back to my dad's as I have training with some strange girl at lunch time." Jason smiled as he left.

Val felt that 'thing' she had for Jason spring into her heart, and then she covered it with a concrete blanket. Now wasn't the time for the love thing to be confusing people, although she had to admit as he walked away that she hadn't noticed until now how very nice he looked today. Maybe he had made an effort for her. She smiled to herself.

"Hello, you may think that what you are thinking right now, Val, is safe in your head, but I must inform you that 'cow eyes' combined with drool tend to inform the rest of the world that you are having wicked thoughts about a boy." Delta patted Val's shoulder as she walked past her holding Val's lunch, which she then proceeded to open and devour.

"Thanks Dr Phil," Val laughed. "Do you think we have a book about this 'Theban' thing here?"

"Not sure and sick of looking. Let's have just one miracle book a day, Alien."

Val had to agree that the whole thing had become quite exhausting. At least they had the zodiac book. Although it was great that Wendy had been able to pinpoint something about the book, Val didn't want to explain to the others how odd she found it that Wendy had arrived when she had. Even Wendy's choice of literature was peculiar. Val was learning to work on the side of caution. She would keep her eye on Wendy from now on and keep her suspicions to herself.

Val made her boxing date with Jason and today they slowly moved through the first four punches. Left and right jabs and head hooks. Val was actually enjoying the boxing more than she had thought she would. It wasn't just because she got one-to-one time with Jason; it also made her feel more confident about protecting herself.

Shane was interested to see the book and whilst Val trained, Delta and Shane sat over it with puzzled expressions on their faces, pointing at a picture every so often and even laughing at one or two, which bothered Val.

When they had finished, Jason gave Val a small towel to wipe her face and a hearty pat on the back. Val wasn't sure if this was one of those 'I'm showing you I like you' pats or 'you remind me of my childhood dog' pats.

"Come and look at this Val," Shane called her over.

"What?" Val pulled up a chair behind Shane's, throwing her sweaty towel in Delta's direction.

"You are so dead." Delta flicked it away.

Val flashed her gloves at Delta and laughed as Jason passed her a water bottle.

"OK kids, let's concentrate." Shane looked at them all with stern, grown-up eyes. "Look at this picture Val. Does anyone seem familiar?"

He showed Val an intricate hand drawing of a group of six adults all standing together and looking happy, as if they were rejoicing at something. As Val's eyes scanned the faces, she took a sharp inward breath.

"Val?" Shane looked at her.

"That's her, the woman from my dreams, but why is she in this book?" Val looked visibly shaken.

"Well, maybe your dreams are more like memories," suggested Shane. "You dream about people you know, so maybe you knew her. I have a friend who is a psychic and she believes that we don't live once, we come back again and again." Val looked at Shane.

"So what you are saying is that I know this woman from a past life, one in which I was possibly into some sort of voodoo or magic stuff?" Val asked, clearly not impressed by the idea.

"Well, yes. Let's not forget, you have the ability to walk through fire, and control air and water with your hands," said Shane.

Val sighed. She knew he was right but she wasn't at all sure if she wanted him to be.

"So when will we know anymore about this Theban thing Wendy mentioned?" asked Val.

"Well, my friend is out today working, but as soon as he gets back I'll speak to him," said Shane still scanning the pages. Jason shot Val a look to remind her of the promise she made not to mention his little slip up. Val gave him a nod and he seemed more relaxed.

"Is that your friend Sam, the one Jason was talking about?" asked Delta.

"Delta!" Val moved swiftly over to Delta and pinched her arm.

"Ow! Why did you do that? So Shane's friend is called Sam." Delta just couldn't stop herself now. "Sam, Sam, Sam." Delta jumped up and started to run around the table.

"I'm so sorry, Jason." Val shrugged.

"It's OK. I should have told you his name. I don't know why I didn't," said Shane.

"I'm sorry, Dad, it just slipped out." Jason hung his head.

"Don't worry son, worse could happen." Shane smiled as Delta came around for her fourth lap of the table still singing Sam's name.

"I'm sure at some point you will meet Sam, but he lives in London and doesn't surface often due to work commitments," said Shane.

"Well at least he has a name now. So how will you show him the book?" asked Val.

"Well, real people in the modern world, Val have something we like to call a scanner," replied Shane with a cheeky grin.

"So, another funny man, that's all I need. I have to go back to work, so I'll see you guys later."

"Don't leave me here. Please take me with you. They might make me fight." Delta jumped to her feet running in a Delta fashion towards Val.

"Bye girls," Shane called and Jason waved a hand.

Val opened the bookshop and the first thing that greeted her was the large wooden crate that Mr Gallymore had had delivered the day before. That was a job she needed to do ASAP, before Mr Gallymore turned up.

Delta attempted to help open the box, but it was Val's brute force that won through in the end. As they lifted the lid, a puff of musty smell came oozing out.

"Oh heavens! Do you think there is something dead in there?" Delta peeped over the top.

"Not unless Mr Gallymore is collecting the classics in the form of dead writers, no." Val let out a giggle taking the top off to reveal a mixture of large, small, old and out of print books. Delta appeared with a pair of large yellow rubber gloves on her hands.

"If they have germs on them as old as they smell and they have managed to survive, then they could possibly have what you Brits call the plague." She picked one out of the crate and carried it down an aisle.

"We will be here all night if you do it one at a time." Val started to pack the book trolley with the new, old books as Delta trotted back for another.

As the day came to a close, Val pulled the last of the books from the trolley and placed them on their designated shelves. All the time she was thinking about the book. It could hold all the answers, but without the key to what it said, she might as well not have found it. Delta had made a sorry attempt at helping, but Val was just glad of the company.

"Time to go," Delta called from the counter, jangling Val's keys.

"OK, be there in two," Val called back. As she looked at the worn book in her hand, she thought about how words, written and spoken, created everything we see, how your life could be shaken by one message or one word, good or bad. Then she placed the book on the shelf and slapped herself lightly on the face. "What's wrong with you?" Making her way back to the counter she grabbed her bag.

"You ready?" Val asked as Delta pushed past her in her eagerness to leave.

"Time to have a little fun. I texted Jason. He's going to meet us at that really nice pub in the village," said Delta.

"The Albion?" Val asked.

"Yes. I like it in there, they always give you peanuts with your drink." Delta pulled her car keys out and the lights on the mini flashed as it opened.

"Do I look OK?" Val asked looking herself up and down.

"Yes Val, you look a picture of elegance." Delta opened her door and got in, not even looking in Val's direction.

"So, when are you going to ask him?" enquired Delta, pulling out onto the main road.

"Ask who what?"

"Jason-on-a-date." Delta spat the syllables.

"Are you joking? He isn't interested in me." Val's voice was now so high it was almost squeaking like a choirboy's.

"Well I don't agree. However, you won't know until you ask."

"Then what? If he doesn't it will get awkward and then we lose two of the most important friends we have. That would be a disaster," she replied, trying to hide how much it hurt talking about it. Val placed her head against the car window and closed her eyes. Hoping this would stop Delta asking any more questions.

CHAPTER 7

Going Underground

"OK, here." Delta spun the mini into the car park coming to a halt next to a really smart Harley-Davidson. The rider was in black leather with a black helmet and mirrored visor.

"Now look at that Delta. Looks good, black, dark and sexy, but I bet when he takes off his helmet a long mane of grey hair will fall out and a sixty-year-old man will shoe horn himself out of the leathers." Val and Delta sat for a moment watching the rider turn off his bike and dismount. Then the dark stranger started to walk towards them. When he got to the side of the car, he flipped up his visor.

"Hello girls."

"Hi Jason. Val was just commenting on how you were a sixty-year-old hippie biker," said Delta.

Val sank into her seat. Could this get any worse? Her heart was pounding, he was now not only her dream guy, he had a fantastic bike and he looked gorgeous in leather.

"Well you should never judge a book by its cover," replied Jason opening her car door and offering her his hand.

If Val's head had been any lower, it would have disappeared into her shoulders. She had no choice but to take Jason's hand. As their skin touched, Val felt a shock flash up her arm. She could hear her heart pounding but this was more than what she felt for Jason. A flickering torch light, reflected in the visor of Jason's helmet caught her attention. As she inspected it more closely, she felt her grip on Jason's hand loosening.

"Jason, put the helmet down."

Jason lowered the helmet to the ground, unsure of what exactly was the problem, but knowing better than to argue with that tone of voice.

"Val what's wrong?" he asked.

"They are trapped underground. I can hear them calling out, and I need to help them." Val stepped forward, then looked back at Delta who was running around the back end of the car.

"Don't wait up." Val touched the visor on the ground and she was gone.

Val blinked then blinked again, she felt confused. Were her eyes open yet? All she could distinguish was intense darkness. She rubbed her lids vigorously, but that didn't seem to help the situation. As she started to adjust to the dark she could hear distant voices calling. After several moments, she spotted a flash of light around twenty feet away, moving around like a lighthouse beam through the mist. Lifting herself to her feet to investigate, she crept carefully towards what she thought was a wall, for guidance.

Outstretching her hand hesitantly, Val felt how cold and wet the wall was. When she pulled her hand back, she realised that it had come with her in the form of dirt. "Nice," Val whispered.

She felt apprehensive. Her idea of mud was the stuff under your feet on a rainy day, not on the walls and over your head. As she slowly edged her way towards the voices, she felt something strike her foot. Leaning down she was surprised to see a large pile of hard hats and jackets.

Val grabbed a thick padded jacket, and put what appeared to be a miner's helmet on her head. She reached up and after a few moments fumbling managed to switch on a small torch that was on the helmet's peak. "That's better, now I can see how dark it is," she said, realising the irony and shaking her head.

Val edged forward. The noise began to get louder and Val could make out a solid beam of light ahead. Following it around a small bend to the right, she came face to face with utter chaos. There were men and women shouting and lifting rocks frantically. Val could see that there had been some sort of landslide and these poor people were trapped.

Hopefully not for long if Val could help. Plus, on a selfish note, she wanted to get back to the pub, to Delta and Jason.

"Who are you? Another one of those useless guides come to panic?" A tall thickset man wearing a ski coat and helmet similar to Val's grabbed her by the arm.

"I'm sorry you must..." but before Val could finish her sentence he was talking again.

"Doesn't matter," the man said dismissively. "Have they got any further forward?" He was now looking over Val's shoulder. "I've been back up to the top but the rescue services won't be here for another fifteen minutes."

It dawned on Val that if he had been out and the people she could see were trying to move the rocks, then someone was trapped on the other side.

"So how many people are trapped?" she asked, trying to look as if she was one of those useless yet confident guides.

"Well, we were twenty-five to start with and there are twenty of us now so you do the maths." The man was really not warming to Val and she didn't want to stay in his presence any longer.

"I'm sure someone will be here soon." She smiled weakly, about to move away.

"Yes, shame no one is able to get through the emergency tunnel, it would have made it so much easier for everyone," the man said.

"What emergency tunnel?" Val asked.

"Well, all of these mine walks have a backup passage. They were originally built by the miners, but now they are meant for emergencies only. Although the top one is open, no one has the key to the bottom door. We think the people who are stuck are directly on the other side of it."

This was exactly what Val needed. "This exit, where exactly is it?" Val enquired.

"Over there." The man pointed to a heavy metal door that was ajar. It had a sign on the outside that said 'Staff Only' in bold red letters.

Val now had a plan of action. She would simply go down the shaft and open the door, releasing the trapped people before the emergency services arrived.

"Thanks." Val patted the man on the shoulder as she passed, pushing the heavy door open.

"You can't go down there. The door is locked so what's the point?" The man seemed agitated by Val blatantly ignoring his words. She really didn't have time for explanations, so she just smiled at him and made her way through the gap.

On the other side of the door, the darkness was even more intense than before, if that was possible. Just when she was thinking about going back and finding another light, the door slammed shut behind her.

"No! I'm in here," Val shouted swinging around and kicking the heavy metal door. After another several minutes of disjointed escape attempts, Val gave in to the idea that she had once again been proven herself a gullible idiot! How could this be happening to her?

"Don't fight it chosen one, you wouldn't want the shaft to collapse in on you," the man's voice called from the other side of the door.

"Who sent you? Was it the coward who hides behind my dreams, not man enough to come out, so he sends his little lackeys?" Val shouted.

"You think I'm going to tell you anything? You will have to kill me to get anything out of me, Val," the man laughed.

"I hope you rot in hell!" Val shouted in anger.

"Thank you. I hear the weather is lovely at this time of year," the man replied sarcastically.

God, where was Delta when you needed a sharp one-liner? Val thought, reaching into her back pocket pulling out her phone. "Oh no!" –There was no signal. Val shoved it back into her pocket. "So once again, you fool, you're trapped not only underground, but inside a tunnel underground," Val muttered to herself turning towards the tunnel to flash her headlight into its murky darkness. "Oh, and smelly too. Well, this just gets better." Val pinched her nose and started to head cautiously down the slimy steps. Within a few moments she could see that the rubble was beginning to pile up. She realised that the reason they hadn't been trying this exit wasn't because there was no key, but because there had obviously been a cave-in here as well. So how long would it be before anyone even bothered to open the exit door again if they all knew that this was a no-go area?

As Val reached the worst bit of the fall, she could just hear the cries of the people who were really trapped coming through the air towards her. She also observed that the nasty smell had not abated. If anything, it seemed to be getting worse. Val slumped onto a large rock for a quick moment of self-pity and to contemplate what Jason and Delta would be doing in her absence.

"It's just going to answer machine." Delta flipped her phone shut, shoving it back into a small Gucci bag.

"Plain or cheese?" Jason asked.

"Plain, please," Delta answered. "I do love your Walkers crisps; they don't do anything as good back home." Jason threw a red packet of plain crisps through the air and Delta caught them at an obtuse angle, obviously to avoid any nail chipping and such.

"So how did you meet Val?" Jason asked as he perched on his bike seat facing Delta who was sitting in the open door of her mini. They had decided that it would be best to position themselves around Jason's helmet.

"Her dad built my house and that's about it." Delta lifted a crisp to her lips. "I think I should text Val's mum and tell her she is staying at mine tonight, just in case she takes longer than usual. What do you think?" Delta asked.

Jason nodded in agreement. "I'll text my dad too," he said lifting his can of coke to take a drink.

Val wondered what exactly she was supposed to do to help these people. Standing up, she started to pace the space available. Picking up a small rock, she tossed it into the air, whilst she considered how warm it was in this jacket. Northern Rock it said on the label. Val continued walking, tossing the stone and listening to the consistent cries coming from behind the door. Why was it, she wondered, that people who were trapped always seemed to scream so much? Did they think their voices would break them free? In a very inappropriate moment, Val laughed out loud.

Then she realised something, the rock she had been tossing in her hand had become substantially lighter. Val looked at the stone for a moment and then threw it to the ground. Grabbing another rock, she tossed it through the air. As it landed in her palm, it diminished in size, releasing a powdery cloud. But how? She wasn't sure what was happening, but she repeated the exercise three times and the result was the same. By the time she had finished, another rock had turned to dust.

If she could keep dissolving the rocks, maybe she could get to the door. She definitely wasn't going to get out any other way. Val took a rock in each hand and started to throw them, then another and another. This was going to take forever, she looked like a circus act and there were far too many for her to work two rocks at a time. To make things worse, the strange smell was seriously appalling and she was starting to feel the effects of being underground.

How could she speed this up? In a flash she got an image of her dad. "What would the builder do?" she asked herself. "Dynamite." Just the right amount of explosive in the correct place could knock down a tower building without touching the surroundings. Could she focus the energy that was breaking up the rocks into one point that was powerful enough crumble the larger rocks? Val started to think it through. She wanted to call through the door and tell the others to shut up; she had never worked well with distractions.

She knew the energy was in her hands, but how could she focus it? Val jumped to her feet. She could hit it as if she was boxing, like she did with Jason. "OK but how hard?"

All of a sudden, Val stopped dead as the reality of the smell dawned on her. It was gas. She remembered the tinny odour from years ago when they had had a leak at home. But where was gas coming from down here? Val flashed her torch around and then she spotted it: a large blue canister resting in the corner. Val walked over to it and grabbed the tap to close it. She was too late. The bottle was already empty and the tap was broken. A little note around it read "boom".

"Very entertaining," Val hissed. The gas bottle's contents were floating in the air around her, no wonder she felt light headed.

So things had changed. She needed to hit the target while not causing a spark on the old metal door or she would be part of the problem rather than the solution. Also, now she knew it was gas, she had to move quickly. There could be more bottles anywhere and she would put nothing past these people.

Val moved in closer and, looking at the rocks, started to focus all her energy as Jason had taught her. She saw herself being pushed around, becoming more enraged as she saw the smug face of today's prat. The pain started like a knot in her stomach and as the energy rose, so did the anger. She could feel herself welling up and then in the blink of an eye, she aimed at the rocks and released a punch directly into the centre of the fall. Her fist penetrated the stone and an invisible shock wave rippled through the air.

As the rocks dissolved, a mass of red smoke rose around Val. She stood completely still, waiting for the air to clear. As the mist began to settle she saw that the door in front of her was almost clear. "Well done you." Val gave herself a victory pat on the back and realized in her moment of adulation that her hand felt as if it was on fire.

"Hello, is there someone on the other side of the door?" a male voice called out.

"Yes, I'm going to get you out of there," Val called back. Within a second, she heard cries of enthusiasm. "Now that's more like it," she thought. Val felt down the cold wet door and found the door handle. However, flashing her torch over it, she saw that it had been damaged in the rock fall.

"I'm sorry, the handle is broken on my side," Val called to the others.

"OK. So what now?" the man called back.

"Give me a moment." Val stood back and looked at the door. "Maybe I could hit the door at an angle?" she said to herself. Looking at the state of her hand, Val decided that wasn't going to be an option.

"Hello again," the man called. "They are saying on the other side that the rescue team is here. We've told them to come down the passage to help you open the door."

"Great news," Val called back, however she wasn't thinking that at all. If the rescue team arrived, she would have the same problem she had had on the beach. She couldn't risk anyone else's safety tonight.

Val was beginning to feel stressed, she needed to get to whoever it was she was meant to be saving, and then get out of here.

She started to look around for a rock or something to bash the door with, and then remembered the gas, so that was a no-no. "Come on, no time, think Valerie," Val muttered to herself.

"Anyone there?" A voice echoed down the tunnel.

Great, here comes the cavalry. The question now was should she answer or not? She decided to remain silent. As she walked backwards and forwards, pacing like a caged lion, she felt a pain rising in her chest. It was similar to the one she had felt before she made the old lady fly and the lifeguard lift off. 'Why now?' Val thought, as her arms started to tingle uncontrollably. She stood still for a moment, sensing the closeness of the others, but unable to control the urge to walk towards the door.

"Stand back!" Val shouted.

"Sorry?" the man's voice called back, but it was too late, Val could no longer contain the power that had grown inside her. She felt a huge surge of energy down her arms and as she placed her palms on the door, a huge pulse shot through Val's hands and the door shook. Val fell backwards and a cloud of dust exploded in front of her.

She waited for the dust to clear once more, but to her disappointment, as the dust settled, nothing seemed to have changed. She stood up, making her way to the door to call out again. Placing her hand on it for support the strangest thing happened. The door seemed to move. Val placed her hand gently on the handle and with one push the whole thing started to fall in the direction of the people trapped on the other side.

"Move!" Val shouted as the door fell. Then she found herself face to face with five very shocked and dirty-faced strangers. "Hello," she said as a large figure pushed her from behind.

"Out the way please. Give us room." A huge man in a yellow plastic suit and wearing a red hat with a torch far larger than Val's, pushed past, followed by two smaller men. "I'm the rescue warden. My name is Tom. Has anyone been injured?" he boomed.

Val wondered if his voice caused caves to collapse, as she watched the five strangers stumble over the door she had just felled.

"We are all OK," called out a man.

"Can anyone else smell gas?" asked one of the women as she made her way past Val.

"Oh heavens!" Val had been so wrapped up in the moment that she had forgotten about that.

"Move quickly up the stairs, do not turn on any new lights or electrical equipment and as you are all able to walk, follow me quickly to the exit," the warden barked at them.

Val had to smile at this man. She was sure he must have 'importancy' issues. She was beginning to feel quite smug. All she had to do now was find the person she was meant to save and give them a pat. Then a half of sweet cider and some dry roasted peanuts would be her reward. As she watched them pass her in the corridor, one by one she patted them on the back. Nothing happened. There was just one man left.

The man stopped as he stepped over the door, looking at Val for a moment. "Are you the person I was talking to through the door?" he asked.

"Yes, I'm Val." Val smiled knowing that with just one handshake he was going to be traumatised for life by the disappearing girl. Ah well, needs be.

"I'm Max. Thanks for trying to help us."

"Come on, let's go." Val offered out her hand to help him over the door.

"This gas smell is strange. In all the years I have been coming here I don't remember anyone talking about gas in this shaft." As Max reached out for Val's hand she pulled it quickly away. That was it! They *wanted* her to shake hands with Max. They, whoever they were, wanted her to cause the blue spark that happened when she teleported so that she would kill everyone in the shaft. Well, she had been a fool once today, but not again.

Max slipped as Val pulled her hand away. "Sorry," Val winced, "I have a cramp in my arm." Val pulled her hand into her chest moving away from Max towards the wall.

"Not to worry. Let's get out of here." Max opened his arm towards the steps to do the gentlemanly thing and Val moved in front of him quickly, hoping that she was the one who had to do the touching not him. At the top of the tunnel where she had initially been locked in, the door was now wide open and the rest of the group had obviously been moved outside as there was no evidence of life.

"Keep moving; it's not far," said the bullish caveman leading them.

Val was annoyed that she was having to do all this exercise. They seemed to walk up hundreds of steps before they reached the final exit. She hadn't signed up for underground exploration; then again, she hadn't signed up for anything. As they reached the top, Val could feel a sense of relief ripple through the others. At least *they* knew where they were.

Coming out into the moonlight was a wonderful feeling and, for a moment, Val stood taking in the large half moon and breathing in the fresh air. As she turned to look for Max, who had been behind her all the way, she was shocked to see him being escorted to an ambulance by a police officer. "Does nothing run smoothly in this world of mine?" Val grouched to herself as she made her way towards them. She heard the officer asking Max questions, so she decided to wait until Max was free. She watched all the others being greeted by family and friends, obviously pleased to be reunited with their loved ones.

After fifteen mind-numbing minutes, Val was losing the will to live. What was this officer doing? Didn't he want to talk to anyone else? Then he turned, and Val managed to see his face. *It was him*, the man who had locked Val in the tunnel! Well, Max was Val's man and she was going to get him. Val walked towards them both with an exceedingly confident stride. No one stopped her.

"Evening constable," Val smirked turning to greet Max with a warm smile.

"This young lady deserves a medal for bravery. I have been an officer in the Navy for a very long time and have rarely seen such determination and courage." Max smiled at Val then turned back to look at the clearly shaken police officer.

Val turned towards the officer grabbing his hand and started to shake it vigorously. "I'm so pleased that people like you are here to help keep us safe," she said. Keeping hold of his hand, she swung back towards Max and held out her hand. "It has been an honour to meet you." As she touched Max's hand the blue spark passed between them, and Val and the police officer disappeared.

Jason and Delta, who had created a teepee out of empty crisp packets, watched as above them the lights in the sky shimmered and distorted. They instantly recognised the signs that Val was returning

"Jason, here she comes! Shame she's too late for a drink." Delta smiled.

Jason gave her the thumbs up. A body was falling towards them, but Jason and Delta stood frozen to the spot. Why had this large police officer fallen through Val's portal?

He landed with a bump, then, looking perfectly composed, he stood up and faced Delta.

"Hello, are you OK?" Delta asked moving in to see how he was coping with what had just happened. His reaction was as strange to them as him coming through the portal was. Pushing Delta roughly out of his way causing her to hit the mini door, he ran.

"Now that was just weird," said Jason as he helped Delta up. However, his good deed was cut short by Val landing on him. Scrambling to her feet and ignoring her friends, put her fists up, as if she was ready for a fight, and turned in circles, looking for her opponent.

"If you are looking for PC Plod, he just ran away," Delta said as she lifted herself off the mini door and dusted herself down.

"Which way?" Val looked at Delta.

"That way." Delta pointed in the direction of the main road. Val jumped off Jason and started to run.

"Hi, would be nice," Delta called after Val.

"Let's go. She has obviously brought this bloke back for a reason." Jason grabbed his helmet off the floor and jumped onto his bike. He sped off after Val, and Delta was left trotting around the mini.

"I wish someone would understand I'm just not meant to run," Delta called out to no one.

As Val ran, she could feel her heart pounding in her chest. The streets were in darkness, only the light of the stupid orange glow-lights the council called streetlights were visible.

At last she caught site of her enemy. He was slowing down. He might be evil but he was not as fit as she was. As she crossed the street onto the main road, all she could focus on was him. She had never felt this burning feeling of determination before. It was like a fire in her stomach and she wasn't going to back down until she got some answers. Then, just as she was really gaining on him, he ran into the local police station.

Val stopped dead in the middle of the road and yelled in frustration. "You coward! Come out and face me. I'm just the chosen one, come on!"

She was been oblivious to the fact that Jason had just pulled up on his bike. When he tapped her on the shoulder, she nearly jumped out of her skin.

"OK Bob the Builder, get on my bike before they arrest you for being very, very muddy and chasing police officers in the middle of the night while dressed as a miner." Jason grabbed Val's arm but felt her resistance, her reluctance to go with him. "Val, not here, not now, please." Val turned and saw the concern on Jason's face. He was right, this wasn't the right time or place, but at least she had the satisfaction of knowing that her enemy wasn't going to have such a comfortable evening.

G . L .   T W Y N H A M

"OK," Val nodded, climbing onto the back of Jason's bike.

Delta pulled up next to them. "My house?"

"Yes, I'll follow you." Jason signalled for Delta to lead the way.

Pulling into the drive behind Delta, Val almost fell off the bike. All the pressure, fear and pure adrenaline had left her exhausted. She slowly climbed off and walked towards the house. She took no more than three steps when her knees buckled. As she fell, Jason caught her, lifting her off the ground like a feather into his arms. She heard him giving Delta instructions to take her helmet and then she faded into a deep and restful sleep.

Val opened her eyes to the sound of intense laughter. Lifting her head off the pillow she instantly remembered the previous day and that, to her relief, she had come back to Delta's house. Another crescendo of laughter came forth and Val could distinguish Delta and Jason's voices. She slowly lifted herself off the bed, feeling every muscle cringe in pain from the earlier day's escapade. She was relieved to see that she was still in her own clothes. She was rather shy and the idea of Delta or Jason doing the deed of undressing her made her shiver.

Making her way downstairs, Val admired the house. Her dad had built it eight years ago and he still said it was his favourite. Val had to admit she would love to live here.

Her feet felt cold on the marble floor as she made her way to the kitchen. Maria, the help, was cleaning a large window and turned to wish Val a "Buenos Dias." Val smiled back. Maria was about all the company Delta had. A lot of the time her parents were trotting around the globe on one mission or another. Val turned into the swing door to the kitchen just as another great roar of laughter erupted. She was surprised to see not only Delta and Jason, but Shane as well.

"Morning all." Val waved as she pulled a stool up to the black marble counter covered in a massive array of breakfast treats.

"Morning Val." Shane patted Val on the back.

"So, all having fun then?" Val asked shovelling a large piece of melon into her mouth.

"We were just talking about the way you looked last night, running off in your miner's helmet and ski jacket." Delta was struggling to keep a straight face.

"Yes, well if you had been where I was, *you* would be glad of a jacket and helmet." Val nodded as another piece of melon went in followed by a piece of bacon.

"So, tell us all about it," Shane said.

"Yes and who was the copper?" Jason chirped.

Val spent the next few minutes telling her tale and listening to the gasps of the others as she hit on the more exciting notes. Then, as she finished, the questions started. Although Val was dirty and still very tired, she didn't mind answering because these people cared about her.

"So now what?" Delta asked.

"Well, we need to work on the book. Any news from Sam?" Val glanced over at Shane.

"Funny you should say that. I received a parcel from him last night," said Shane.

"What was in it?" asked Delta, obviously hoping for a gift.

"Something for Val," Shane smiled.

"Me?" Val said surprised to say the least. Val had never met Sam and he was sending her gifts.

"Yes Val. Sam is very interested in your adventures and he is possibly in a position to help you." Shane smiled at Val.

"In what way?" Val asked.

"Well, he doesn't work for anyone in particular, he is more of a freelancer. He helps whoever needs him, a little like yourself." Shane grabbed another muffin.

"Great, so what has he sent her?" Delta interrupted almost annoyed that Val hadn't asked yet.

"Don't know. It's in a large box back at the shop," Shane replied.

"Well, let's go and look," said Delta impatiently.

"No, I need a bath, and I need to tell my parents when I'm coming home." Val stood and turned to leave the kitchen, then paused at the door. "Is about thirty minutes OK with you?" She smiled at the others and they all started laughing.

"Yes, I suppose father-son bonding can wait till next Sunday." Shane shrugged his shoulders in Jason's direction and Jason grinned back, relieved that their Sunday morning fishing had been cancelled.

Val ran up the stairs and into Delta's very nice en-suite bathroom. In record time she showered and dressed in clothes she borrowed from Delta. Although Delta dressed like an A-lister most days, she did possess a few normal clothes in her large collection.

Delta was waiting outside in a shiny metallic blue Lotus.

"Where's the mini?" Val leaned down to open the door.

"Maria says it needs a clean." Delta genuinely looked confused.

"And this little beauty belongs to who, your mum or your dad?" asked Val as she climbed in.

"It's Maria's little runabout." They both laughed as they sped out of the drive, waving to Maria who was watching from the doorway.

As they made their way to the tattoo parlour, Delta explained about all the wonderful things this car could do and Val listened in awe. Although Delta played it blonde a great deal of the time, her head for facts and figures was impressive. "Where are your parents today?" Val asked.

"Well, Dad's flying over Europe, some big deal and a little golf's going down. Mum is back in the US having some body part made to look younger than a five-year-old's,"

Delta's expression never changed, but Val knew how lonely she got sometimes. Delta's situation made Val appreciate her parents even more than ever. For all the money Delta could lay her hands on, she had no one to share her joy with. Val grabbed her mobile phone and called her mum. There was no answer, and then Val remembered: it was Sunday so her mum would be in church and her father would be worshipping the gods of the golf course. She left a message.

"Hi, Mum and Dad. I'm staying at Delta's again tonight. Her parents are away so we are going to have a wild party with many male lap dancers."

"Hello Mrs. Saunders, that's not true," shouted Delta as Val laughed.

"OK, just a few lap dancers. I'll go to work on Monday from her's, so I'll see you Monday night. I love you both very much."

The High Street was completely deserted and it seemed strange not to see an array of two-wheeled vehicles parked outside Shane's shop. Delta pulled up and Jason came running out to greet them.

"Wow, you would think we hadn't seen him for days," Delta said as she stepped out of the car.

"Is this really a Lotus Supercharged Elise SC?" stuttered Jason. Val was disturbed by the way he was looking at the car, with love in his eyes and his tongue struggling to stay in his mouth.

"Yes, here, take it for a spin." Delta threw him the keys. At this point Jason almost fainted. Before the girls could say goodbye, he had jumped in and was speeding off down the street.

"Does he have a driver's licence?" Val asked Shane who was just coming out of the front door to see his son disappear at speed.

"Slightly late to be asking that question isn't it girls?" Shane replied.

"So let's go and open Val's present," said Delta.

"This way ladies"

They followed Shane into the gym to find a large brown box on the table. Val picked up a card that was on the top of the box. Opening it with great trepidation, she read:

Dear Val,

I know it won't make much sense to you why I'm giving you these things or where they originate from, but try to forget that point and just use them. I want to help you on your journey, although nothing comes for free.

Val felt herself tense up at the idea that these gifts would cost her something.

I need to know from you how they work, if they work and if not, how I could do it differently.

Val sighed; well at least he didn't want money.

I will ask Shane to pass on the results and I will try to help you any way I can in the future. Stay safe.

Regards, Sam

Val passed the card to Delta and opened the box. Inside she found several smaller boxes, the first containing what looked like a small brown earplug with a label attached: Covert cellular communications. With it came a silver necklace in what seemed to be a Celtic design with a honey yellow gem in the centre. Attached was a label that said: Tracker.

"I hope these things come with instructions," Val commented.

"That one in your ear and that one round your neck, not exactly rocket science," replied Delta flippantly.

"OK Sherlock." Val pushed Delta affectionately.

"She's right. Pop it in your ear," Shane said.

Val tentatively placed the small brown pill into her ear, unsure if it was going to disappear into some magic hole she had in her brain.

"Next!" Delta handed Val a small brown cylinder.

Val opened the end cautiously and tipped the contents out just as Jason returned from his escapade in Delta's car. Dropping the keys in front of Delta, he grinned at her like a boy who had just opened his first Scalextric on Christmas morning.

"OK, so what is it?" Delta pushed Jason out of the way.

"Well, it's a small piece of metal." Val held the shiny silver cylinder out towards the others. In that moment lights flashed under Val's fingers and the whole thing sprang to life. With a whoosh, the end extended to just over a meter long and a silver guard swivelled in a circular movement to enclose Val's hand. Val gaped at it, unsure what move to make next.

"Oh how cool." Jason murmured. "It's an épée."

Val realised she was still pointing it at them and slowly lowered her hand.

"Give it here." Jason reached out and Val gladly handed it over, but when Val's fingers left the sword and Jason touched it, it retracted into the cylinder again.

"That's not fair." Jason stood with the cylinder in his hand.

"Val, take it again." Shane suggested.

"OK." Val took the cylinder, but nothing happened.

"Hold it out, like you did before," said Jason.

As Val held it towards the others, it extended, reaching its full length in less than a second. In a moment of bravado, Val pointed the end directly at Jason.

"I wouldn't do that Val," Delta warned. It was too late. A bolt of white light hit him straight-on. Jason dropped like a rag doll and was left convulsing on the floor.

"Oh my God I killed him!" Val threw the sword to the ground where it instantly retracted. She joined Shane at Jason's side.

"Don't worry it's only temporary; it says here it should last about five to ten minutes depending on the size of the person," called Delta waving some instructions at the others.

"Is this Sam a nutter?" Val screamed at Shane who was now sitting on Jason's chest.

"No, he just wants to keep you safe." Shane was actually smiling which Val found disturbing.

"Leave him here. He'll be OK." Shane waved a hand at Val to move away. Jason had stopped shaking and was now just lying very still.

"How do you know this Sam? Why does he have such dangerous things and why is he sending them to me?" Val asked.

"He used to work with me before I left the army. We have been in some tight situations together. I got too old to do the jobs but he stayed on. That's about it, Val." Shane grabbed Val's arm gently. "Come on, let's look in your last box; it's the biggest."

Delta was already leaning over it like a child waiting for a jack to jump out. Val made her way to the table looking back at Jason, still worried about him, and then at Shane, shocked that he wasn't bothered that his son had been knocked out by a piece of metal.

Val opened the last box. "If anyone else gets hurt I'm going home," she said.

Shane and Delta nodded impatiently.

Inside were a laptop and four mobile phones. Val already had a phone but it looked nothing like these. They were green and black and seemed to be larger than your average Nokia with a clasp on each one. Val slipped the one with her name on, onto her belt. As she pulled the laptop out and placed it on the desk, Delta collected the phone with her name on it.

"What in sweet baby Jesus's name is this?" Delta held the phone up to Val's face.

"Well, it's your phone," Val said trying to look past it and start up the laptop.

"I'm not carrying this thing around with me! Forget it." Delta placed it back in the box. As the laptop sprang into life so did the phones, all bleeping at once. Val looked down at hers and on the screen she saw a GPS map (Val knew all about these as her dad had one for his golf courses). There was a bleeping spot in the centre.

"What do you think that is?" Val showed Delta the screen.

"I don't know," Delta shrugged. "You know, I'm sure James Bond had much better looking gadgets than these." Delta walked off towards the coffee machine in disgust.

"Looking at these notes Val, the bleeping is you," said Shane making his way over with a sheet of paper. "The laptop is for us to track you through the necklace." Shane handed Val the necklace from the table. "I think you need to put this on."

Val pulled the chain around her neck and closed the clasp.

Jason was starting to come round, rubbing his head with one hand and trying to keep himself upright with the other. Shane glanced at him them, looked back to the notes.

"The note also says that the earpiece is connected to all the phones and the laptop. That means you can talk to us as long as you have your phone with you. The épée, or sword, is a tazer. It will program itself to your finger-print and not work for anyone else," said Shane.

"Lucky I didn't pick it up first then isn't it?" said Delta sarcastically. Although everyone had to admit it was true. They needed to take their time with these things.

"There is a book for each of us explaining how our pieces of equipment work. If you want to know where

Val is, Delta, you will have to carry the phone." Shane offered Delta her phone again and she took it as if it were covered in worms.

"I'll be accessorising, you do understand?" she said pointing her finger at the others. Jason was now back on his feet.

"You OK, son?" Shane smiled, patting Jason affectionately on the back as he arrived unsteadily at the table.

"I've felt better," Jason said, grabbing his new phone with a look that said *I'll let you off zapping me if I get a toy to play with*. He sat down at the table, politely moving Val away from the laptop.

"Hey, I was looking at that," Val protested.

"Yes, and looking is all you need to do. You may have super powers, but I'm the computer expert."

Val sighed, and moved away, relieved not to have the responsibility of it all.

Jason and Shane spent the next hour huddled around the laptop whilst Val listened to Delta complaining about her ugly phone and she really wanted to go and do some retail therapy to get over the shock.

Val sat looking at all the things she now had to carry around with her. Was she expected to constantly have the phone thing in her ear, and what if she lost anything? It must have cost a fortune. This Sam guy was obviously in a good position to do this, or maybe it was all stolen. So many questions.

"Hey Val, are you feeling OK?" Jason called across to her.

"Yes, why?" Val responded unconvincingly.

"Cool. Let's start your fencing practise." Jason jumped up from his chair grabbing Val's hand as he walked past.

A fluttery feeling flooded her whole body and Val was unable to stop her legs following the first guy she thought she had ever truly fallen in love with.

"OK, these are your jackets." Jason handed Val two white jackets.

"Why two?" Val asked as she slipped them on.

"More protection. And here are your cups." Jason held out two full moon plastic cups. "Slip these in the front of your jacket to protect your chest." Val could feel the heat rising in her cheeks as she slipped them in.

"Can I ask why it has this dangly piece in-between my legs?" Val asked giggling.

"Yes, you do that up on the back of your jacket so I don't slip my foil up the side by accident," Jason responded, pointing at Val with his foil.

"Oh, OK." Val bent down to do it up.

As they moved on, Jason positioned Val's legs. It was almost like boxing but the opposite way round.

"The first thing you need to learn is that you must always salute the person you are about to enter into combat with." Jason raised his foil to the right of his face and lowered it with a swishing motion to the ground. Now he really looked amazing. "This is your foil." Jason handed Val a very bendy sword. It was over a meter in length with a cup to protect her hand. Holding it was harder than she had imagined. She started to giggle and then felt uncontrollable laughter rising inside.

"What seems to be the problem, Val?" Jason asked impatiently.

"Mine is broken," Val said bending the sword backwards and forwards almost as if it were jelly.

"It's supposed to be like that so we don't hurt each other," Jason replied, sharply tapping her foil with his.

Val stopped laughing as if a bucket of cold water had been thrown in her face. He must think she was a complete idiot.

"Salute," Jason instructed and Val lifted her foil up and down as Jason had shown her. "Right, here is your mask. Put it over your head after you have saluted, and never before."

They both donned their masks. Val thought she now knew what it felt like to be a fly. Looking at Jason, she knew he meant business; she quickly took the position he had shown her, and concentrated on her lesson.

After two hours, a large amount of sweating and several sore muscles, Val felt she had done enough for the day.

"That's it, I've finished." Val pulled off her mask. Jason tapped Val's mask with his foil and pointed to her head. "I'm sorry, didn't you understand?" Val replied.

"You finish when I say you can," Jason said seriously. "Now, en garde." Val prepared herself. "Advance, extend arm, now lunge."

Val was tired and really had had enough, and Jason knew it. He called out, "Salute."

Val lowered her arm and raised her visor.

"That's it for today," Jason said as he shook Val's hand.

"Control freak," Val murmured under her breath as felt relief rushed through her body. She was pleased with what she'd learned from Jason and looked over at Shane and Delta for approval. They were so completely engrossed in the laptop, they hadn't even been watching. So, no longer the chosen-one, she had been shoved to one side by a Dell.

"Sorry, does no one have any interest in my progress?" Val asked as she took off her jacket, allowing her plastic cups to spill out onto the floor.

"No. Shane has found this really interesting news on AOL about a disappearing girl. You need to look at this." Delta beckoned Val over. "There has been a sighting of you vanishing near a mine in Devon. Some Naval Officer called Max Phillips says you and a police officer disappeared before his very eyes," Delta giggled.

"Hey Dad, don't we have family in Devon?" Jason asked.

"Yes, your Aunty Pauline lives there."

"Well I'm pleased for you both. Maybe next time I teleport there I could sleep over," Val said sarcastically. "Even better, you can now Google me. Maybe we could eBay my services."

"Do you think people would pay?" Delta asked in a serious tone.

"No." Val grabbed a bottle of water from Delta's hand and sat down. Jason sat next to her giving Val a pat on the arm.

He was sitting so close they were actually touching. Val's stomach fluttered. She leant forward to pick up the sword from the table. "I suppose I will be carrying this epée everywhere, is that correct?" Val looked at Jason for confirmation. He nodded back at her. As she picked it up her arm flinched. "Do you think this thing is safe?" she asked.

Jason shrugged his shoulders and moved away like a child who had just been burnt.

"I promise I won't do that to you again." Val smiled sheepishly.

"Look at what it says here." Delta pointed at the screen. "They are bringing in some man called Derek Acorah who is a medium to make a connection with you." At this point they all burst out laughing.

"Do you think he will?" Val said, unable to catch her breath.

"Well if anyone can, Derek can," said Shane. Val's arm twinged again and she noticed she still had the sword in her hand. Maybe it was letting off small shocks. Val pushed it into her back pocket.

"Well I need the little girls' room, so excuse me for a moment." Val stood up and made her way towards the toilet.

As she passed the gallery area, Val spotted one of Shane's pictures shift. She stopped and moved in closer to inspect it. It wasn't actually the picture; it was as if an image was appearing on the glass. It was swirling, like water going down a plughole at speed. Val could sense its darkness and she could actually smell disinfectant oozing out of the image. She heard the faint call of a woman and felt compelled to touch the image. Placing her hand on it, she once again found herself slipping into the darkness.

"Did you hear that Dad?" Jason asked looking up from the laptop.

"What?" Shane turned to see Delta. He could tell from the expression on her face that something was very wrong.

Delta pointed in the direction of the Gallery. "She was heading for the toilet. She bent to look at that picture and the light took her." Shane patted Delta on the shoulder. "Come on, she'll be OK." He beckoned her to follow as he walked towards Jason and the laptop. "OK son, let's find her."

Jason started tapping in the codes that Sam had sent with the instructions, and then leant back in his chair.

"Well?" Delta asked impatiently.

"She hasn't arrived anywhere yet, but when she does we'll know where," said Jason, smiling confidently. They all huddled around the screen like children at Christmas staring into Hamleys toy store window at the array of tempting treats.

'Bleep.'

"There she is!" said Jason.

CHAPTER 8

Up, Up and Away

Val opened her eyes to be greeted by a silver bowl containing blue water, which was spinning into an abyss in front of her. A hideously strong smell of detergent violated her nasal passages. She lifted herself up, and instantly realised that she was looking at a tin toilet.

"Great, toilet. My favourite," Val said as she surveyed her surroundings. She recognised that this was the sort of toilet you would find on a train or a *plane*. There was a sudden, violent shudder and Val fell backwards towards the mirror unit. Quickly placing her head between her knees and her hands over her head she started to pray as she rocked backwards and forwards.

"OK, so I have lied a lot recently, God, and I know I need to pay more attention to my parents, but please, sweet, kind God, if you care about me at all, make this a train not a plane," Val cried into her knees.

"Hello Val," a quiet voice whispered into her ear.

Val looked up. "Hello. Is that you, God?" She looked around her tin prison for a sign; nothing would surprise her any more.

"No." Then she heard giggling. "It's me Jason, son of Shane." Then she heard uncontrollable laughing.

"Well, I'm so pleased you people think this is entertaining," Val huffed.

"Sorry Val, I didn't realise you had a fear of flying," Jason responded.

"So, am I on a plane?" Val whimpered.

"Well, unless you are on a train thirty two-thousand feet above the tracks, yes, you are definitely on a plane." There was silence.

"I can't be on a plane. I want to come home now." Val started to shake. "Where exactly is this plane?" she asked.

"Well, from what this computer is telling me, there are lots of numbers and figures, but in plain English you are flying over the North Sea, 15 minutes away from Norfolk," Jason responded. He could tell by the silence that Val was struggling with this whole situation. "Val, I'm here, so keep talking to me. What do you normally do now? Jason hoped this would get Val moving.

"Well, I suppose I assess the situation and go and look for whoever needs me," Val replied as she started to get up.

"Good, OK. Where exactly are you?" Jason kept his voice very calm.

"I'm in the toilet. I think I can hear an airhostess talking outside. I need to get out of here without drawing any attention to myself." Val now felt slightly more focused.

"I'll talk to you as you go along. Let's get going Val." Val felt a warm feeling all over; she was so pleased to not be alone.

She flicked the catch and pulled open the door to come face to face with a very grumpy, balding, sweaty, over-weight middle-aged man in an expensive suit, who was obviously in need of the service she had been hogging.

"Sorry," Val apologised, looking at the ground as she passed. The man grunted and walked past her into the toilet. Val got a strong whiff of his warm aftershave, which made her stomach slightly more nauseous than it had been before, if that was physically possible.

Unexpectedly, the plane lurched to one side and Val felt her heart jump into her throat as she grabbed the edge of the nearest seat. "If we were supposed to fly I'm sure we would have wings," Val hissed under her breath. When she looked up, she saw the full extent of her problem. "Oh bums, this plane is massive."

"Val, how many seats from one side to the other?" Jason's voice resounded in her ear.

"Only four seats in each row in this section but I can see through the curtains and they are sitting three, four, three. It's huge." Val looked around to make sure she wasn't drawing too much attention to herself as she slowly started to make her way down the plane.

"Hello," a young female stewardess in a red suit greeted Val as she passed her. Val smiled back weakly. She needed to keep moving and could see that there were at least four sections up ahead and hundreds of people. How would she know who to help? Maybe she could stand by the door at the end of the flight, like the captain, and shake everyone's hands.

She assumed from the champagne flutes that passengers were holding that she was in first class. They seemed to be mostly businesspeople who were clicking on their laptops or, in the case of the women, reapplying their lip-gloss.

No one here looked in imminent danger so Val headed for the next section. A man who was walking backwards towards her while talking to a stewardess turned. Val instantly recognised his face.

"Hell, no," Val whispered, throwing herself clumsily into an empty chair.

"What's wrong?" Jason's voice rang in her ear.

"Delta, your dad's here," Val whispered under her breath hoping that they would hear her.

"My dad! He's coming back from the States today. Well, now I can tell you you're on the VS2343 from Kennedy airport to London Gatwick arriving at eight p.m. our time." Delta finished with a grunt of satisfaction, as if she had added the secret ingredient to the cake mix that was Val's life.

"Great! Just pray that he doesn't see me. That would be just too much explaining." Val reached forward to grab a magazine to cover her face. When she peeked over the top, Delta's father was seated a few rows in front.

"OK, I'm going to make a move." Val held the magazine up in front of her face as she headed towards the curtains.

"What can you see now?" Jason asked.

"Richard Branson."

"What?"

"I have a magazine in my face and there is a picture of Richard Branson. He looks really good for his age," Val said.

"Get serious," Jason snapped.

"Yes sir." Val smiled for the first time, starting to relax. As she moved through the next section, the difference in the passengers was apparent. Most people were casually dressed, and the quality of handbags dropped dramatically. Delta had taught Val a lot about distinguishing classes by accessories and she felt quite sad that she knew these unimportant pieces of trivia.

"I have moved to economy," Val said. "I haven't made contact with anyone, good or bad, yet."

"Keep your eyes open," replied Jason.

"Will do, Captain," Val chirped.

Val was only a few steps into the economy section when a petite blonde woman sprang to her feet about five rows in front of her.

"He's got a bomb!" she screamed, jumping into the aisle and starting to run, screaming as she went.

Within seconds the whole section was on its feet. Like a cattle stampede, they all tried to follow the woman into first class. Val had just enough time to jump into an empty gap from where she observed the full extent of the hysteria. Not only was everyone running, she also had Jason shouting into her ear.

"Did she say BOMB?" he yelled, repeating it about five times.

"Stop, shouting!" Val bellowed back at him.

"Sorry, I didn't think you could hear me. So, did she say bomb?"

"Yes," Val replied abruptly. If her stomach was jumpy before it was now tied in painful knots. Her heart was hammering, she could barely breath and her knees were actually knocking together. She bent down for a second to catch her breath before rising again to take in the full extent of the situation. How, she wondered, was she expected to deal with a bomb?

Next to where the blonde woman had been sitting, was a thirty-something dark haired man in a blue shirt and slacks. Unlike the other passengers, he hadn't run for his life, but was now jumping around hysterically in his seat. Val found it even more bizarre that he didn't seem to be making any noise. If he was a terrorist, he was a very quiet, very well-dressed one.

Stepping out into the aisle, Val composed herself and slowly made her way towards him.

"What's going on, Val? Please speak to me." Jason's voice was cracking under the pressure.

"I'm OK. Give me a minute. I think I have found the person I was looking for," Val replied calmly. She edged closer and all of a sudden the man spotted her. He seemed even more distressed than the other passengers. This made Val think that maybe he wasn't the bomber the woman had made him out to be. As Val moved closer he became still and she saw that he had one hand hand-cuffed to the seat.

"Wow, these people get dirtier every time," Val whispered, trying not to scare the man who was still like a rabbit in headlights looking at her.

"Who is dirty?" Jason asked, perplexed by Val's comments.

"Shh," Val snapped. "Hello, my name is Val." She was now only two aisles away and this whole section of the plane was empty, but she knew they would only have a few seconds alone. The man started to make strange signs with his hand on his chest.

"He isn't talking to you. What's going on?" Jason wanted to know. Jason obviously wasn't going to be able to keep quiet during this situation, so Val decided she would just ignore him.

"Are you OK?" Val smiled as the man carried on beating hand signals onto his chest with his free hand.

"Can you talk?" He shook his head violently. "OK," Val smiled.

"Is he a mute?" Jason called out as if he had guessed the answer to a quiz question.

"Jason, if you don't shut up I will cut you off," Val responded smoothly.

"OK!"

"Can you help me? I know you don't have a bomb," Val said. The man nodded vigorously. "Do you know where she put her bag? Maybe there are some keys for your cuffs?" Val was now next to the man. If this was a set-up then this would be his moment to attack. She gently placed her hand into her back pocket checking that her sword was there. As it brushed her fingers she felt slightly more secure. The man pointed to the overhead luggage compartments. Val smiled again, hoping to reassure him. Reaching up and releasing the door handle, she quickly pulled down all the bags. The man pointed vigorously at one of them; it was brown leather, like the ones Val had seen doctors with. As she picked it up he became very agitated, shaking his head and stamping his feet. Val dropped the bag and took a step back.

"Has this got a bomb in it?" Val asked him. He shook his head and Val felt the relief wash over her body. She picked the bag up again, more carefully this time. There was a large tag on it: '*Name; Paul Brown – speech impaired*'. Val smiled and pointed at him. "Are you Paul?" The man nodded with tears of relief in his eyes.

Val placed it down. "Do you see the woman's bag?" Paul nodded again pointing to a red leather handbag. Val picked it up and tentatively opened the zip. Before she had time to look inside, Paul sat down abruptly, and was looking even more petrified. When she looked at him he pointed past her head.

"What do you want to tell me?" Val asked, but before she could get any more out of him, a deep Texan accent came from behind her.

"Ma'am, I'm Sky Marshal Lewis. Please raise your hands and move away slowly."

Val turned around, gently placing the red bag next to Paul. Behind her, a man in blue jeans, white shirt and a black bomber jacket was aiming a gun at Paul's head.

"No! Stop! You don't understand." Val raised her hands towards the man, trying to block his view of Paul, in the hope he would listen to her, aware that Paul was now fumbling through the red handbag with his free hand. If she could get him a little time, maybe he would find the keys.

"I won't tell you again. I'm an armed sky marshal and if you do not leave that man right now I will have to assume that you are his accomplice." The man was edging forward. Only three or four rows separated them now. To her horror she realised that he was pointing his gun directly at her head. Val saw Paul pulling out a set of keys. "Stay calm. This may still work out," Val told herself. Then, behind the marshal, she saw the woman who had originally raised the alarm. She stared at Val, then gave her a little teasing wave.

Val would have been more annoyed if she hadn't just seen Paul undoing his cuffs.

"Please, this man can't speak. See, there a label on his bag that tells you that. That woman handcuffed him to his chair and…" Before Val could finish, the woman grabbed the unsuspecting sky marshal's hand and was pulling at his gun. As he struggled with the woman, the gun went off. Val's instincts kicked in. She leapt through the air, her hands reaching out like a goalkeeper's, her body pushing in front of Paul with no thought for her own safety.

Val focused all her energy on deflecting the flying bullet with one hand. It felt like she was bending the air with her hand. The power that surged through her was similar to the energy she had used on the lifeguard. With her other hand, she grabbed Paul's jacket and pulled him to the floor. There was aloud thud just millimetres above her head as the bullet penetrated his chair. Val knew that she had saved Paul's life.

As they lay on the floor, chaos reigned overhead. Time to go. She looked at Paul, smiled and grabbed his hand.

Val felt the blue spark, and a deep sense of relief to be off the plane. She landed hard in front of the painting, to an instant explosion of cheers from her adoring fans. As she stood up Delta started hugging her, thanking her profusely for coming back, and for saving her dad. Shane was visibly moved by the whole experience. Jason grabbed Val and lifted her off the floor and into his arms before planting a huge kiss on her cheek.

"You are my hero," he said into Val's ear, lowering her gently to the ground.

"Wow! I wish I could have taken you lot with me before." Val smiled. This felt amazing; at last her friends could see what she had to go through.

"I feel a celebration is in order." Shane waved his arm in the air almost like a general calling his troops together.

"Don't you think Val should have a rest?" Delta said.

"No, I'm fine. Let's party." Val was loving this.

As they closed the shop and packed away all the goodies, Val looked at the others, feeling a sense of satisfaction, as if she was now part of a team. Today she actually liked her life, even if it was the strangest life possible.

Arriving at the 'Snakes and Ladders' burger bar, Val was filled with excitement. Jason had kissed her! OK, only on the cheek, but hey, she wasn't complaining. So where should she go from here? She saw marriage maybe two years down the line and then three children, although she did want to do a little travelling before then.

"Come on 'Val the amazing' let's get you some meat."

Val snapped out of her daydream as Delta grabbed her arm and they waltzed into the bar.

The smell of burgers frying and the sixties music playing made this place one of Val's favourites.

"This place, it reminds me of home," Delta said, looking pensive. Val forgot that Delta was away from her home and her other friends, with whom she spent considerably more time than she did with Val.

When the waitress brought their drinks, Delta called for silence. "I would like to make a toast to the bravest, and most courageous person I know," she said, lifting her sparkling water. They all raised their drinks.

Val thought that she might pass out with the feeling of sheer contentment in her heart, and she hadn't even eaten her favourite double burger with pineapple yet.

"To Val," they chorused.

"Shh," the barman shouted over in an annoyed tone. He was staring very closely at a large flat screen TV over the bar.

"What's going on?" Shane asked him as they all turned to look at the screen.

"Plane crash. They say it's a blood bath; no chance of survivors," he replied.

In the silence of the moment, Val heard Delta's glass smash on the floor. She got up from the table with an expression Val had never seen before. Val rose and followed her as she moved to the bar. The TV screen showed a burnt-out plane. What was left of the tail was sticking out of the ground, resembling a bleak gravestone. The Sky news reporter was grim. "Gatwick airport is not releasing any information until the families of crew and passengers have been informed. We are unsure of the number of casualties. Looking at the devastation, the situation doesn't look promising." As she finished speaking a trilling sound broke the silence.

"Delta, it's your phone," Shane grasped Delta's hand, thrusting a glossy pink phone into it.

Delta opened it in a dream like state. "Yes," she nodded. "OK, I'll come home now." Delta closed the phone and started to walk towards the exit without even turning to speak to the others.

"Wait! I'll drive you," Jason called out.

"Let me come too, Delta." Val followed.

Delta turned around with tears welling in her eyes. "You have done enough damage. Please stay and celebrate your great success." She turned and ran through the doors, leaving the others silently watching.

When Val started to follow, Shane grabbed her arm. "Not the best time, Val. Leave her to go home," he nodded gently at Val.

"But she needs me." Val now had tears streaming down her face. "This is all my fault. I should never have got any of you involved." She started to pull away from Shane's grasp and he instinctively knew to let her go.

"Delta will be OK," Shane called as Val followed Delta.

"Oi! Someone has to pay the bill," called the barman angrily.

"It's OK, I'll pay you now!" said Shane making his way back to the bar. Jason stood looking between his dad and the door, almost unable to decide what to do.

"Leave it, son. They'll be OK and there's nothing we can do right now. Come on, let's go home." Shane passed a bundle of notes over the counter and, putting his large arm around his son's shoulders, led him out.

Delta had already left the car park by the time Val pushed through the door; she knew there was no way of stopping her now.

Val knew she couldn't go back in; the pain of seeing those pictures on the screen again would be too much. What had she done wrong? Why had it crashed? Was it the bullet? She started to run, needing to get home. As the tears started pouring down her face, she felt ashamed for celebrating at the cost of her best friend's father's life.

As Val ran, she screamed abuse into the darkness at whoever thought it was a good idea to give her this curse. Then she shouted at herself for letting all the others in on her secret. She finished off with a despairing bellow for being such a loser.

When Val eventually stumbled towards her house, it was lit up like a Christmas tree. She reached the door and pounding at it with her fist. The door opened. "Val!" Mike's voice was the best sound she had heard all day.

"Dad." Val reached out and grabbed her father's neck as he bent down and pulled her in close.

"Are you hurt? What's wrong? Val, please speak to me." Mike was inspecting Val for visible wounds. "Susan, come here now! Val's hurt!" Mike shouted towards the kitchen.

Susan was at their sides within a second, and wiping her dirty hands down her apron, she ordered, "Get her to the sofa, Mike." "Mum! It's the plane. It crashed," Val blurted through snot and tears.

"Get her a brandy." Susan pointed at the cabinet. Susan sat at Val's head and stroked her sweaty hair, making a deep shushing noise. She asked Val no questions, just sat waiting for her to talk when she could.

Val took a deep and controlled breath. "Mum, Delta's dad was on the plane; he's dead." As the last word came out, she started to sob again.

"Mike, put on the TV please," Susan asked calmly.

The huge flat screen TV on the wall sprang into life. Mike quickly switched to Sky News and was met with horrific images of burning metal and fallen trees.

"Dear God!" Susan breathed.

"Mum, it's all my fault." Val kept crying.

"How can this be your fault?" Susan asked.

"It just is." Val needed to stop talking or things would be said and she would put her family at risk.

"Val, where is Delta?" Mike asked.

"I don't know. We were all having a burger at the 'Snakes and Ladders' and she saw the news and ran."

Val was slowly calming down and her father passed her the brandy.

"Who is all, Val?" Susan enquired.

"Just me and Delta." Val looked up at her mum who was still stroking her hair.

"Have you called her?" Mike asked.

"No, I just ran home."

"You ran the five miles from the 'Snakes and Ladders' to home? Wow, no wonder you couldn't talk!" Mike exclaimed. "I'll give her a ring."

"Where is your mobile, Val?" Susan started to look around.

"It's in my back pocket." Val reached down and realised that she still had an assortment of gadgets about her body. She reached in and pulled out what now seemed like a very plain and unexceptional mobile from her pocket, trying to leave her telescopic sword behind.

"Call her then," Susan said as if giving instructions to a toddler. Val pressed her speed dial but it went straight through to answer machine.

"How are you doing, Mike?" Susan called through.

"Engaged at the moment, but I will keep trying," he shouted back from the kitchen. All of a sudden, Val saw something in her mother that she had never noticed before. She had an inner strength that was helping her cope in this very delicate situation. For a moment, Val just looked up at her mum in appreciation and then the phone started to ring.

"Yes, just a minute," Mike said as he walked into the lounge. He handed the phone over to Susan.

"Hello Patricia. Yes, Val is home. Is Delta with you?" There was a silence. Patricia was Delta's mum. Sometimes Val had mistaken them for each other, which had been slightly disturbing. "OK, I'll tell Val. If you need anything, please call me. Bye." Susan switched off the phone.

"Val, he's OK." Susan now had tears in her eyes.

"Really Mum?" Val started to sit up.

"Yes, Patricia said it was a miracle. Some man called Paul Brown helped to get Jeffrey out of the plane. It seems that one of the engines exploded as the plane was landing. Patricia says Jeff mentioned a bomb." Susan looked into Val's eye with that heartfelt emotion only a mother and daughter have. "He's OK, Val, don't worry, and Delta is safely at home."

Val nodded. Paul had saved Delta's dad. So, that's what it had all been about. For a second she felt a little relief from the pain, then she just lay back down, letting the tears roll down her face. Her mum slowly stroked her hair until she slipped into the world of sleep.

When she opened her eyes, Val saw the trees and the path leading to her dream village. It was dark and damp and she felt the coolness of the wet grass between her toes.

She could sense the presence of the one she was growing to know as her adversary, although she didn't know where it was emanating from.

"Come out coward. I know you're hiding!" Val shouted. She no longer feared him. Her best friend had walked away from her and possibly hundreds of people had died tonight because of her actions, so what had she got to lose?

"Scared of a little girl are you?" she baited him, sensing the anger vibrating in the air. "Too scared to face me, you have to send your little followers to get me." Val was now spinning in circles as she shouted. Then she spotted a shadow moving across the body of a huge oak tree. "You do know only pussies hide in trees?" Val didn't get time to see what struck her; it was far too fast. It smashed across her face and she felt the blood spurting from her mouth. She coughed as she fell onto her knees.

"Well I must say, you are brave." Val wiped her bloody lip and laughed. She pulled herself back to her feet as another blow caught her from the other side and she collapsed again.

"You will give up child," mocked a voice that almost didn't exist. It was a cold voice that left Val, not only in pain, but shaken to her bones as she pulled herself onto her feet again.

"Never, I will never let you beat me and if you ever try to hurt anyone I know again, I will kill you." Val spat blood onto the woodland floor.

"Kill me, you pathetic creature? You can't even see me. How do you expect to kill me?" the voice mocked her. "Gather your soldiers, child. I will enjoy killing each and every one."

Val felt another strike from behind and this one held such force that even as she fell, she knew he had damaged her.

Hitting the ground with a thud, she immediately heard her mother screaming. Opening her eyes, she understood why. She had been thrown from the sofa where she had fallen asleep, onto the glass coffee table and had managed to smash it. As Val took in the extent of the situation, she noticed large amounts of blood on the carpet and in the broken glass, which was now only inches away from her throat. Val felt herself being lifted into the air. The arms that held her were strong and steady; she knew they were her father's.

Her mother told Mike to put her back down on the sofa. He lowered her slowly and Val started to feel the full force of the blows she had just received. This meant that the injuries he had inflicted upon her in her dream had somehow manifested themselves in the real world.

"Val, tell me where it hurts, honey?" Susan had a chequered tea towel at Val's face. "I don't understand what happened. We left you sleeping and the next thing we knew, you'd fallen through the coffee table." Susan was shaking and Val could tell from her expression that her face must be a mess.

"I was having a bad dream, Mum. I'm sorry about the mess," Val said, terrified that this thing that was tormenting her had crossed over into the real world.

"Don't worry, we can clean this up. It's your face that's worrying me." Susan held Val's chin gently in her hands looking at both sides. "I swear, if you hadn't been sleeping here just a minute ago I would say you had been in a fight." Susan placed a kiss on Val's head and handed her the tea towel. "Let me get you some ice." Susan stood up, walking around Mike who was removing the broken glass.

"Mike get the car started, we'd better take her to accident and emergency."

Mike nodded.

"NO!" Val shouted through the pain. The last thing she wanted was to be asked loads of questions. What if they wanted x-rays and she had to get undressed? What if they saw the tattoo? Add the excitement of some unexpected teleporting, and she would be locked up before the clock struck twelve.

"Val, I know you don't like hospitals, but you have some nasty cuts. They may need stitches." Susan had her serious look on, and Val knew she was going to have to work hard to convince her.

"I'm not going. Call Uncle Julian, he can sort me out," Val pleaded. Val's uncle was a local GP and at least he wouldn't ask her to get undressed.

Susan sighed, then reluctantly agreed. "OK. I'll give him a bell, but if he isn't there you are going to the hospital."

"OK." Val crossed her bloody fingers.

Luckily for Val her uncle was there and he came around straight away. Val played her pain down as her uncle inspected her face. He was concerned by Val's wounds but after her insisting that she felt wonderful, he agreed that she needed nothing more than the few steri-strips he had applied, and time to heal.

Julian patted his sister's shoulder. "Susan, she will be fine, but be prepared for her to look a hell of a lot worse in the morning." He smiled at Val and handed Susan some painkillers. "Give her two every couple of hours. She will be sore for a few days." He gave them both a salute and went into the kitchen to talk to Mike.

"Beer time then." Val grinned at her mum as best she could.

"Yes." Susan placed two tablets in Val's hand and gave her a glass of water. "Take these. Let's see if there are any updates on the news about the plane crash." Susan switched on the TV and as Val had expected it was still all over Sky News. But now the breaking news was different.

"They are calling it an act of God. Looking at the wreckage, no one can believe that anyone could have survived. However, I'm here today as a witness to the fact that every man, woman and child has walked off this plane alive. There are some minor cuts and bruises, but everyone is hailing the staff on this flight as angels. There is talk of an explosion inside the economy section of the plane. Nevertheless, the pilot had enough time to land safely and get everyone clear before the right side engine blew up." The reporter kept turning and pointing at the wreckage that was still smouldering. "In my career, I have never witnessed anything quite like this. If I hadn't seen those passengers being bussed away I would have said it was impossible." The young male journalist was clearly shaken by what he had seen.

"Well would you believe it?" Susan just sat shaking her head. "All those people and not one dead! It is an act of God like that man said." Susan looked towards the ceiling in an awed manner.

"That's fantastic news." Val could feel the effects of the tablets starting to overwhelm her. As her eyes closed she felt that maybe, at last, she was on the right path.

"Have a good sleep, honey." Susan tucked Val under a blanket and stood up to go and see her brother in the kitchen.

"Ow," Val hissed as she opened her eyes. The pain in her face was excruciating and she dreaded what her reflection might reveal. She could hear her mum humming some strange tune in the kitchen and, as she started to get up, a whoosh of pain hit her head and she had to spend a few minutes gathering her thoughts before she could get to her feet.

"Mum," she called out weakly. Susan's radar hearing picked up Val's whimper quickly enough.

"Hey, morning." She said rushing into the lounge.

"Mum, what time is it?"

"Oh, you look much better than I thought you would. It must be because you're young." Susan smiled at Val.

"Thanks...I think. Now what's the time? I need to get to work." Val tapped her wrist.

"You aren't going to work, honey. I've already called that lovely Mr Gallymore. He said to take as long as you needed." Susan smiled at Val.

"How did you call him?"

"Well, I know where you work, so Yellow Pages and presto, he was on the other end of the phone." Susan led Val towards the kitchen.

"Was he at the shop?" Val could feel herself getting stressed. She would surely get the sack for this.

"Yes, he said he was here for a few days and that he would call to see how you were doing. He seemed so sweet." Susan shrugged, unsure why Val was still asking her stupid questions.

"Have something to eat and I'll run you a bath." She patted Val on the shoulder, pulling a chair out, and placed a large English breakfast in front of her. Val's stomach flipped.

"I think I'll skip the food for now, Mum, thanks. Maybe some juice..." Val winced.

"OK, but you will have to eat at some point." Susan pulled the plate away, not wanting to upset her.

At that moment the front doorbell rang. Val felt the whining noise go through her whole body like a chainsaw. How long this would last she wasn't sure, but she wasn't going to hang around to feel sorry for herself. She had a job and she was going to do it.

Susan opened the door and Val heard a chorus of women's voices. It must be her mum's gossip group. Val grabbed a glass of juice and some painkillers and made her way discreetly towards the bathroom, praying no one would stop her with questions. She was sure her mother would be filling them in anyway.

As she entered the bathroom, the full horror that was her face stared cruelly back at her from the mirror. "So much for not looking too bad," Val whispered. She realised her mum had been trying to be kind. Her cheeks were black and swollen with bruises and there was still dry blood on her lips. Val wanted to cry. She had never, in her life, felt so low. Her best friend had abandoned her, she had caused so much pain, and the worst part was the lying. She couldn't even go to hospital when she was wounded.

Stuffing two tablets in her mouth and taking a painful gulp of juice to wash them down, she started to run the bath water as her tears rolled down her sore cheeks. She needed to sort this out and it couldn't wait. She needed to get away from all her friends, old and new, until this was over, and go it alone. As she stripped off, she saw the reflection of the tattoo in the mirror, the same way she had just a week ago. Yet this time it was different. There were no longer thirteen symbols; now there were only six. "Well, not much longer to go," she thought. She had better get sorted before someone called for her from downstairs, or maybe even further away.

Val felt better after getting into fresh clothes and was ready to face the world again. She shoved her sword and all the rest of her gadgets into the various pockets of her jacket. She would give them back to Shane to return to Sam, and then they could get on with their lives.

As she made her way downstairs, she could hear the women in the front room making appropriate noises as Susan told them all about the previous night's goings on. Val loved her mum, but she had never understood why women spent hours over coffee talking about things that weren't going to change. She wondered for a moment what would happen if all these people thought about world peace. 'Maybe not,' she grinned making her way to the front door, like a mouse escaping a fat, sleeping cat. She opened and closed the door and was free. The air hit her face like a soft kiss. She hadn't realised how cooped up she had felt. Val checked her watch. "OK, next bus in ten minutes, time to get there."

As she walked, the mixture of sunshine and fresh air made her feel a lot better. This feeling instantly disappeared as she arrived at the bus stop where a woman holding a baby let out a gasp when she saw Val's face. She had forgotten how bad she looked. Val pulled up her collar and tried to keep to the shadows until the bus arrived. Then she waited until everyone else had boarded before running for the door.

"Hell!" the bus conductor blurted as Val boarded.

"No, just a return to Arcsdale, please." Val's voice was quiet yet stern enough to tell the driver she wasn't in the mood for staring.

"There you go." The driver passed Val her ticket without even making eye contact. Val moved down the bus searching for a seat on her own, which she found, pushing herself as close to the window as possible.

As she watched the view, she felt the stares burning her back. Still what did she mind? These people would never live through what she was living through, so who cared what they thought.

Val jumped off the bus with every intention of making her way to Shane's, but something stopped her. She couldn't face him just yet; she would go after work. She pulled out her mobile and switched it off. She didn't feel like answering questions today. It was bad enough that she had missed one morning on only her second week at work; she didn't want to prolong the pain of getting to work late any longer.

Arriving at the bookshop, she was greeted with an open sign and a nice crowd of people just exiting, waving goodbye to Mr Gallymore as if they actually liked him.

"Morning Mr Gallymore. I'm so sorry to get here late." Val had her face down; she felt it would be safer not to make eye contact.

"Miss Saunders, you do look lovely this morning. I take it that you feel my customers want to be served by someone who looks like they have been ten rounds with Randy Turpin." Wallace moved back over to the counter and put down a book he was holding.

"I'm so sorry, but I don't know who Randy Turpin is." Val shrugged.

"A boxer. World class, back in the nineteen fifties. Not to worry. You can sell books, Miss Saunders, but you obviously aren't taking advantage of the facilities to broaden your knowledge," Wallace finished.

"Oh, I do look at some books," Val responded. If only he knew how important his books were.

"Well, let's make a decision before you talk more of my precious existence away. Are you staying to work?" Wallace stared at Val.

"Well, if you don't think my appearance will offend the customers too much, I would like to, if that's OK?" Val tried to smile at the end of her sentence, but it must have looked quite odd. She felt like she had been to the dentist and been injected on both sides of her mouth. She wouldn't be surprised if Wallace pointed out that she was dribbling.

"I employed you so I didn't have to do this, so you make an educated guess," Wallace snapped. Before Val could respond, he had grabbed his tweed coat and was heading for the door. "If you feel unwell, close the shop. I have just had another crate of important books from all over Europe delivered. It's at the back of the shop. Please make sure these books are put out on the shelves *ASAP.*" He turned and was gone.

"Bye. Yes I will be fine, thank you," Val mumbled under her breath. She turned and looked at the shop. Why had she taken this stupid job anyway? Oh well, no point in moaning. She grabbed a glass of water from the still mangled cooler and headed down the shop to check on the new books.

The bulky and aged looking crate sat by the window only feet away from Val's first teleporting spot. As she started to open it, Val noticed how old and dirty it seemed considering it had just been delivered. The crate opened with ease and as she started to grab the books and place them onto the trolley, she saw that most were in foreign languages.

Val hadn't yet got to know the shop well enough to be able to pinpoint a specific sub-section without spending at least an hour looking for it, so she simply grabbed a few books and started looking.

Val moved swiftly up and down the aisles com-pletely engrossed in searching for her language section. Coming to work had definitely been a good idea. At least she wasn't thinking about the pain from her stupid face. At last she spotted a small brass plaque with the words *Foreign Languages* embossed on it. "Cool," she exclaimed to herself. Three rows away from the crate on the left hand side. She would get the hang of this eventually, if she didn't get the sack first.

Val had started to unload her books when, directly in front of her, she spotted an aged brown book spine with the word 'Theban' embossed on it in gold lettering. Val grabbed it and pulled it from the shelf. She leafed through it and immediately recognised some of the symbols, which were the same as the ones in the zodiac book. However, this book would be of no real help to her because, to her dismay, the text was gibberish. How was she supposed to read it?

As she started to push it back onto the shelf, a small folded piece of paper fell out. Val slowly and painfully bent down to pick it up. It wasn't as old as the book, but the edges of the paper were slightly brown and it seemed to have been folded for a long time. Val was careful not to rip it as she opened it out. On the page were the hand-written words: Theban alphabet translation. Underneath were images of the English alphabet and below each letter, a symbol. "Excellent!" Val said gleefully. Then she spotted something that left her cold. The symbol that represented the letter V was the symbol in the centre of Val's tattoo. As if she was having a flashback, she remembered what the woman had called her during her dream: it was 'V'. That was her name. Val closed the paper and shoved it into her pocket.

She realised that the enemy was closing in. She didn't care if it took her all night, she would now be able to translate the book, and find out about the people who were in it. Maybe, just maybe, there might also be a clue to why she was *the Chosen One*- whatever that meant.

She moved with more confidence now, loading the books with an urgency to get her job done, as she had

promised Mr Gallymore. She certainly didn't want to
upset him; two of the clues to who she was had come
directly from his shop so, in some strange way, she was
linked to this place.

Once Val had finished, she was ready to start working out the puzzle. She would close at five, head for
Shane's shop and collect the book, which she had left for
Shane to scan for Sam. Then she would leave the gadgets
and head home for some serious translation work. No
one else would be hurt, or even involved.

As Val started to get ready to lock up, the doorbell rang
with its annoyingly sunny disposition, and in walked
Wendy. Val sighed. This was the last person she wanted
to see.

"Hi Val, sorry to call in so late, but I need another
book." Wendy gave a weak squeaky sound. "Is it OK?"
She smiled at Val who was holding the door open with
her foot.

"Yes sure. Come in." Val managed to grimace a
smile.

"Thanks. I know what I want, so I won't be long."

Val nodded as she went behind the counter to make
sure she had all her belongings. As she bent to get her
handbag she felt a sharp pain shoot up her arm. The pain
was again reduced in ferocity, as if with each of the
symbols disappearing, so the pain lessened.

No! Not now! And especially not with Wendy just
two feet away. She already had her suspicions about
Wendy's peculiar literary tastes and her ability to turn up
at the worst possible moments, and it was very strange
that she didn't seem to be the least disturbed by the state
of Val's face.

"Wendy, I don't like to rush you, but I must really be going." Val's voice was strained.

"OK, I have it. Sorry for the delay." Wendy came trotting up to the counter with an old looking leather bound book. Val grabbed it and went to check for the price on the inside cover. To Val's dismay there was none. This meant that it was a book that Val had to look up. These prices were in a special book that Mr Gallymore called his 'worthy books'. The ones that only true readers would buy. Val didn't have time for this and she needed to get rid of Wendy now.

"Wendy this book has no price in it. Could you please come back for it tomorrow?" Val smiled, holding the book tightly, as the pain continued to shoot up and down her arm.

Wendy started to protest. "I need it tonight; it's important." She reached out to grab it from Val. Val was surprised that Wendy was being so stubborn. The book must be important.

"OK. Take it, but promise to pop in tomorrow and pay for it." As she spoke, Val heard the distant whimpering of a small child.

"Thank you. I promise I will be here at nine a.m." Wendy smiled, slowly prising the book from a now very distracted Val.

"Yes sure. Bye." When Val turned to let Wendy out, she was in an almost dream like state. The noise was getting louder and she really didn't have a clue where it was coming from.

"See you in the morning," Wendy gushed, waving as she left.

Val was no longer listening. She shut the door behind Wendy, turned the key in the main lock, then headed back into the shop. The sounds of the little child's whines were now beginning to annoy her. She made her way behind the counter and slipped on her jacket as she tried to pinpoint the direction of the noise.

"Come on, where are you?" Val mooched around trying to get closer to the sound. It was almost like a game of 'Hot and Cold' without any help. At the back of the shop, she heard another cry, and then she spotted it. There was a movement in the silver light switch on the wall near the closet. Even when she moved in closer, she could only just make out the silhouette of a child.

"You people really are scum, picking on kids now," Val called out as if someone should be listening. Val looked around for a second to make sure she had closed the shop then placed her hand on the light socket. "Lights out," she said. The shop was thrown into darkness except for a small flicker of blue static as Val slipped away.

CHAPTER 9

Pick on Someone
your Own Size

Val was met by gloomy shadows, and a bitter odour. It was as if she had been sent into the local Italian restaurant's wheelie bin. She pinched her arm to make sure she hadn't knocked herself unconscious in the process of teleporting and this was just a dream. "Ow," she whimpered. Nope, she was definitely awake.

Her thoughts were broken by a child's cry from the other side of what she could only imagine was a wall. It was impossible to see her surroundings in this darkness. Val dropped onto her knees and crawled towards the noise, feeling the floorboards as she went. Reaching hesitantly out, she found that there was what seemed to be a wall in front of her. Pushing her hand slowly up it, she realised it was not a wall at all, but a door. Val had never known a room as dark as this and even wondered if maybe she had jumped through time as well as place because, when she left, it was daylight outside the shop, yet now it felt like the darkest of nights.

Shuffling closer to the door, she spotted a crack, small, yet large enough to peek through. As she pushed her eye to it, she could just make out a dingy, dirty look-ing room. On the other side and in the corner, was the silhouette of a child. She was wearing dungarees and looked about seven or eight years old. Then it went dark again. Val strained to see. Then it dawned on her that her view was being blocked by a human form on the other side of the door. Val held her breath as she reached into her pocket, glad that she hadn't given back her sword just yet. She slowly pulled it out.

Within seconds, the little girl began screaming. Val felt a sick churning at the bottom of her stomach as the figure moved forward in large cumbersome strides. Val waited until she could see a shimmer of light again and then she couldn't quite believe what she was seeing. The man on the other side was huge. He was larger than the very first man she had been entangled with in the bookshop; he made Shane look like one of Snow White's little helpers.

The girl was whimpering like a small dog, clearly terrified. Val had heard quite enough. She stood up, feel-ing her way up the door to the handle. With her other hand she flicked out her sword, hoping it would be a silent event.

'Whoosh,' it crackled. "Note for Sam, sword too noisy," Val mumbled, grabbing the door handle. It was now or never. The thug's ears seemed to prick up; he had heard Val's sword and was heading back towards the door. Val pulled it open and, as he came towards her, she stepped out raising her sword into the salute position.

"I think you need to pick on someone your own size," she said, almost choking on the words. The fear was freezing her vocal cords and she sounded like a cross between Mickey Mouse and Bart Simpson. The thug stopped in his tracks and for the first time Val could clearly see the little girl in the corner of the room. She looked dirty and scared. Her hair was still plaited although it was messy. She had obviously been here a while. As she looked back up at the giant, he started to laugh. It was a deep and gruff laugh, like a typical maniacal movie villain's snigger. This annoyed Val.

"OK, I warned you." She lunged forward and the tip of her sword made contact with his exposed belly button. The thug was caught by surprise. He had a confused expression on his face as the white sparks began. Val held her sword against his body for several seconds, and she was starting to worry that he wasn't going to fall down. Then she remembered Delta saying that size did make a difference. Just as her brain was scrabbling for a plan B, he slowly started to topple, vibrating, to the floor. A cloud of dust rose around him and he appeared to be unconscious. Val knew she wouldn't have long so she flicked the sword to close and shoved it into her pocket.

Jumping over the now motionless body, she ran towards the little girl.

"Hello, I'm Val." She smiled as she began untying the child's hands. "What's your name?"

"Lottie," the girl rasped. She had obviously been crying for a while.

"That's a lovely name. Best if you don't talk. I'm going to get you out of here, OK? Take my hand." Val stretched out her hand and Lottie's small hand gently grabbed it. She could see the bloody marks on her wrist from the rope. "Let's go." Val pulled her up and they were almost out of the room when she felt a pull on her ankle. The thug was already starting to wake up and had a hold on Val's leg.

"Run!" Val screamed at Lottie, as she stamped violently on the thug's hand. "Get-off-me-you-animal." Val spat each word in sync with her thudding boot. The thug howled in pain as Val jumped over him towards Lottie who had managed to get to the door. Val threw herself at the handle and the door sprang open.

Grabbing Lottie once again, she started to make her way along the darkened corridor that opened out in front of them. There was no wallpaper on the walls and, as Val felt her way, she noticed that they seemed to be weeping some sort of slime. Although the corridor wasn't in complete darkness the whole house seemed to have no natural light. It was as if they had fallen into a black and white film. As they reached the top of the staircase, Val heard their aggressor hot on their tails.

Val turned. "Hold on," she said as she lifted Lottie off the ground.

Luckily for Val, Lottie was very light and Val knew she could move quicker with her off the ground. Val made her way down the stairs cautiously, feeling every step with her toe. When they eventually reached what felt like the bottom, Val was met by more doors and more darkness. She was starting to feel panicked and very disorientated.

She couldn't work out the layout of the house because there were no open windows to see if she was even on the bottom floor. She was also very aware of the fact that they were being followed, which was making her grab at every door handle in the hope of some escape route. As she did, Val felt splinters from the rotten wood thrusting into her hand. Adrenaline stopped the pain, for now.

As she made her way to the end of a corridor she heard loud banging. How had the giant managed to get in front of her? Or was the noise coming from behind? She stopped for a second to get her breath, and then the banging started again. It was growing in volume and frequency. Val didn't know which way to look.

Grabbing her sword and lowering Lottie to the ground, Val placed her index finger to her lips signalling for Lottie to be quiet. Two large eyes looked back at her and she nodded her head. "Whoosh," the sword was extended and Val was ready once again to go into battle. She had made her mind up; whatever it took, she would save this little girl. Then a bang like a gun went off and streams of dazzling daylight hit them both in the face. As a thick cloud of dust rose, Val braced to defend her charge.

"God, this place is filthy; you can't expect me to go in there."

Val would have recognised that voice any time and any place. "Delta!" Val screamed as the dust started to settle. Grabbing Lottie again under her arm, she ran towards the light. "Run!" she yelled as she pushed past the silhouettes in the doorway without even stopping to acknowledge them.

She ran over a junkyard of a garden, through a broken gate and came to a standstill next to Delta's red mini. She gently lowered Lottie and then bent down gasping for breath.

As she started to recover, she stood up to find herself face to face with Delta and Jason who had done as they were told and run behind Val to the car.

"First things first, what are you doing here?" Val questioned, looking confused. "And secondly, where are we?"

"I was trying to contact you all day but your mobile was off. Therefore, I was looking for you on the laptop.

I saw you jump, so I called Delta. When I realised that you were so close, we had to come and help," Jason replied shrugging his shoulders.

"When you say close, how close?"

"Six miles from the shop," Jason said. Val felt a tug on her sleeve. Looking down she was met by a scared little girl's face.

"Sorry Lottie. These are my friends. You can trust them. This is Delta." Delta offered a small wave to the little girl who smiled back. "And this is Jason."

"What on earth happened to your face?" Delta winced in Val's direction.

"Long story. I'll fill you in later," Val replied.

"OK boss, what now?" Jason asked.

"Well, I'm pleased to see you both, but the story is this: the man who just attacked us was *massive*. He had Lottie as a prisoner and I'm just happy to be out of there. But I don't think it's over as I haven't done my vanishing act yet." Val looked at Lottie.

"Do you think there is anything else you need to do?" Delta chirped up.

"Excuse me." Lottie's timid voice broke their conversation.

Val turned and bent down to Lottie's height. "It's OK, we will get you home to your mummy soon," she said rubbing Lottie's arm.

"But the man has my mummy in there." Lottie's eyes filled up with tears as she pointed to the house. "He took her when we were out shopping and then he came back for me."

"Right." Val stood up and grabbed Delta's arm. "Get her in the car, Delta. Talk to her about fashion or handbags, I don't care, just do it." Delta nodded at Val.

"So Lottie, do you know about Jimmy Choo?" Delta asked as she opened the door and helped Lottie into the passenger's seat.

"Jason, I need to go back in. Her mother is in there and I have to get her out." Jason looked at Val and smiled.

"You're truly the most amazing person I have ever met, but I'm coming with you," he said.

Val started to shake her head in disagreement. "Jason, I don't have time to argue. It's not safe." Val's words fell on deaf ears; Jason was already heading back across the garden to the house. Val threw her arms in the air in submission and turned to wave at Lottie and Delta who were already looking at a copy of Cosmopolitan.

Val caught up with Jason. "Listen to me, this man is twice the size of your dad, the house is pitch black and I don't know where her mum is."

"If we work together we should be OK." Jason smiled as Val pulled out her sword. "See, we have a weapon on our side," Jason said smugly.

Val smiled back, thinking it better not to tell him that it had worked on the thug for a total of about a thirty seconds.

They made their way back up the hall that had given Val and Lottie their escape route. Jason positioned himself back-to-back with Val and she could feel his warm body pressing against hers. Then she got a waft of his aftershave. "Get a grip! Now isn't the time to be having inappropriate thoughts." Val shook her head. Reaching the stairs, Val felt Jason pulling on her hand.

"What?" she whispered.

"Up or down?" Jason asked, pointing with his nose in both directions.

"Well, Lottie was upstairs and I didn't see her mum there, so I suppose we should go down." The thought filled Val with dread. Cellars rarely had more than one in and out door.

"You lead." Jason moved in behind Val. She made her way towards the furthest door and turned the handle. It opened first time and quite smoothly. Inside, Val instantly heard a muffled noise.

"She's here," Val whispered, looking at Jason. The two drew closer and took one step at a time. Val could feel the sweat dripping down her hand onto the sword. As they reached the bottom step, they saw a faint glow around the end of the staircase.

"Well, he isn't behind us, and it doesn't sound as if he is in front, so let's go," Jason said.

Turning the corner they emerged into a dimly lit room, in the centre of which was a gagged woman who was tied to a chair. When she saw Val, her eyes filled with tears. She was labouring to breathe with the gag tight around her mouth and getting so emotional didn't help. Val hurried straight over to pull it off.

"Please, don't leave me," the woman sobbed.

"We won't, I promise. Are you Lottie's mum?" The woman's face went pale as she looked at Val.

"He has Charlotte, here?" "Yes, she was tied up upstairs, but she is safe now. We have her outside." Val spoke to the woman as Jason frantically tried to get the woman's hands free.

"I was shopping when he grabbed me, but Charlotte was in the car and I thought that he wouldn't find her." The woman was shaking and obviously deeply traumatised. "How did you find me?" She looked from Val to Jason with a puzzled expression.

"We heard Lottie from the street and came to investigate," Val said in such a convincing tone she nearly believed it herself.

"Is it day or night? I can't remember. I don't even know how long I've been here." The woman was looking around her as if disorientated by the whole situation.

"Look at me. I'm Val, this is Jason, and it's Monday the 11th about 5.30 p.m. Now, let's get you out of here. How's it going Jason?" Val looked to Jason for support.

"I think this bloke is a sailor. I can't get these knots undone," Jason answered without shifting his eyes from the rope.

"Well at least we're alone." Val smiled at the woman.

"No we aren't!" she screamed at Val, but it was too late. The thug had crept up on them as they were talking. He was not only large, but agile as well. Val didn't have time to turn before she was pulled off the ground, causing her to drop the sword, which instantly retracted. The next she felt was the wall that stopping her flight through the air. The breath left her body as she dropped to the floor.

When she managed to get back on her feet, Jason was hitting the man around the chest area; he couldn't reach any higher. Val was on the move again. She needed her sword back, but it was on the other side of the room, and between her and it, were two men fighting. It didn't last long. Val looked on in horror as the thug lifted Jason off the ground and shook him like a puppet, before he throwing him across the room. Jason lay motionless on the ground and the thug was on his way towards her again.

"What now?" Val thought looking around her, frantically searching for an escape route. Spotting a furnace in the corner behind her, she ran to it. Looking through the glass, she could see a small flame burning. Maybe, just maybe, she could use it. She opened the door and placed her hand into the flames.

Val focused intensely and when she pulled her hand out she had what looked like a tennis ball of fire resting on her palm. She waited for some sort of pain, but nothing happened. If she hadn't been quite so scared she would probably have thought that this moment was extremely cool, but there was no time for that. Turning towards the moving thug, she raised her hand and smiled at him. He stopped, wary of her, astonished by what she was doing. The woman, who was still on the chair, was now clearly in a state of shock, and Jason hadn't made the slightest move.

"OK, we can do this the easy way or we can do it the hard way." Val waved the ball of fire at him. The thug registered what she was saying for a second or two then burst into gut-wrenching laughter.

Val lifted the ball to shoulder height and threw it with all her strength. Watching the ball fly through the air gave her a wonderful sense of satisfaction that she was at last taking some control of her powers. The thug, still laughing, moved very slightly; the ball of fire flew past his head and hit the opposite wall. Val thought she was going to die of embarrassment and the thug could now hardly stand up due to laughing so hard.

Val wasn't going to have this. The woman needs to be rescued and reunited with her daughter, and Jason needed an ambulance. She had grown tired of this man. She turned once more and reached into the furnace. With the anger now raging through her body, she pulled out another ball of fire

"What now?" The thug taunted her. "Remember, three strikes and you are out."

As Val started walking, it became very apparent that her temper was directly linked to her powers. The flames began to caress her, skipping up and down her clothes as she made her way towards the now not-so-cheerful thug. By the time she reached him, her whole body was on fire.

"Stop!" he screamed.

"Did Lottie say stop? Did her mum say stop?" Val asked, pointing a flaming arm at the woman who was sitting very still in the chair. "I told you once and I won't tell you again: pick on someone your own size." Val smashed both her flaming hands onto the thug's pounding chest, and he was on fire. He turned to run. She struck him again from behind. His look was beginning to resemble Val's, although *he* wasn't flameproof.

The thug pulled away from Val's flaming grip and ran from the cellar leaving Val with the woman still tied up, and Jason out cold on the floor. Val ran to Jason's side, picking up her sword on the way.

"Jason, Jason, wake up," Val cried. As she reached out to touch him, the flames petered out and she was once again back to normal.

"What?" Jason said shaking his head and starting to lift himself up.

"Are you OK?" Val grabbed his arm and started to pull him to his feet.

"Where is the man?" Jason looked around.

"He's gone and you need to get out of here too, with her." Val pointed to the woman who was still sitting open-mouthed.

"What about you?" Jason grabbed Val's hand. "What happens to you?"

"I need to go back the way I came." Val smiled as she held her hand out to the woman. "This will definitely freak you out, although I think the damage is already done," "Give my love to Lottie." The spark flashed and she was gone.

Val landed back at the shop in time to hear the clock chime six. "Wow, that was quick. I must be getting good at this." Val grinned as she walked towards the front of the shop. Making her way to the counter, she grabbed her handbag and pulled out her phone, switched it on and started to dial.

"Hello Shane," Val said, unsure of his reaction after last night's episode.

"Hello! How did it go, did the others find you?" Shane obviously hadn't heard from Delta and Jason yet. Teleporting *was* the quickest form of travel.

"They did find me, and we are all OK. Jason may need a few bandages, but between us we saved a little girl and her mum." Val felt a lump form in her throat. It had been quite an emotional hour and although she was glad they were all OK, she still had issues to resolve with the others. "I will come over in a few minutes; I just have to finish off here." Val closed her phone and slipped it back into her bag.

Glancing down at the necklace, she realised she had forgotten that this was what they had used to find her. Maybe she wasn't supposed to be alone. Maybe they were a team and, as much as Val wanted to run from them, they were going to keep on following her. She had to admit that she like that idea and Jason, Shane, Delta and Sam were big enough to make choices for themselves.

Val prepared to close the shop for a second time. Locking up behind her, she turned to walk down the steps and was greeted by Delta who was sitting on the bonnet of her mini and smiling.

"How did you get here so fast?" Val looked surprised.

"Well, while you and Jason were doing Starsky and Hutch, I got Lottie to call the cops. They arrived just as the crazy man came running out of the house covered in flames. Good job by the way," Delta gave Val a thumbs up. "They raided the house and found Jason and Lottie's mum making their way out of the cellar." Delta jumped off the bonnet and opened the door for Val. "Val, stuff happens and we all make mistakes. This has been a learning curve for us all and I want to say the 'S' word for how I behaved last night, but I can't." Delta stood back and opened her arm to invite Val to get in.

"Do you mean sorry?" Val smiled as she jumped in.

"No, it was 'S' for shopping, but if you want to say sorry, then thanks." Delta started the car and pulled away in a screech of tyres. "We need to get to the hospital."

"What's wrong?" Val tensed up. "Is it Lottie?" "No, Lottie and her mum will be fine. It's Jason. He was having problems breathing when he came out, so the police were dropping him off at the hospital and Shane was going to meet him there. I thought maybe you would like to see him."

"Delta, what do you think Jason thinks of me?" Val asked, not looking at Delta. She kept her eyes firmly on the view out of the window of the car.

"Do you want my opinion?"

"Yes."

"OK, when he called me about you, he was in a really bad way. He couldn't get to you quick enough and I could tell it was more than just a friendly 'let's all go to the pub together'." Delta looked at Val and smiled. "I think he likes you. Why don't you ask him and find out?"

"What if he doesn't like me? Maybe he just feels sorry for me. I couldn't cope and then I would lose a friend who means a lot to me."

"Val, you need to make that decision for yourself. I can't answer that one." Delta changed gear as they slipped onto the motorway. "Now tell me all about your lovely blue cheeks, Alien."

Val let out a laugh. She could never have left Delta; there was no-one quite like her for making the biggest problems feel silly.

As they sped along, Val's mobile started to ring. It was her mother.

"Hi Mum," Val answered. "No, I won't be home for tea. Me and the Yank are spending some quality time together if that's OK?" She smiled at Delta. "Yes, I will be home, but not till later. Love you too." Val flipped the phone shut and sat back to think exactly how she was going to tell Jason just how she felt.

"Jason Walker please?" Val said to the woman behind the desk at Accident and Emergency.

"Take a seat. He is being seen to now," she said, not even lifting her eyes from the screen in front of her.

"Thanks." Val grabbed Delta and they went to sit down.

"Maybe you could get them to look at your face while we are here. You know, a bit of foundation would cover that up." Delta kindly offered Val a pot of brown liquid from her bag, which Val tactfully turned down.

"Coffee?" Val asked, pointing to a vending machine in the corner of the waiting room.

"No, it's not." Delta shook her head and they both giggled together.

Val sat on her plastic chair, working through in her mind what she was going to say. She went through a few scenarios and decided that she would wait until everyone had left and they could be alone, so she could tell him exactly how she felt.

"Hey girls." Val looked up to see Shane standing over them. Jumping to her feet, she grabbed him. Shane led them into the ward area, peeling Val off. "Jason has a few broken ribs and I think a bruised ego because he wasn't awake while you beat up the big guy, so don't be too hard on him." Shane smiled at Val.

She was starting to get a deep churning feeling in the pit of her stomach. Her nerves were going to get the better of her.

"He's in here, just don't make too much of a fuss, OK?"

The girls found Jason sitting on a bed with a bandage around his chest.

"Hello Jason." Val walked over, so she was closest to him.

"I'm so sorry I wasn't more help, Val." Jason looked at the floor.

"Hey, you kept him busy while I set myself on fire," Val said playfully, hoping this would make him feel a little better.

"Hi Jason. Hope you feel better soon. I need to get a drink." Delta turned, winked at Val and walked out of the room.

"Bye Delta, thanks for visiting, I think," Jason said, looking up just in time to watch Delta exiting.

Val could feel the heat of embarrassment starting to burn her cheeks so she decided to go for it before she passed out.

"Jason," Val said gently.

"Yes Val?"

"I need to talk to you about something important." Val's heart was now lodged in her throat.

"Is everything OK?" Jason said.

"Yes fine, I just need to tell you something." Val took a step towards Jason and then she heard a noise. The toilet in the room was being flushed. Shane and Delta were outside so who was in there?

"Val, what do you want to talk about?" Jason didn't seem bothered that the toilet door was opening and so the bells started to ring in Val's head.

"Jason, when can we go home, baby?" said a female voice from behind the toilet door.

"In a minute, Fran. Just talking to my mate Val," Jason replied.

Mate! Did he just call me, mate?' Val could feel the anger in her heart as a super model came from behind the door.

"Val, I have heard so many nice things about you, I'm Francesca," she said offering Val her hand.

"I have never heard anything about you," Val retorted. Fran uncomfortably pulled her hand back. Val watched aghast as this girl, with her perfect auburn hair and amazing good looks, sat down on the bed next to Jason. For a split second, Val imagined setting her on fire and then blowing her up.

"Val, this is my girlfriend, Francesca. She is here on holiday."

Val just looked at them.

"She arrived as a surprise today," Jason explained.

Who was he trying to convince that he didn't know she was coming? Val thought.

"Well, I will leave you two love birds to it then." Val turned to walk out of the room.

"I thought you wanted to talk to me?" Jason called after her.

"It can wait," Val replied despondently. As she reached the door, the tears were already welling in her eyes.

"Bye Val. I hope we meet again soon," Francesca called. Val carried on without responding. She knew it would have shown in her voice that she was crying.

Delta was waiting at reception with Shane. Val could see straight away that Delta had been informed of '*its*' arrival.

Val composed herself and said to Delta, "I think I would like to go home now."

Delta nodded.

"Will I see you tomorrow, Val?" Shane asked.

"Yes, we need to do some translating. I found some information I think will help and I need you to pass on a message to Sam for me," Val said in a more businesslike tone.

"See you in the morning then." Shane went back towards his son's room.

As Val left the hospital, she thought it ironic that she had arrived with a healthy heart yet was leaving with a broken one.

Delta grabbed Val's hand and squeezed it hard as they left the building. They only released each other as they reached the car. The journey home was in silence as Val stared out of the car window watching the world pass her by.

"Here we are Val. I'm so sorry about what happened. If it's any consolation, I think you are way cooler than whoever she is." Delta leaned over and looked up at Val as she exited the car silently.

"It's OK, Delta. He never said he liked me and he never said he didn't have a girlfriend. It's just my luck." Val turned away, shutting the car door before Delta could make any more attempts at making her feel better. "Hi Mum!" Val shouted up the hall.

"Hi honey. How are you feeling?" Susan called back from the kitchen.

"Great. Where's Dad?"

"He has had to work late. This new client of his wants his house building double time. Your father reckons it's a bit odd, but he has paid cash so who would say no?" Susan had made her way to greet Val at the front door. "What's wrong?"

"Nothing, just my face is a bit sore." Val looked at her mum as the tears slowly started to roll down her cheeks.

"Come on, let's get some hot chocolate." Susan put her arm around Val's shoulder and led her into the kitchen. Five minutes later Val was served a piping hot chocolate with whipped cream, marshmallows and chocolate sprinkles, while her mum told her all the church gossip.

It was nice just to listen to the inane goings on of the local women. It distracted Val from the pain in her heart for a while.

"Well, your dad is obviously going to be very late, so I'm going to retire," Susan said. Val nodded in agreement and they said their goodnights as they walked upstairs.

"Val was relieved to be in her own familiar environment. Taking off her clothes, she slipped on her pyjamas. Had she really been that close to making a total fool of herself, of letting someone who called her 'mate' break her heart? "Stupid idiot," Val hissed at herself as she climbed into bed. As she pushed the button to set her alarm, she wasn't sure what her sleep would bring, but she had a tight hold on her sword. If she was getting beaten up in her dreams, maybe she could try and take her weapon with her. Val closed her eyes and after a long day, she was fast asleep within seconds.

She woke with the bleating tones of the alarm and, for a change, she felt completely rested. It was a glorious morning and even though the previous day's events were pretty hideous, she was prepared to let it go and get on with her weird and wonderful life as 'Val the defender of something'.

She was pleasantly surprised at how quickly her face was healing. As she headed out of the house and made her way to the bus stop, her mobile started to ring. It was Delta. Val didn't feel like talking just yet, so she let it go to answer machine.

As she arrived at the shop, her eyes were met by a sight she really could have done without today: Wendy.

"Morning, Val. I said I'd be here at nine and here I am." Even her chirpiness made Val feel nauseous.

"Hi Wendy. I was sure you wouldn't skip town," Val smiled wryly.

"Well, I just want to pay for my book." Wendy looked down at her as she climbed the steps and for a second Val sensed something odd or different about Wendy today. She couldn't pinpoint it, but she had changed.

"Come on in." Val opened the door and moved to switch off the alarm.

"You are so lucky to have a job here. I don't think I would be able to get my head out of the books." Wendy passed Val and headed down the main aisle.

"Well, I try to stay focused." Val dropped her bag behind the counter and looked for her pricing book. "What was the title of the book you took yesterday Wendy so I can work out the price?" Val called out but there was no answer.

"Wendy, I need the book's title?" Val came around the counter and started to walk down the aisle after Wendy. When she reached the end there was still no sign of her, so Val turned and walked back to the counter. "Wendy?" Val called out again. There was no response. The door-bell rang and when Val looked around, the person who walked in nearly made her faint. It was Wendy.

"Morning Val. Sorry I'm a little late, but the bus got stuck behind an accident on the main road. Did you see it on your way into work?" Wendy looked at Val, slightly concerned with the fact that Val was now making her way towards her shaking her head like a deranged goat.

"Everything OK, Val?" Wendy asked, eyeing Val up and down.

"You just arrived?" Val stood so close to Wendy that she could smell the coffee that Wendy had had with her breakfast.

"Are you OK? Do you want me to come back later?" Wendy started to move backwards towards the door.

"No. Just pay for your book. Which one did you take?" Val started to move back around the counter never taking her eyes off Wendy.

"I took a signed first edition. Kate West's 'Dedication for the Solitary Witch'," Wendy said in a hushed tone. It was different when you just paid for a book. Vocalising it made it sound odd.

"Yes, Kate West. Just a second." Val bent her knees, not letting her gaze leave Wendy for a second and grabbed the special book of prices. She flicked from page to page looking at Wendy between turns.

"That's forty-six pounds please." Val forced a grin at Wendy as she got her money out to pay.

"I know I have strange tastes, but I'm harmless," Wendy said passing the money over and starting to make her way out of the shop.

"Wendy, can I ask you something?" Wendy turned to look at Val.

"What?" Wendy responded.

"Do you know anything about dreams?"

"Only what I read in books, Val. If you go down the middle aisle there is a very good section on dream interpretation." She paused. "Is that it?"

"Yes, thanks." Val waved feebly at Wendy and she was gone.

"Oh my God! What just happened?" Val walked down the centre aisle, looking for the dream interpretation section. Val knew she had seen Wendy come in with her and then disappear, and come back again. Maybe she was trying to make her go insane. Wendy was buying every book the shop had on witchcraft and Val knew now, from her own personal experience, that everything we see isn't always what it seems.

"Could Wendy have cast some spell on me so that I would see her more than once?" Val wondered. "Well, it will take a lot more than that to freak me out when

I can teleport from one place to another." As Val started scanning the books, she spotted one called 'Astral projection for beginners'. She had heard of this before on the TV, something her mum had been watching. Val took the book back to the counter.

She needed to find out how this aggressor was attacking her during her sleep and if she could protect herself. If he could cause effects in the real world, then maybe she could attack him in the dream world. It had to be worth a try. Val also wanted to know how Wendy the witch had just pulled off that little stunt. However, Wendy didn't pose any physical threat to Val, so she was going to study the more dangerous of the two first.

Val was reading behind the counter with a cup of coffee when she heard the peeping of Delta's horn outside.

Val made her way out of the shop to greet her.

"So, you ready to go?" Delta shouted out of the car window.

"Where?" Val responded with a blank expression on her face.

"To town. I left you a message this morning about going into town during your lunch break, and, if you didn't reply, I would take it that we were on and I would pick you up at twelve." Delta was starting to look annoyed and as Val was feeling a slight hunger pang in her stomach, she decided that a lunch out couldn't hurt.

"Let me just lock up and I'll be with you." Val turned and ran back into the shop. Within a short space of time, Val and Delta were on their way to the shops and Val was telling Delta about Wendy's visits.

Delta seemed uninterested in what Val had to say and, as they arrived in the car park, she sprang from the car shouting, "Let's shop" as she danced into the shopping centre.

"You're happy today," Val said sarcastically.

"Well today I'm going to fulfil my dreams." Delta was still spinning when they reached the coffee shop they both loved. Val made a straight line to the counter almost falling over ballerina Delta.

"Latte?" Val shouted over to Delta.

"Uh huh, skinny please." Delta came to a standstill leaning on one of the shopping centre pillars, posing like a model ready to be photographed.

"Your friend seems happy," someone behind her said. It took her a moment to recognise the girl standing there, then she realised it was Francesca.

"Hello." Val forced a parting of lips that possibly resembled a smile.

"How are you? I just decided to come and do some shopping. Jason is in Boots getting some pain killers." Francesca pushed past Val to the counter.

"Oy!" Val protested.

"Jason has told me all about your little problem and I think you should be locked away and studied, but who am I to say what freaks get to walk this planet?" Francesca turned her back on Val who was standing with her mouth hanging open with the shock.

"Excuse me! Who the hell do you think you are?" Val grabbed Francesca's arm and pulled her around.

"I'm your worst nightmare." Francesca turned and grabbed Val by the throat, lifting her several feet off the ground. Val could feel the breath being squeezed out of her body and she was unable to fight.

"People like you make me sick. Did you really think I wouldn't be able to tell that you fancied Jason, that you had been trying to keep him all to yourself?" Francesca was now moving across the open cafe towards the middle of the shopping centre. Val was floating a foot of the floor hanging on the end of Francesca's hand. She could see Delta, but she was still busy doing Swan Lake and didn't seem to have noticed the goings on. There was no chance of her screaming; she couldn't even breathe. Just then she spotted Jason running towards them. "At last," Val thought to herself.

"Let her go, Francesca," Jason called out.

"Never, you will never love her the way you love me," Francesca spat back.

Jason was by their side in seconds and the first blow was enough. His fist struck Francesca square in the back and she dropped Val, who fell to the floor gasping for air.

"I'll kill her, she's mine," Francesca hissed as started to run away.

"Are you OK, Val?" Jason gave Val his hand to help her up.

"I think I'll survive," Val said brushing herself down.

"Why did she do that?" Val looked to Jason for an answer.

"Because I told her last night that there was never going to be a *me and her*." Jason moved in closer to Val putting his hands gently around her waist.

"Sorry?" Val spluttered.

"Don't you get it? I never told you about her because I didn't want her to come here. I thought it would just be me and you." Jason brought his face closer to Val's.

"Well, that's not nice." Val was trying to feel sorry for Francesca, but it was hard.

"I want you, Val," Jason whispered in her ear. What happened next was so fast Val didn't have time to stop it.

Jason had his lips on hers and her whole body was shaking, and shaking and shaking. What was going on?

"Val, come on honey. You slept through the alarm, wake up." Susan was rocking Val's body into consciousness. "You will be late for work." Susan stood up and walked out of the room, leaving Val pondering on the only revenge she would ever get on the girl who had stolen her man.

CHAPTER 10

Tickets Please

Val was unenthusiastic about getting out of bed, but she was already late so she couldn't delay for long. She sat up taking a gulp of the tea her mum had left and swivelled her legs out of bed. Once she got going, she moved swiftly and was ready to leave in time to catch her bus.

"See you later, honey." Susan kissed Val on the cheek and passed her lunch.

As Val made her way to the bus, Delta rang her. "Morning," Val answered.

"Hi, would you like to meet me for lunch?" Delta said chirpily.

"OK, same time as usual," Val answered.

"Cool." Delta hung up.

When Val arrived at the shop her jaw nearly hit the ground. There was Wendy waiting in the doorway, in exactly the same stance and clothes as in her dream. As a matter of fact, the phone call from Delta had been at the same time in my dream Val realised, although, in the dream, she hadn't answered it."

"Morning Val. I said I would be here at nine and here I am," Wendy said as Val made her way up the steps.

Val quickly made herself come to terms with what she was seeing, and responded. "Morning Wendy," she said, unlocking the door. "Well, I just want to pay for my book," Wendy said pursuing Val. "You are so lucky to have a job here. I don't think I would be able to get my head out of the books," she added, following Val closely.

Val moved around the counter to safety and sat down. She didn't want Wendy to see how shaken she was with the whole dream repetition situation.

Wendy headed off down the main aisle, just as she had the night before in Val's dream. At this point, Val got out of her chair and headed towards the door to see if 'Wendy two' was on her way.

Testing to see if her dream was more of a premonition than a reverie, Val turned her head back towards the shop and called out, "Wendy, do you know the title of the book you took?" Testing "Yes, it was 'Lunar Cycles of importance from 1645 to 1945'," Wendy called from the centre aisle. Val breathed a sigh of relief. That wasn't what she had said to her before. And as far as Val could see from the door, she wasn't going to magically re-appear from anywhere.

"OK," Val replied moving behind the counter to find the book of prices. Wendy returned to the counter after a few minutes perusing the aisles.

"So, how much do I owe you?"

"Twenty-five pounds. You have expensive tastes in reading, Wendy," Val smiled.

"Well, I believe that the books you read define who you really are, don't you?" Wendy pulled the cash out of her purse and looked Val straight in the eyes. Val was frozen to the spot for a second. She remembered that in her dream, Wendy had been different, something had changed, and here she was looking at the same change once again.

"Thank you," Val said almost in a whisper.

"No, thank you." Wendy picked up the bag from the counter and walked out.

Val stood for a few seconds wondering what Wendy had meant with the book comment. Did she know about the Zodiac book? How could she know?

Val remembered asking 'dream Wendy' about dreams and subsequently finding a useful book that was in the centre aisle, so she decided to investigate. She walked down the aisle, quickly finding the spot she was looking for. There in the centre was 'Astral projection for beginners', the book she had picked up.

Val tried desperately to rationalise what was happening. Maybe she had seen it before and her dream had just reminded her of its place. "Yes that's it," she said to herself while nodding convincingly. Val opened the front page and took it back to the counter sitting down to read a little.

The next thing Val knew, Delta was outside beeping her horn. Val jumped. Putting her book onto the counter she quickly locked up and made her way outside.

"So how did you sleep last night?" Delta asked as soon as Val was in the mini.

"Fine, though I had a bit of a weird dream."

"So, indulge me in your fantasies." Delta grinned back at her. Val told her about the double Wendy scenario and how Delta was had been ballerina, finishing with the Francesca situation.

"Wow, that's a busy dream." Delta looked slightly concerned. "Take my advice Val, don't let the Francesca thing bother you."

"If you are concerned that I'm going to set her on fire, I won't - unless she really is a baddie." Val made kung fu arms as if ready to attack.

They parked the mini, making a mad dash into the shopping centre through the rain that was now pouring down.

"Latte?" Val called to Delta who was grabbing them a table.

"Uh huh. Skinny please." Delta did a quick ballet turn to her chair. Val wished she hadn't told her about the dream; she would be making fun of her all week.

"Your friend seems happy," a voice came from behind her. Val's skin turned to ice. This time she wouldn't mistake that voice.

"Francesca, hello." Val turned smiling at the girl behind her. "How are you?" "I bet Jason's in Boots," Val responded smugly.

"No, he's back at the shop; they are expecting a visitor." Francesca looked slightly confused by Val's comment. Val realised this wasn't her dream and she needed to act slightly more normally.

"Would you like a coffee?" Val asked.

"Are you sure?" Francesca looked at Val, clearly puzzled. "Yes, I'm sure."

"I would love a hot chocolate with cream please, oh, and call me Fran. Only my nan and granddad call me Francesca. I keep thinking you are going to tell me off." Fran smiled and Val knew it was going to be hard to dislike her.

"Go and sit with Delta and I'll bring them over," Val told her.

Val made her way over with the tray to the sound of laughter from the other girls. "What's so funny?" she asked.

"Fran was just explaining how much Jason had moaned about his ribs hurting in hospital," Delta responded.

"Yes, he was like a little girl," Fran smiled. "Though, he was so brave really, saving that little girl and her mother. It was such a lucky thing that Jason and Delta were around at the time." Fran smiled at Delta. "Shame you missed all the fun, Val. What's it like working in a bookshop?"

Val's mouth twitched; they hadn't told her she was there. The cheek! "Well, I try to keep busy." Val tapped Delta's leg under the table. Delta smiled back shrugging her shoulders. As they sat telling each other their life stories, Val unexpectedly felt an intense twinge in her arm, almost making her spit out her mouthful of mocha.

"Anyone want another one?" she spluttered.

"I never say no to chocolate," Fran answered.

"Do you have time?" Delta looked at her watch.

"Yes, all the time in the world." Val turned and headed to the counter. "One skinny latte, one chocolate and one mocha please."

Val winced as the pain intensified. She discreetly lifted up the sleeve on her sweater to reveal that two of the final five symbols were bright red. "No wonder it hurts so much," Val thought. She turned to see Fran waving at her.

"Five pounds twenty please," the girl behind the counter said.

"What?" Val could see her lips moving, but the sound of grating metal drowned out her words.

"Five pounds twenty," the girl repeated impatiently.

Val could now hear screams. This was pure terror. She turned around and felt herself being drawn away from the coffee shop. As she started to walk, she made sure her earpiece was in place and that her trusty sword was in her back pocket.

Val was oblivious to the chaos she had left behind her. Delta, realising instantly that something was wrong, stood up and made her way to the counter where the waitress was shouting about Val walking away without paying.

"Shut up!" Delta snapped putting the money on the counter.

"Is there anything wrong?" Fran was hot on Delta's heels.

"Not now, Fran." Delta could see Val heading toward the shops almost like a bloodhound on a trail.

The screaming was becoming unbearable. Val kept walking until she felt that she was getting closer. Finally she stopped in front of a door – to the ladies' toilets.

As soon as Val opened the door, she knew this was the place; the noise was now excruciating.

Luckily for Val, the toilets were empty. She found herself facing a huge mirror that covered the whole wall. Slap-bang in the middle, she could see the backs of a dozen people, all looking down at something and screaming. Val hesitated for a moment, wondering whether she shouldn't be questioning what she was about to do, but there just wasn't time. "Here I go." Val placed her hands on the mirror and vanished.

The door to the toilet flew open and Delta ran in just in time to catch the last of Val's spark. Fran ran into the back of her.

"Where's Val?" Fran looked around. All the cubicles were open and there was obviously no one in there. "Delta, where's Val?" Fran grabbed Delta's arm.

"Be quiet!" Delta snapped, at Fran as she got out her very sparkly accessorised military-style mobile and started to dial. "Hi Jason, Have you got her?" Delta stood silently listening, as Fran looked on in amazement, then said, "Yes, she's here," and nodded at Fran.

"Does he want to talk to me?" Fran reached for the phone. Delta pulled it away.

"Well I don't have much choice, do I?" Delta said. "No, I'm sure she won't be happy, but what else can I do?" Delta hung up. "You'd better sit down we could be in for a long wait, and what I have to tell you may leave you unable to stand."

Fran did as she was told; she could tell Delta was serious and in that mood she was also quite scary.

Val felt a strong breeze rushing through her hair and the first thing she saw was clouds. She realised that she was seated, and that the music she could hear to was more 'rave' than she would personally have chosen.

To her astonishment, Val had arrived on a rollercoaster ride. She was at the back of a half a dozen of carriages, which were now stationary. The other passengers were crowded at the front. Val was surprised and shocked to see several of them standing up. She took in the panorama for a moment. The sea was to her right and to her left was an ocean of caravans. As she stood up, ready to investigate, she heard a familiar voice.

"Hello mate," said Jason.

'And on with the mate,' Val thought. "Hello, do you have any clues as to where I am?" She spoke quietly, trying not to draw attention to herself.

"You are in Lincolnshire, somewhere called Ingold-mells," Jason responded.

"OK. Well, I can see the sea from up here because I'm on a rollercoaster." Val looked again towards the sea where several large tankers were visible on the horizon.

"Google says the only rollercoaster there is in a place called Fantasy Island," Jason said.

"Well that's great, thanks," Val nodded.

"What's going on?"

"Everyone has moved to the front. They're looking at something. I think I'm going to have to climb to them. Luckily they are all so distracted that no one has seen me arrive."

"Be careful." Jason sounder worried.

"OK, *mate,*" Val responded.

As she stood upright, a gust of wind almost knocked her back down. Gritting her teeth, she climbed over the first gap between carriages. Val knew it would be OK as long as she didn't look down.

The music stopped suddenly. She heard cried from below and, risking a glance down, she saw that everyone had stopped what they were doing, and were looking up at the roller coaster. It didn't take Val long to realise why. The very first cart had come off the tracks and was hanging precariously over the side. That was scary enough; the fact that it had two people trapped in it made the situation much worse. Val knew that these were the two people she had been summoned to help, but how would she get past the rest of the people and save them without drawing attention to herself? This was going to be impossible.

She scrambled over the last gap between the carts. She was now close enough to talk to the other passengers.

"Hello," Val said cautiously, addressing the woman who was nearest to her and who was obviously in a state of shock. The woman looked at Val blankly.

Val needed to get past her to the front. "Excuse me," Val said confidently, giving the woman a gentle push.

The woman moved back. Val was now stuck between her and the next victim.

There was an unexpected scream as the cart dropped another few inches, causing the other carriages, to which it was still attached, to tilt dangerously to one side. Val needed to work quickly. She remembered the man she had met in the cave with Max. He had looked and sounded official, and had had no trouble in getting people to obey his instructions.

"Hello!" Val shouted over the whimpers of the stranded passengers. They all turned to look at her. "I'm a trained rescue warden. Please let me through."

The crowd parted, seeming relieved that someone was taking charge.

When Val got to the edge, she could now see that a woman and man were trapped in the cart, which was dangling, swaying gently in the wind, a hundred feet above the ground. The unfortunate couple were pinned in their seats by their harnesses, which, unlike everyone else's, hadn't opened. If they didn't escape soon, they were going to fall to their deaths. How on earth was she going to get them out?

"Jason, can you hear me?" Val shouted.

"Here," Jason responded immediately.

"I need to get two people out of a rollercoaster cart. They are trapped by their harnesses. Any suggestions?" Val questioned.

"What powers did you use to get the people out of the cave?" Jason responded.

Val replayed the scene in her mind and saw herself shocking the door so that the hinges broke down.

"I punched the door and disintegrated the rocks, but if I do that here the whole thing will fall down."

"Could you maybe focus your power on the harnesses?" Jason replied.

"Yes, I think I could." Val smiled.

"OK you two." Val addressed to heavily built men who were standing behind her. "I want you to hold my waist with one hand each. I'm going to hang over the edge to reach the cart." The men nodded. "With the other hand I want *you*," she pointed at the first man, "to grab and hold the woman's hand." "And you," she pointed at the other man, "do the same for the man, do you understand?" Val sounded very confident and once again they nodded in agreement. "OK, let's do it."

Val turned towards the petrified couple who were looking up at her. The men lifted her over the edge, to the horrified screams of the crowd below. "Hi, I'm Val." She fought a moment of intense nausea as she looked down at the gathering crowd who looked like ants. "Take these men's hands." They did as she said; she seemed to be the only one here with a plan.

"I'm going to make the cart shake, but not too much." Val could see the fear on their faces. "I need to do this quickly or we are all going to fall so hold on to those hands really tightly." Val placed her hands on the cart and started to focus her energy onto the harnesses.

As the cart began to shake the couple instinctively tightened their grips. Looking down again, Val saw that there were camera flashes going off and a few video cameras were aimed at them.

"This isn't enough, Jason, it's not coming apart," Val said. The couple looked at her, the panic on their faces growing. She did her best to smile back.

"Try harder. You need to shake the whole thing apart," Jason replied tensely.

"I'm going to make it a little rougher, guys," Val shouted back to the men.

Now Val pushed all her energy into her hands. The whole cart began to shake, slowly at first but as Val built up momentum, it became more violent. The woman was crying, but Val couldn't stop. At last the cart started to come apart. Nut and bolts, and rivets rained down on the spectators below, who starting yelling angrily.

"Nearly there. Hold on." Val warned, seeing that the cart was on the point of total disintegration. "Be ready to drag them up." Val was beginning to feel faint from focusing her energy for such a long period of time. How much longer could she keep this up?

When she was on the point of exhaustion, there was a large bang and the cart started to fall. There were more screams from the crowd below and Val found herself and the couple hanging over the edge, held in mid-air by the two men.

Val let her arms hang loose as she took a breath. She could feel herself fading out of consciousness, but she knew she still had to touch the couple. As they all hung precariously above the onlookers, Val reached for the woman's hand, which sparked. Then she turned to the man and tried to grab his hand. She couldn't quite reach him. Looking up again, she noticed that one of the men who was holding them was smirking at her. "Damn!" Val thought as he let her go and pulled in the woman. Val slipped. The other man was also grinning in Val's direction, and she knew her time was up. Two people to help; it added up that there were going to be two villains.

There was no way she was going to get out of this one. She was hanging mid-air and there had been no second blue spark. Then the second man released her waist and she began to fall. As she tumbled past him, the man who had been trapped in the cart just managed to grab her hand. She felt the second spark and, once again, started to fall.

Val landed violently on the hard tiles of the toilet floor. She opened her eyes to be greeted by Delta's familiar smile.

"Hello Alien."

"Hello Yankee. Miss me?" Val let her body relax for a second. "I'm lying on the floor of a public toilet, aren't I?" Val said feeling completely grossed out.

"Yup," Delta laughed.

"Uggggh!! OK, let's get out of here." Val stood up, then realised that Fran was keeping people out of the toilets by holding the door shut with her foot. "Oh! Hi." Val said lamely. "It's OK. She knows everything." Delta walked past Val and tapped Fran on the arm. "She's one of us now."

Fran's expression told a thousand words. She had just seen Val reappear through an electric rip in time and land on a toilet floor in front of her.

Val forced a smile. "Welcome on board." Fran pulled her foot away from the door and a woman burst in. She looked at the girls, tutted and then disappeared into a cubicle.

"Are you OK?" Fran asked Val as they walked.

"If I'm honest, I could do with a rest." Val's shoulders slouched.

"Delta told me that they know where you are and that you can communicate with Jason."

Val nodded. She hadn't thought about how this would make Fran feel. The truth was Jason hadn't told Fran about any of this and that must hurt.

"Fran, I'm sorry that Jason hasn't told you about me. He was sworn to secrecy." Val felt uncomfortable.

Fran grabbed Val's hand. "It's OK, Val," she said warmly.

"Thank you." Val knew it was going to be impossible to dislike Fran.

"Right, let's go." Delta waved the girls towards the lift.

"What time is it?" Val realised she needed to get back to work before she did anything else.

"One-thirty," Fran replied.

"Great, I'm late." Val pushed both girls into the opening lift.

They travelled back to the shop in silence. Val was aware that this was a lot for anyone to understand and she couldn't think of anything to say to make it easier; it just was what it was.

"Shall we come with you?" Fran asked from the car as they pulled up.

"No, I just need a little time on my own, but I promise if anything happens I'll call you, OK?" Val smiled.

The girls agreed to meet Val at Shane's when she had closed. When she opened up, she was greeted by a phone ringing. Making her way behind the counter she found her mobile phone buzzing away, her mum's name flashing on the front.

"Hi Mum," Val chirped, thinking it was lucky that she had got there just in time to answer the phone.

"Don't you dare '*hi Mum*' me, Valerie Sheridan Saunders," Susan hissed. "What's wrong?" Val was worried. Her mum never called her by her full name unless she was in serious trouble.

"Where have you been for the past few hours?" Susan yelled between sobs and shouting.

"At work," Val replied.

"Don't you lie to me!" Val could hear her mum's voice cracking. "Your father is going to collect you as soon as he can get there. Don't you dare leave the building. Do you understand me?" Susan shouted.

"Mum, please tell me what's wrong?" Val was close to tears. She couldn't remember a time in her life when she had heard her mum so mad.

"I'm watching you on TV. Valerie. Girl falls from rollercoaster and disappears. So now do you want to tell me why my daughter, and I know it was you, is being filmed falling off a rollercoaster in God-forsaken Skegness?"

Val could hear her mum sobbing on the other end of the phone. She couldn't lie any longer. Val knew there would be repercussions to this but how could she hide the truth from her own mother?

"You're right, it was me. We need to talk." Val knew this wasn't going to be easy but it had to be done. "Mum, I'm closing the shop now and heading home. I will explain everything, I promise." Val's throat had tightened up and she didn't feel that she could say another word.

"You had better have a good explanation," Susan said. Then, after a short pause she asked, in a softer tone, "Are you OK? Did you get hurt? It looked painful. What was that shaking thing you were doing? How did you get to Skegness and back so quickly? Is it my fault?"

"No Mum, this isn't your fault. There is so much to tell you. I'm fine, a little tired and I could do with some food." Val knew this would soften the blow. "So I'll see you in about forty-five minutes, OK?"

"Alright Val. I love you." Susan was crying again.

"And I love you too, Mum, to the stars." Val closed her phone and stood in silence, trying to imagine what it was going to be like explaining everything to her parents.

She locked the shop. She didn't care about books today, and she definitely didn't care about what Mr Gallymore might say. She grabbed her things, but as she left the shop, she decided she needed to see Shane before she went home, just to explain that she might never see the light of day again.

As she arrived at the tattoo parlour, she was greeted by Delta's mini and Jason's bike. She took a deep breath and headed in. There was no sign of the girls and Shane was just taking some money from a client. Val gave him a feeble wave and went to rest on one of the waiting area chairs. Shane ushered the large and hairy customer towards the door and locked up behind him.

"Well, you are definitely news today." Shane walked over to Val who had her head down. "Come on, I have someone I want you to meet." Shane grabbed her hand and pulled her up.

"I can't stop long. I have to get home to my mum. They know what they saw on TV so I have to tell them the truth." Val sighed thinking how odd it was that Shane wanted her to meet someone at a time like this. Well, she would be a rat in a lab as soon as someone outside her family recognised her, so what difference would one more person make?

Shane walked in first and Val was greeted enthusiastically by Delta and Fran, who grabbed her, one on each side, giggling like little girls.

"You guys, I'm not really in the mood for fun. I have to go home and explain everything to my parents," Val told them.

"They will be fine, and you're not leaving until you meet our new friend." Delta pulled Val along, grinning disturbingly from ear to ear. "How could they be so oblivious to my situation?" Val thought, walking into the gym where Jason was waiting with a serious expression on his face.

"I know you want me to meet someone, so can we just get on with it," Val said wearily. "I really need to go home." "I just wanted to know how you are. Are you OK?" Jason seemed taken aback by Val's attitude.

"Forget about moody boy and come over here." Delta pulled Val towards the laptop. Val didn't spot the head until she was nearly on top of it and the stranger stood up. Val felt her breath catch in her chest.

"Hello Val. I'm Sam." He held out his hand. She hadn't pictured him this way. She had assumed that because he was Shane's friend he would be old. He wasn't old, and he was the most gorgeous man Val had ever seen. No wonder Delta and Fran were almost skipping. Val held her hand out towards him. He grabbed it, shaking it powerfully. Val just stared at him. He was Italian looking; with perfectly gelled spiky jet-black hair; his eyes looked completely black, if that was possible, and his lips said *kiss me now*. Sam smiled at Val as he gently let her hand go. Val's arm slapped against her side bringing her back into reality.

"Well hello, I'm pleased to meet you," Val said, still unable to get her breath out or in.

Jason sighed loudly and rolled his eyes. "Yes, this is Sam and you are Val. Now, let's talk about what happened on the rollercoaster." "Oh…Yes…OK," Val got her head together and followed Jason back to the others, who were now drinking coffees and cokes at the table.

"So Val, do you like our new boy?" Delta winked at Fran and the pair dissolved into helpless giggles.

"I have to admit he is very nice." Val said, flushing a deep, glowing red.

"OK, girls, we need to talk" Shane said. They all managed to calm down before Sam dragged his chair over and joined them.

"Right, Val's face has been all over the news. We need to keep her safe until this dies down a little," Sam said. Everyone nodded in agreement.

"I know you all have my best interests at heart, but I'm not so worried about the daylight episodes; it's what happens to me in my dreams that concerns me. This thing is hurting me in a time and space I can't control, and in a way the government wouldn't even think of." Val looked to the others for some reaction, but they all looked as blank as Val felt.

"Maybe this will help you." Sam held out a bound manuscript to Val.

"What is it?" Val asked.

"It's a translated copy of your book." Sam also gave her the zodiac book. "I managed to make a program to translate the pages from Theban to English," Sam said.

The girls all looked suitably impressed by Sam's impressive skills, while Jason huffed into his coffee.

"Thank you. I really can't thank you enough for everything you have done for me." Val placed both books into her bag. Her pocket started to vibrate; Val pulled out her mobile "It's a text from my dad; I really do need to go home. My mum and dad have seen the news too and they are worried sick. I've got some serious explaining to do. Can you take me Delta?"

Delta nodded her head.

"Can I talk to you again?" Sam asked.

"Will you still be here tomorrow?" Val responded, hoping he would say yes.

"Yes, I'll stick around for a few days. I've got a new gadget for you too."

Val felt her heart skip and then the buzz at the excitement of receiving more goodies.

"Right, see you here tomorrow then, if I haven't been taken to area 51." Val walked towards the door with Delta in tow.

"You have training tomorrow, Val," Jason piped up, passing Val a cap. "Hide your face for now."

"Thanks, and I'm sure I can do both, *mate.*" Val waved back at Jason. As she walked away, she felt a slight feeling of satisfaction.

Delta did what Val expected and got her home faster than the bus, actually probably faster than an F-16 jet. She made her way towards her front door ready for a strained evening.

Susan opened the door before Val could get her fingers on the knob. "Get in now." Susan looked up and down the street.

"Mum, there is no one out here." Val rolled her eyes taking off her cap.

"Not yet." Susan grabbed Val by the arm and led her into the lounge where her dad was sitting in his chair nursing a whisky and looking rather pale. "Hi Dad." Val sat where Susan positioned her.

"Hello honey. You OK?" Mike broke his trance-like stare to make eye contact with his daughter.

"The truth," demanded Susan, "that's what I want. Are you taking drugs or mixing with the wrong sort of people or what? How the hell did you get to Skegness and how did you disappear? Was it a TV stunt?" Susan took a breath and Val knew it was now or never.

"Mum, please let me speak, it will make all of this quicker and easier for all of us."

Susan grabbed her drink, glared at Val, then said, "Go on then, but the truth, Val. Make sure it's the truth."

"It all started a few weeks ago. I had these strange dreams and then, on the day before my birthday..." Val proceeded to tell them everything: the shop the book and even the tattoo. She didn't hide a thing and it felt liberating. It took almost an hour to explain. Nonetheless, Susan and Mike listened in silence until Val had finished.

"Show me your arm." Susan said. Val showed her mum the three symbols left on her arm.

"Why you, and why now?" Mike chipped in as Susan tried with her tea towel and a little spit to rub the tattoo off.

"Dad, I don't know. I can't tell you anything more than I already have."

"Why didn't you trust us enough to tell us before now?" Mike asked.

"Why did you go to a stranger?" Susan pitched in.

After all she had told them, Val realised they seemed more upset that she hadn't felt she could speak to them from the start.

"Because I wanted to keep you safe," Val answered.

"That's not your job, Val. It's our job, as your parents, to keep you safe," Susan said and Val knew she was right.

"Whatever is happening to you? We are your parents. That isn't a part time job. We made a decision a long time ago to make you; we brought you into this world and from that day to this it has been our job to look after you. I know how clever you are, I know we have done a good job when I look at the person you have turned into, but we are still your mum and dad and as such you must trust us." Susan put her hand on Val's.

Val's eyes filled with tears. "I'm so sorry, Mum," she sobbed. Susan moved in to hug her and Val slowly released all the tears she had been holding in. Mike stood up and walked out of the room.

"Is Dad angry?" Val asked Susan.

"Give him time. He was really worried about you. You are our only child; all our hopes rest on your shoulders." Susan wiped Val's eyes. "What happens to you now?" she asked.

"Nothing, until I get a calling. You know, like I told you, I hear noises, see images in things and then, puff, I disappear." Val smiled.

"Oh yes, puff and disappear," Susan said with a troubled tone in her voice.

"When the last three symbols have gone, I think this will all be over."

"How do you know?" Susan asked.

"I don't, but I can hope." Val sighed, suddenly terribly tired. "Mum, I'm worn out. Would it be OK if I went to bed?" Val stood up, still holding onto her mum's hand.

"Yes. If you need me, call," Susan said. Val made her way upstairs. She was surprised to find her dad sitting on her bed.

"Are you OK, Dad?" Val asked.

"No, I'm not OK, Val. You have just told me something that, in my life, I have only seen on TV or read in books. You have kept this secret and now I can't even protect you. You have been bobbing in and out all over the world and this man, this Shane, didn't think that your father needed to know." Mike was looking at the floor and Val felt his pain. "You don't know when or where you may disappear again, or what danger you might face. So, no Val, I'm not OK. But one thing will never change; no matter where you are and who you are with, if you need me, call me and I will be there because I love you." Mike stood up. As he walked past Val, she saw tears in his eyes. Never in her eighteen years had Val seen her dad cry. She didn't like it.

Val dropped her clothes and for the first time in nearly two weeks she didn't have to worry about anyone catching her. The hiding was over. It wasn't what she had wanted, but considering all that her parents had just had to listen to, they had taken it reasonably well. Val snuggled into her bed with the translated copy of the book. She opened the first page and within seconds was out cold.

Morning came too quickly. As Val opened her eyes to the daylight, she was shocked to see her mum sitting on the end of her bed.

"Morning Mum," Val said.

"What are you going to do today?" Susan asked hesitantly.

"Well, I have to go to work." Val sat up.

"What if someone recognises you and takes you away?" Susan looked concerned.

"I work in the most boring place in Britain and I have no friends who don't already know what I can do. No one came knocking our door down last night, so I think we are probably in the clear. You need to relax a little, Mum." Val patted her mother on the shoulder as she walked over to her wardrobe. The truth was that Val was as worried as her mum that someone would recognise her, but she couldn't let her mum see it.

"That's not easy, Val. This is all so...so bizarre, so out of control. The news people will be trying their best to find out about you. And until all those signs have disappeared, you will still have more of these...these..." She trailed off, lost for words, but her expression spoke a million words.

"Mum, I promise you, if something happens to me today, I will contact you straight away and if I can't, Delta will, OK?" She hugged her mum reassuringly.

Susan nodded and reluctantly let Val go.

Val got ready and headed to the kitchen "Where's Dad today?"

"Still doing that cash job; he left for work early. Give him some space; he needs more time than me to get use to the fact that you're special." Susan gave Val a kiss and handed her a packed lunch. "Thanks Mum."

"I don't care how special you are, you still need to eat. Maybe it's all the healthy food you have eaten that has helped you with these things you can do." Susan smiled.

"Well, I'll keep an eye on that one, Mum." Val smiled back at her as she closed the door.

On Susan's insistence, Val wore a baseball cap and dark glasses on her way to work, to avoid being recognised. To her amusement, she attracted far more attention wearing them than she did when she took then off.

Val had put the book and her translated copy in her bag. Today she was going to find out who she really was, or so she hoped. The bookshop was becoming part of Val's life. She knew her security code off by heart. She had started to recognise some of her regulars and she felt relaxed. After opening up, she sat down with a coffee and opened the front cover.

This book is written for the eyes of the thirteen only. The chosen ones and the star child, the sisters and brothers sent to guard the doorway, never to allow him to return.

Val felt strange; was she one of the thirteen and who was the star child? She would need to make notes and Google was definitely going to come in handy. And who was this *him*?

The thirteen must be protected. They must live again and 'V', daughter to the star man and moon mother must lead us home to safety.

"Right. Star man and moon mother, weird," Val muttered to herself. She remembered that she had been called 'V' in her dream. Could it be that she was the one the book was talking about? But then how did her mum and dad fit in? They couldn't be the star man and moon mother; they were too ordinary for that! And she knew she was their daughter; she had proof of that in the form of some very graphic pictures of her birth. Val felt confused. Whilst she sat trying to digest the information she was reading, the door opened. It was Fran.

"Morning," she greeted Val cheerfully. "So this is where the mighty Val works, and there was me thinking that you worked the local carnival as a rollercoaster repair woman." Val stuck her tongue out at Fran and they both laughed.

"What are you doing here?" Val went to the kettle and flicked it on.

"Boys talking geek is so boring." Fran started to look at some of the books on display.

"Was Sam there?" Val didn't turn around; she wasn't going to let her emotions get the better of her again.

"Do you mean that sexy hunk? Oh my goodness, I thought I had died and gone to heaven. How good looking is that guy?" Fran stopped for breath.

Val made hot chocolate and passed one to Fran. "Well, he was nice, but I need to focus on what is going to happen to me now that I have been, and am still, on the news." Val walked back to the manuscript.

"What does it say?" Fran leaned over trying to look.

"Gibberish at the minute. Something about a star child, and a star man and moon mother." Val looked quizzically at Fran.

"Can I ask a question?"

"Shoot" Val answered, smiling at Fran.

"How do you know this book is right? That what you are reading is true or meant for you?" Fran asked.

"Well the book's zodiac has changed in direct relation to my arm so I am sure it does have something to do with me." Val shrugged her shoulders.

"OK, so what…" Fran was cut short by the entrance of Delta.

"Morning ladies." Delta floated elegantly into the shop then leaned on the counter. "How is my favourite alien this morning?" "Wow! Now we're all here, it's like the three musketeers have returned," Val chirped waving her arm as if she was holding a sword.

"At least you have a weapon," Delta retorted, "but what do we do now?"

"We wait." Val looked at them with a determined expression. "What for?" Fran asked.

"Well, I still have two zodiac symbols and the V on my arm, so I'm guessing this thing isn't over yet."

"Yes, you're right, it will only be a matter of time before you pop off again." Delta clicked her fingers.

The girls exchanged a look of agreement as the doorbell rang.

Val stood up. To Val's shock and horror, in walked Mr Gallymore.

"Well, I will get that book for you if you wouldn't mind waiting." Val smiled at Delta.

"What book?" Delta looked at Val confused.

"Mr Gallymore, good morning! How are you?" Val walked round the counter to greet her boss.

"I thought you were going to get a book for this young lady."

"Yes." Val started to turn.

"I hope you can find it and fast." Mr Gallymore walked around the counter and, unlocking the private door, disappeared as fast as he had arrived.

"Wow, not only is he attractive, he also has a million dollar personality." Delta let out a little girly squeal as Fran struggled to hold herself up against the counter.

"Shush, he might hear you." Val punched Delta in the arm.

"Right, I'm going shopping with my mum while she's here for a few days in-between lifts." Delta pulled her face up tightly. "If you need me, call." "I have to go as well and help Jason prepare some torture he has planned for Val later on today, plus I get to look at Sam," Fran giggled. "Bye-bye for now." the two girls left together and Val was alone again.

Val desperately wanted to read the manuscript, but didn't want to risk Wallace catching her and asking awkward questions, so she busied herself with her usual organising and cleaning.

Val heard the doorbell ring and went to the front of the shop to greet her customer. To her surprise, Wendy was back.

"Goodness, you must read very quickly," Val commented.

"I'm not here for a book." Wendy seemed more serious than normal.

"I'm sorry I can't do coffee today. My boss is in his office and he doesn't like me drinking, or even breathing, while I'm working," Val said.

Wendy snorted a laugh. "No, that's not what I want either," she said.

"So what do you want?" Val asked, suddenly feeling uneasy.

Wendy smiled coldly. "I saw you on TV yesterday," she said. "And I want to know what you are going to do about it."

CHAPTER 11

Disco on Ice

Val managed to keep her expression blank as she looked at Wendy. Inside she was panicking. She hadn't even taken Wendy into consideration. She had been too busy worrying about her friends and family to be concerned with anyone else.

"You're wrong, but I'm not surprised. Even my mum commented how much that girl looked like me." Val grinned, turning away from Wendy.

"Val, I have been looking at you for thirteen years, I know it was you. So what are you going to do about it?"

Val realised that there was no point in denial. "Look Wendy, you are walking into something that really isn't what it seems." Val was imagining knocking Wendy unconscious with a large book and making a break for it.

"You are not listening to me. I don't want to cause you a problem, I want to help you." Wendy's expression changed and she stepped closer to Val. "I know you think I'm odd; I know you don't want to be my friend, but I have knowledge that could help you." Wendy was searching Val's face intently.

"The only things I know is that your name is Wendy Whitmore, you have a very odd taste in books and that I don't need any more people involved in this." Val walked behind the counter using it as a barrier between them. "If you are prepared to keep my secret, then thanks; if you aren't, then get out now." Val pointed towards the door. She felt very vulnerable. Everything she had tried to keep secret was being shown to the world and she had no control over who wanted a piece of her. Maybe her mother was right; maybe she wasn't safe at the bookshop.

"I know you don't trust me and I know you don't like me much, but you must listen to me, just for a few minutes, please," Wendy pleaded.

"I don't seem to have any choice, do I? You have me cornered," Val replied angrily.

"Thank you." Wendy relaxed. "Witchcraft has been in my family for generations. There is a Whitmore family legend that says my family line goes back to the Essex witch trials of sixteen forty-five; that my great, great, you get the idea (Wendy waved her arms) grandmother was murdered for protecting other sister witches from the Witchfinder General." Wendy took a breath.

"OK," Val said, slightly interested despite her antipathy towards Wendy.

"The witches are said to have rewarded my family with the gift of clairvoyance, which means clear of sight or fortune teller." Wendy moved her hands around her eyes dramatically. "In the books passed down secretly from one generation of Whitmore women to the next, were stories of a coven in Essex. It was destroyed, but they left guardians to protect the 'chosen one'." Val caught her breath and Wendy touched her arm lightly. "Val, I was brought here as a child by my mother. She wanted me to go to only one school and she wanted me to make friends with only one girl." Wendy was now making Val uncomfortable with her closeness and Val took a step back. "That child, Val, was you. She talked about you all the time and I tried so hard to get close to you but it was impossible." Wendy was staring pensively at the ground. "I failed and now I have an opportunity to come to you with it all. Val, I'm your guardian." For a few seconds Val could only gape at Wendy. "Are you telling me that you have always known that I was different and you didn't tell me?" Val felt a tightening in her chest and her anger was written all over her face.

"I was sworn to secrecy." Wendy was the one now walking backwards.

"*You* are my guardian? What a joke! Do you know what I'm capable of?"

"It doesn't make any difference. Whether you like it or not, it's a fact." Wendy was now almost at the door with Val's face only inches from hers.

"So, what's your special power, Guardian? What can you do to protect me? Can you walk through fire, cause earthquakes or breathe under water?"

"No, that's not my job. I'm here to teach you the ways of the craft." Wendy was at the door, and pulling it open in fear of Val's anger.

"How dare you even consider yourself worthy of being anything to do with me! How do I know this isn't a trap? How do I know you don't work for the other side? Get out, go on, get out! Ha! I bet you didn't see that one coming clearly, Miss Clairvoyance." Val pushed Wendy.

Staggering backwards, she slipped down the steps onto the path.

"Val, there is a traitor coming. I'll come back when you're calmer." Wendy turned to walk away as the shop door slammed behind her.

Val was seething; she couldn't believe what she had just heard. She had always known that Wendy was weird, but what an outrageous story. How dare she try and scare her like that? Who did she think she was?

Val walked around the shop feeling like a caged bear. Mr Gallymore hadn't left his private room, so she couldn't be seen sitting down. She wanted to go to Shane's at lunchtime to see Sam, and the others of course, but how could she leave the shop? It would look terrible. So, she continued to mooch around until the last customer left and she could close at five.

As she walked towards the tattoo parlour, she made a quick call home to check in with her mother who had been texting her all day.

It went straight to answer machine. Val giggled to herself as she listened to the long, rambling message her mother had left. At last the tone sounded and Val left her message. "Hi Mum, I'm going to the tattoo parlour then I'll come home," she said and then hung up.

No one seemed to be paying her any attention on the street so she felt relaxed as she made her way to Shane's. When she arrived she saw that the shop was already shut. She peered through the glass and was about to knock when Shane came to let her in.

"Hello, how's your day been?" Shane asked locking the door behind her.

"Well, apart from Wendy confessing to being a witch and my guardian, it's been very boring," Val answered.

"Goodness! How did that come about?" Shane sounded intrigued. They entered the gym to find Jason, Fran and Sam all talking at the table.

"She gave me some stupid story about some witch trials in Essex in sixteen forty-five and how her relative had helped a coven, and now they are the guardians of the chosen one," Val smirked.

"Just a minute, that's right," Sam told her.

"What!" Val exclaimed.

"Yes. There were massive witch trials in Essex at that time. The pictures I sent you were originally from that area. Do you remember the woman with the tattoo that matched yours?" Sam rummaged around in his bag. "This one." He waved a picture at Val. "And I don't think you are in any position to disregard anyone at this moment in time, do you?" Sam looked Val straight in the eyes.

Val felt slightly ashamed that she had forgotten these facts and chased Wendy from her door.

"She said that a traitor was coming. What do you think she meant?" Val looked for support.

"Call her and ask," Fran chirped up.

"I don't have her number," Val replied.

"Well, let's go to her house." Jason grabbed his motorbike keys from the side.

"I don't know where she lives." Val was now pushing dust around on the floor with her shoe, hoping this line of questioning would soon be over.

"So, let me get this straight. This girl tells you all this information and also says that she is here to help you, and you kick her out." Sam put his hand on Val's arm, which under different circumstances would have been pleasant.

"Yes," Val said, "but I still have my suspicions."

"And what are they based on?" Sam asked, still holding her.

"She is the one who, out of the blue, turned up at the shop and told us the book was Theban. I think she's on the other side." "Why would she give you such a valuable clue if she's on the other side?" Shane asked, shaking his head as though he could hardly believe what he was hearing.

"OK, putting aside the fact that you have probably scared off an ally, do you think she will come back?" Sam smiled kindly at Val.

Val nodded. "She said she'd come back." Val wasn't sure that Wendy would come back after the way she had treated her.

"Well then, we will just have to wait until she does." Sam patted Val gently on the arm. Val nodded, Sam was stronger than he looked; his gentle pat had hurt her arm.

Val went to get herself a drink. "Can anyone hear music?" she called out to the others who all turned, shaking their heads. As the music got steadily louder, Val raised her sleeve and saw that one of the remaining symbols was red. She looked around, searching for the image that would send her to her next mission. She returned to the others and saw, in the middle of the glass table, something that looked like a circle of ice, almost as if the centre of the table was frozen.

"She's going to go." Jason warned, grabbing Sam who was moving closer to Val. "Don't touch her or you will get dragged along."

Sam stood and watched.

Val was now focussed on the image. "See you soon." She smiled, touched the table and was gone.

The next thing Val was aware of, was the bitter cold. She was sitting on the floor, with a view of a wooden barrier and a row of plastic chairs. She quickly pulled herself up and was greeted by a full size ice-skating rink. Val fumbled in her pocket, pulling out her earpiece just in time to hear Sam's voice.

"Val, can you hear me?"

"Yes," Val replied scanning the area. "I'm at an ice rink. I've never been skating."

"What's happening?" Sam asked.

"There doesn't seem to be much going on at the minute. I'm not even sure that this place is open." Val looked around her.

"Do you have your light sword with you?" Sam asked.

"Yes, I've got everything. There's just no victim at the moment." Val sat on one of the chairs prepared to wait, confident that the she would soon find out what she had to do.

Then it started. Several doors all around the rink suddenly crashed open and the music got louder. People rushed in, like a small herd of buffalo heading to water. A huge, reflective disco ball lowered itself over the ice rink.

"Is that Abba I can hear?" Sam asked in Val's ear.

"Sam, I do believe it's seventies night," Val giggled.

"What's so funny?" Sam asked inquisitively.

"It's fancy dress disco night. There must be a hundred John Travolta look-alikes." Val was now mesmerised by the dancing on ice extravaganza unfolding before her.

"Anyone look in trouble?" Jason chirped up from the background.

"Not the sort I can help them with." Val laughed. She was now leaning on the wooden barrier, tapping her foot to Dancing Queen. Her attention was suddenly caught by one of the lycra-clad men.

"Wait a minute, something's wrong." Val realised that he was the only person not swinging to the music. "There's a guy who looks as if he's up to no good. I need to investigate." Val edged her way round the barrier and placed a tentative foot on the ice. "Oh dear God I'm going to die!" she exclaimed as she wobbled into the disco slipstream. Trying to keep her eye on the guy while not falling over was becoming harder by the second. "This is impossible. I'll never get him like this," Val moaned, falling with a thud that rattled her whole body.

"Val, you OK?" Sam hoped his voice wouldn't betray the fact that he was grinning. They had all heard the thud and grunt as Val hit the ice.

"Well, if dignity is a feeling, I'm wounded." Val pulled herself onto her hands and knees. "It's amazing how cold this ice is." She lifted one hand off and blew on it. She got onto her knees, wondering how on earth she was going to stand up. Each time she tried, she lost her balance and fell back onto the ice and now she was a couple of feet away from the barrier. She was seriously considering scooting to safety on her backside when she felt a pair of hands going under her arms. As she slid forwards, she was lifted onto her feet.

"Hello Alien."

"Delta!" Val squealed, holding tight to her friend and gliding like a swan on the ice.

"Stay calm, princess. I was shopping in the nearby mall with my mum when Jason called, so I came to give you a hand, although I didn't expect it to be literally."

Val hadn't stopped grinning. "Thanks goodness for you! I don't know how to stay upright on this ice."

"So what are we doing?" Delta asked.

"I spotted this guy moving suspiciously. I want to get to the centre of the ice to check him out. Look, there he is." Val pointed towards the man.

"OK, let's do it." Delta started to move in receding circles towards the centre. As Val watched her quarry, she noticed that he seemed to be moving in on an Olivia Newton John look-alike who was dancing with another girl, directly under the disco ball. The song had now changed. Val didn't recognise it but the effect was that all the skaters had slowed down, and were moving towards the sides in couples.

"Delta, get me in as close as you can, then let me go." Delta nodded. The guy, Val had been watching seemed oblivious to Val's presence and this gave her the advantage.

As she got closer, she saw that he was pulling an implement from his pocket. "Delta you need to get to safety, OK?" Val pulled herself up straight and with a final push, Delta sent Val off in the man's direction.

The girl was still dancing completely unaware of the events unfolding around her. Val was now almost behind him, she slid to a stop, the momentum gone. She was still five feet away, but could now see that he was brandishing a knife.

Val knew that he was going to get to the girl first and was at a loss as to what to do next. For the first time, she wasn't doing well.

Val's next move was purely instinctive. "Hey you! Stop!" she shouted at the top of her voice. The music was so loud that no one heard her.

"Val, can you hear me?" Sam was calling in her ear, but she didn't have time to chat right now. Val tried to run and ended up on her knees, scrabbling across the ice.

The man was already raising the knife. "Please stop!" Val screamed again.

"Val!" Sam was yelled into her ear, but she couldn't answer. It was too terrible to watch. She was going to fail and that poor girl was going to die.

What followed happened in slow motion.

The guy was moving in on the girl who was still oblivious to her fate. Val knew what was going to happen next. She really couldn't bear to look. She was about to turn away when Delta appeared from nowhere. She moved like a swan, gracefully, every movement controlled. Val froze. The blade thrust forward. NO!!!

The pain in Val's body was something she had never felt before. It started from the pit of her stomach and rumbled up inside her, and her whole body started to shake. She could feel the ice below her cracking. Then she was at least an inch above the frozen ground and moving towards the body lying on the ice. Val could no longer hear the music and the people around her were screaming. It was like watching the TV with the volume off. All she could see was Delta's still body and the blood that was slowly spreading out around her.

The assailant was already skating away, but Val put an end to that within a second. Her head snapping in his direction, she pointed her finger at him. He lifted off the ground and smashed into the solid concrete wall, then lay still.

As she got closer, Val saw that her friend's eyes were shut. She let out a howl of despair, like an animal in pain. In a split second the dazzling disco ball turned to dust and filled the air with a thick coat of glitter.

Val collapsed onto the ice, managing to crawl close to Delta and then throwing herself on her like a protective dog, snarling at anyone who tried to get close. The woman who had been the original target, approached Val warily.

"I need to help your friend, I'm a nurse." She edged a little closer, visibly terrified of Val.

"If you touch her I will kill you," Val hissed, still under the influence of her anger.

"I don't want to die, but I don't want her to either." The woman moved another step closer and was almost in touching distance.

Val breathed deeply. She could sense that she was trying to help and she was also immensely brave after what she had just witnessed. Val slumped backwards onto the ice and the girl moved in. She examined Delta quickly then turned to Val. "She's going to be OK. I promise I won't leave her." She placed her hand on Val's, then jumped back with a scream as Val vanished.

Val landed on her feet in the gym.

"Val!" Shane rushed over to her throwing a blanket around her shoulders as she proceeded to collapse to the floor.

"Delta got stabbed and I couldn't help her." Val was shivering.

"Jason and Fran are already on their way to the ice rink. We'll know in a minute what's going on." Shane hugged Val.

"Delta was bleeding. I think she's dying." Val was deeply frightened. It had gone too far. The thought of losing her friend was too much to contemplate.

"Sorry to change the subject, but what the hell happened to you back there? You have completely messed up the computer and all our kit." Sam came over to Val on the floor.

"I don't know. I lost the plot. I was so angry I couldn't control my powers. It was as if they were controlling me." She shuddered with the memory. "Get me to the hospital, please Sam."

Sam gave Val his hand and pulled her to her feet.

"Are you sure you are OK to travel?" Shane interrupted like a protective father.

"I need to get to Delta, Shane. Don't worry, I'll be fine. I'm not the one who has been stabbed." Val moved towards the door. "Let's go." She opened it and Sam followed her.

"Sam, take care of her, mate," Shane called.

"Aren't you coming?" Sam asked.

"No, I have things to do here," Shane responded.

Jason arrived at the ice rink to be met by ambulances, police and hysterical people. Fran grabbed one woman by the arm. "What's happened?" Fran asked her sternly.

"That girl off the TV was here. She just went mad. She's not human. She was floating off the ground." The woman was shaking and trying to get out of Fran's grip, but Fran wasn't ready to let her go.

"What happened to the girl?" Fran demanded.

"She blew everything up and threw this guy across the rink. I think he's in an ambulance and a girl got stabbed." The woman stopped to breathe.

"Who got stabbed?" Fran tightened her grip, dreading the answer.

"Some blonde girl." The woman felt Fran's grip loosen for a moment and took advantage of it to run.

"Jason, I think we have a problem. I think Delta's hurt," Fran called to Jason. He grabbed her hand and pulled her through the crowd, which was moving in the opposite direction.

The full extent of Val's anger was apparent the moment they entered the rink. The ice had been completely cracked from one side to the other. There was a crater in the wall, which they could only assume was where the man had hit it.

"I think she may be getting more powerful." Fran gave Jason a concerned glance.

"Look at the ice in the middle." Jason pointed to a large pool of blood. Fran put her hand to her mouth.

"That's a lot of blood," Fran whispered. They headed back outside trying to find out what had happened. "Hello strangers. Come to rescue me?" said a voice from behind Jason.

"Delta!" Jason exclaimed, spinning around to come face to face with a paler than usual Delta.

Delta smiled back at him.

"Are you alright? You're very pale. What happened?" Jason put an arm around Delta's shoulders, as a man pushed past her.

"It's just a long graze." Delta pulled at her top to show an elongated bandage around her upper back. "It's nothing, but look at the lump on my head. Do you think it will be worse tomorrow?" Delta pulled up her fringe to show a small egg on her forehead.

"But there was so much blood." Fran looked confused.

"Can't answer that one, sorry. I was out cold." Delta looked around. "Where's Val?"

"She left from the tattoo parlour so I assume she will be back there by now. Let's give her a ring and find out." Jason pulled out his mobile.

The speed at which Val moved was disturbing. It was only when Sam managed to catch her up and informed her that she had walked past his car a few moments earlier, that she snapped her out of her shocked state. She stood still, looking lost and vulnerable.

"I need to get to Delta, Sam," she said, her voice breaking on a sob. "She's my best friend. I can't let anything happen to her." Sam grabbed her hand and led her back to his car.

"Wow, it's so small and green and cute." Val stood next to Sam's car.

"This is Sandy; she is a Racing Green Sagaris TVR. She goes from zero to sixty in three point seven seconds and her maximum speed is one hundred and eighty-five miles per hour. She is not cute. We will never have this conversation again and check your shoes before you get in." Sam got into the car without looking back at Val who was standing on the curb not sure whether to laugh because Sam's car was called Sandy or cry because he was truly a geek. She did neither, just checked her shoes and got in.

On the way to the ice rink, Val received a call from Jason. She was relieved to hear that the blood had looked worse than it was. She sat back and relaxed as she chatted to Jason. Then she spotted something that made her look back.

"Stop, now!" Val shouted, shoving her phone in her pocket and cutting Jason off. She could feel Sam's body tensing up as he slammed on the brakes. Val jumped out of the car and ran across the road.

"Wendy!" Val yelled, but she was already too far away, entering a shop about fifty metres down the road. Sam was now hot on Val's heels. They burst into the shop together to find a startled Wendy and shop owner gaping at them. Val felt a flush coming over her; they looked like Miami Vice on a bust.

"Wendy, I need to talk to you, please. I am so sorry for the way I acted earlier on. I just don't know what's going on and who I can trust. Could you please tell me exactly what you know."

Wendy was still looking at her in shock. As Val got closer, it dawned on her just how much the woman behind the counter looked like Wendy.

"This is my friend, Sam." Val turned and Sam waved a hello. "He backed up the story you told me. I was under a lot of stress; I should have listened to you. I'm sorry." Val gave a meek grin and touched Wendy's arm. Wendy still hadn't spoken and Val was starting to think she had burnt her only bridge.

"Hello Sam." Wendy smiled meekly at Sam. "Val, this is my mum." Wendy moved over to let the woman through.

"Val, I'm so honoured to meet you at last." Wendy's mum came around the counter slowly as if she was meeting the Queen.

"Hello Mrs Whitmore, please accept my apologies for not listening to your daughter." Val walked over and shook hands with Wendy's mum who was now almost in tears.

"We have waited for so long: all my life and my mother's, and her mother before. We just didn't know when you would arrive. All we knew was that we had to believe you would get here eventually."

Val was amazed. This woman seemed quite ordinary and yet her whole life had been spent waiting for someone who might or might not appear.

"All I can say is thank you and I hope I won't disappoint you."

"How did you know who Val was?" Sam asked.

"We had charts of the stars. We waited for them to align then we moved to the place where we knew she would be born." Wendy's mum smiled warmly at Val. "I was at your birth. We found your mother when she was pregnant and we stayed with you. I moved Wendy closer to you when she was school age in the hope you would bond, although that wasn't to be."

Wendy looked at the floor as though ashamed.

"But that doesn't matter any more now you are here." She patted Val's hands.

"So what do I need to know?" Val glanced over at Wendy, almost expecting her to flip out a PowerPoint presentation.

"Well, first I really need to know what you do and what you are struggling with, and then we can fill in the blanks. I can teach you all the basics of the craft, like spell work and potion preparation, phases of the moon and how to work in alignment with the elements."

Wendy would have carried on but Val's mobile was ringing. Val apologised, pulling it out to see that it was Delta calling.

"Hello," Val said mouthing to the others that it was Delta on the line.

"Yes, we have been lucky enough to run into Wendy. Sorry about cutting you off," Val responded. "Well yes, we can meet you there in about ten. Alright, bye for now." Val closed the phone.

"Delta has to go and be checked out at the hospital so we need to get over there. Wendy we need to talk, but I need to help my friend right now, so maybe you could come with us to the hospital?" Val raised an eyebrow and Wendy looked to her mother for approval. The woman nodded and Wendy joined Val and Sam heading for the door.

"Slight problem ladies," Sam butted in as they got out onto the street.

"What?" Val questioned.

"My car only has two seats," he whispered.

"Sorry, did you say Sandy only has two seats?" Val giggled.

"I told you never to mention that again, but yes, she does only have two." Sam was puffing his chest out at the girls in defence of his seat deficient car.

"We can take mine if you like," Wendy offered.

"Then it's sorted, we go in Wendy's car." Val was pleased with her organisational skills. "Where is it?" Val asked as they moved along the path.

"Here." Wendy indicated what looked like a little boy's toy van.

"It's a Morris Traveller." Sam stood at the side of the road and for a moment Val wasn't sure he was going to get in. Wendy went around unlocking the doors.

"That is a very cool van." Sam nodded as he walked around it. Val was pleased he had said that, even though she wasn't sure he meant it.

"Well thank you. It's sort of like a family heirloom." Wendy placed the key in the ignition and it turned over first try. They all climbed in.

"Was it your mum's?" Val asked genuinely interested.

"No, it was my dad's," Wendy responded emotionlessly.

"Oh, where is he?" Val asked.

"He couldn't cope with the family quest so he walked out on us. The only thing he left my mum was this car, so I have it as a reminder of my mission in life." Wendy turned a corner and, as she did, Val sat quietly, feeling humbled by all that Wendy and her family had given up for her.

They arrived at the hospital slightly slower than Val was used to, but safely. Val ran into the hospital reception and breathlessly demanded to know where Miss Troughton was. They were directed to a side room. As they entered they were greeted by all the others.

"Took your time then. And Wendy is here because?" Delta said pushing her nose into the air like a rejected top model.

"Delta, you can sulk and moan all you like, I'm just so pleased you're OK, and I'll tell you all about Wendy in a minute, but first I have to hug you." Val moved over and grabbed Delta. She wasn't taking a 'no' for an answer and it felt great.

"Hello you." Fran smiled at Val. "Going to introduce me to your new friend?" Fran waved at Wendy.

"Sorry. Wendy, this is Fran, she's Jason's girlfriend." Val patted Fran as Wendy waved back. "OK, does anyone know what happened to the guy who did this? Did he get away?" Val looked at Jason and Fran.

"Val, he's critical," Jason replied.

"What? He can't be, he ran away." Val looked from Jason to Delta for confirmation that they were wrong. "I wouldn't hurt someone. I'm the one who protects people." Val sat down on a plastic chair next to the bed.

"From what I could find out, Val, you flipped. You threw the bloke almost through a solid concrete wall and

273

then cracked the ice in half. I could go on, but by the expression on your face I don't think I need to." Fran fell silent.

"Why would I do that? This has never happened before." Val looked at Delta.

"You lost it when I got stabbed and I don't remember any more." Delta raised herself from the bed and stood up. "Val, you did what you had to, whether you think it was right or not. That man stabbed me." Delta started to walk towards the door. "I have had enough of your precious NHS for one day, let's get out of here."

Val felt a prickle in her arm. She could see Delta was still speaking, but she wasn't sure what she was saying. "What did you say? All I can hear is a woman moaning." Val knew none one else could hear it. Was she going to teleport again? And if she was, where to?

"I think I'm going," Val called out. Everyone stopped moving as Sam locked the door. Val walked searched for the portal, but there seemed to be nothing. "I can't find anything."

"What's happening?" Wendy asked looking at the others.

"She's screaming and it is getting louder." Val was spinning in circles. "There!" Val shouted and they all watched her run towards a tin bowl on the shelf. She placed her hand on it and was gone.

"What!" Wendy stood with her jaw hanging open.

Jason pulled a chair up behind her and helped her onto it. "I think we need to do a little catch up with our new friend," he said.

Val landed with a groan as she hit the pavement. "So much for cat-like reflexes," she moaned to herself.

The scream hit her ears instantly, but the bigger shock was that she was outside the bookshop. Her mobile started to ring.

"Hello," she whispered.

"Where are you?" Jason whispered back.

"Outside the bookshop," Val responded. "Why are you whispering?" "I don't know," Jason laughed. "Stay there. We'll come to you." He hung up.

Val knew she couldn't wait for them, however nice the thought was; the screams were getting louder; the woman was obviously in serious trouble. Val move past the shop, following the direction of the sound. Looking around the corner of the building carefully, she spotted the woman. It was the last thing she expected: the cries were not because she was being threatened or attacked, but because she was in labour. She was lying on the ground giving birth in the alleyway next to the book-shop. Val quickened her movement, but stayed acutely aware of her surroundings alert for any danger.

"Hello," Val said to the woman quietly, trying not to scare her. She jumped anyway babbling in some strange language that Val couldn't understand. "I-am-Val." She sounded out each word slowly, finishing with an exag-gerated smile.

"Eva," the girl said smiling back between gritted teeth.

Val knelt down beside her. She wanted to get her into the shop without scaring her too much. Suddenly Eva had hold of Val's hand and was squeezing like a mad woman. She started screaming in Val's face, it seemed to last a good ten minutes and all Val could think was that this was a great advert for contraception. She was defi-nitely never going to have a baby; it really did hurt. After

Eva had come down from the contraction, Val pointed at the wall next to them. "My shop," Val said. The girl seemed to understand and seemed relieved at the idea of going indoors.

Val helped her to her feet and they shuffled towards the shop. Whilst they made their way, Val was struck by the fact that this was her last but one tattoo and then it would be over. She also wondered what use Wendy would be to her; she had arrived a little late in her adventure – unless she was a trained mid-wife.

They turned the corner to be greeted by Sam, Jason, and Delta exiting Delta's mini.

"Hello people, this nice lady, Eva, is having a baby. We need to get her into the shop." Val welcomed the men helping her as Eva was quite heavy. "Delta, are you sure you should be here?" Val questioned.

"I wouldn't miss this for the world." Val unlocked the bookshop and they all passed inside.

"Call an ambulance, Delta."

"Will do." Delta reached for her phone.

Eva grabbed Val's hand as another contraction started. As she did, the spark passed between them and Val found herself back at the hospital with Wendy still in shock and Fran passing her some water.

"Hello," Fran said. "I'm surprised to see you so soon."

"Well, that was crazy! There was no baddie Fran, just a pregnant woman who was in labour." Val scratched her head in confusion. "She wasn't at risk, she was just having a baby in the street. As soon as I got her into the shop I came back. I just don't get it. Has Wendy been like this since I left?" she asked Fran who nodded back at her. "Wendy it's OK, I'm back," she said, kneeling in front of

Wendy who now seemed to be almost chanting. Just then Wendy grabbed Val violently by the arms. Val was petrified at her strength. She was trapped in her grip. More intimidating was the fact that Wendy's eyes were completely white. Fran stumbled backwards falling onto the floor as Wendy started to talk.

"You have failed," she shouted in Val's face. Val didn't like what she was saying, but she remembered what Wendy had told her about being clear of sight. Maybe this was what she meant.

"What can you see, Wendy?" Val asked.

"Baby's still in danger. The evil one is coming and the traitor is in position." Wendy slumped on the chair releasing Val and lowering her head between her knees.

"Things just get weirder," Fran said from the floor.

"Fran, we need to get back to the shop *now*. That baby is in danger and the evil one is coming." Val grabbed her phone and dialled Shane's number.

"Hi Shane we need you. Meet us at the bookshop." Val hung up and started to dial Delta's number. "Delta, you need to protect that baby. I'm coming, but so is the evil one. Tell Sam and Jason to be ready." Val put the phone into her pocket. "OK ladies, we have a job to do, let's go."

As they all jumped into Wendy's Morris Traveller, Val wondered if they would ever get there. Wendy revved the car and they set off for the shop.

"OK, when we get there, let me deal with the big evil, please girls. You need to stay safe," Val shouted over the noise of the engine. Fran and Wendy nodded in agreement. As they pulled up outside the shop they could see the others inside.

"Let's go." Val jumped out of the car with Fran and Wendy following. Making her way up the stairs, she could hear the cries of the woman who was still in the throes of giving birth.

Jason saw the girls arriving and opened the doors to let them in. Val came flying past. "No time to stop." She was followed by Wendy and, as Fran entered, Jason grabbed her and gave her a hug.

"You OK?" he asked.

Fran nodded. "I will be when this is all over and Val is safe." She let go of Jason and moved towards the girls on the floor. Val was already sitting by Eva's side.

"Miss me?" Val smiled. Eva's expression was one of fear and confusion, but the pains of labour were obviously scarier than Val's disappearing act. "Where is that ambulance?" Val called out.

"I called Val. I don't know what's keeping them," Delta said as another contraction started.

"Where's Shane?" Val asked.

"Is he coming?" Sam wanted to know.

"I called him. He should have been here ages ago." Val looked concerned. "Get some hot water," she ordered. "Our coats will keep her warm." Once again, Val felt in her element.

Eva gripped Val's hand as another wave hit her.

"Do you have any family?" Val asked Eva as she started to breathe more calmly.

Eva nodded. "Away." She made flying signs at Val.

"Where?" Val asked trying to keep Eva distracted whilst she wondered what to do next.

"Mexico." Eva's eyes were filling with water.

"That's lovely. Do you know anyone here?" Val didn't want to ask about the baby's father, just in case it was a sore subject.

Eva understood the question. "Si." Another wave hit just as Val's phone rang. It was her mother. Val knew she couldn't lie to her, so she let it ring.

"Who was it?" Delta asked.

"Mum. I'll call her as soon as this is done. I can't lie to her so I'm better off waiting." Val turned to see a message pop up on her screen.

Hope you are OK. Luv you to the moon and back, Mum.

Val pushed her phone back into her pocket.

"Ow!" There was an intense pain in her arm. She saw that the final tattoo, the one that symbolised V, was glowing red. "Not now!"

"What's wrong, Val?" Delta asked.

"My last tattoo is glowing; I think I'm going again. Hey, it may be the last time." Val smiled, standing up and walking around the others. "Fran, you sit with Eva. Jason, I need you to protect her, I don't know where I'm going or if I will make it back in time." Jason nodded. Val turned towards Delta. "Look out for Shane; he must get here soon." Delta moved towards the door. "Wendy, don't have another turn until I get back OK?" Wendy blushed and Val patted her on the back as she passed.

"What about me?" Sam asked.

"You are coming with me." Val smiled as she grabbed his hand.

"Val, you know what happens if you take someone with you," Jason said sounding panicky.

"Yes, but you all have jobs to do, and you more than anyone need to be here, Jason." He had to agree she was right. "And if I need someone to get me back here, Sam is an even faster driver than Delta."

"Well, I'll have to be the judge of that myself," Delta said.

"Positions everyone." Val walked over to Eva. "I will return." She smiled kindly at her and then turned to look for what was to be her last journey. She moved with definite purpose around the bookshop, looking for the place, with Sam hanging onto her hand. Strangely, there was no distinguishable sound and there seemed to be nowhere to touch. Was this last tattoo different to the others? "Val I'm starting to get dizzy." Sam pulled Val to a halt at the main door. Val looked out through the glass door in the hope of seeing Shane, who still hadn't arrived. All she could see was the reflection of the highly lit up bookshop.

"Let's take a look outside," Val suggested.

"OK," Sam agreed.

Val pushed the door open and, in a flash of light, they were gone.

CHAPTER 12

When a Child is Born

"OK, they've gone and we need to get on with things." Jason moved around Fran and headed to the door to check if anyone was coming.

Eva was in a complete state of shock having watched not only Val disappear twice in one day, but now Sam too. Her contractions seemed to have eased a little and Fran was talking to her to keep her calm. Wendy was just standing very still, obviously trying to take it all in.

"Where do you think they are?" Fran called over to Jason.

"I don't know, but here comes Dad," Jason said relieved.

"Hello son," Shane greeted him as he opened the door. "Where are Val and Sam?" he asked. Before Jason could answer, there was a flash of light and the rip by the doorway opened. Out stumbled Val, still holding hands tightly with Sam.

Val leapt into her ready to go position and Sam just managed to get onto all fours before he was sick all over the floor.

"Well, at least someone else knows how it feels." Delta declared as she threw over to Sam a bunch of tissues from the box on the counter.

"What are we doing back here?" Val stood up straight, stretching her back and looked at Shane. "And where have you been?" Val looked confused and annoyed.

"I had a job to do," Shane said hugging Val. She rested her head on his chest, comforted by his strength.

"Hello, man down, in need of medical attention here," Sam called from the floor. They all ignored him. Eva screamed and started to push, and that grabbed everyone's attention.

"If I'm here, that means someone in this room needs my help." Val felt confused. She had already helped Eva, so it wasn't her. She walked around, touching everyone's hands.

"What are you doing mate?" Jason asked.

"No one needs my help, so why am I here?" Val was getting nervous.

"Sorry to stop the party, but I can see something coming out." Fran looked pointedly in Shane's direction. "Do you know what we should be doing?"

"OK, let me through." Shane started to roll up his sleeves. "Jason, lock the door," he ordered. Eva was now screaming.

"Olla, mi nombre es Shane." Shane employed his best holiday Spanish and bent down to have a closer inspection. He could see the baby's head was coming. "OK, I need you to push really hard; the baby is nearly here." Eva nodded. Shane's calm attitude made her trust him.

"So Shane, did you learn midwifery at tattoo school?" Delta called over sarcastically.

"No, but I delivered Jason," Shane responded, not looking away from Eva.

"Don't ask for details please," Jason said his face flushing crimson with embarrassment.

"Isn't anyone slightly even concerned that I have disappeared and ended up back here again?" Val asked the group who were all busy witnessing the miracle of life.

"I can see its head," Fran squealed with her hands up to her mouth.

"One more push," Shane told Eva.

She nodded in agreement, gripping his hand tightly. As she let out the final scream everyone stopped moving. Even Val paused to take in the moment, as Shane lifted the baby up.

"It's a boy," Shane he said, wrapping the baby in Jason's jacket. "Pass me your knife, son." Shane raised his hand and grabbed Jason's knife.

The group stood mesmerised around Eva who was absolutely exhausted. Val moved closer to see the baby. She had never seen a birth before and now she was truly impressed. Not just with Eva and her baby, but that they had managed to bring this new life safely into the world. No big bad, no traitors. Maybe Wendy wasn't as good a clairvoyant as she thought, although the white-eye thing was scary.

"Hey Delta, do you want to have a look at the baby?" Val asked her. She noticed that Delta had moved away while everyone else had moved closer.

"No thank you, but I think it's time Daddy got to see it." Delta walked behind the counter and, to Val's shock, pulled a key from her pocket.

"What are you doing Delta?" Val asked, feeling fear coursing though her.

"Something I have waited a long time for." She pushed the key into the door marked Private and slowly opened it. Val stood up.

"How did you get a key for that door Delta?" Val walked towards her.

"Master, your child has arrived," Delta called through the gap.

"Who are you calling? Stop it! You're freaking me out."

Delta lowered her head and out walked Mr Gallymore. Val nearly burst out laughing. What was Delta doing, calling Mr Gallymore master? For heaven's sake, he couldn't master a large gust of wind. And what had she meant by 'it's time to meet your Daddy'? Eva was far too pretty and young to be seen dead with anyone like Wallace.

"Delta, whatever you are doing it's not funny." Val's raised voice had caught the attention of the others who were all turning to look at the counter.

"Mr Gallymore, I'm really sorry you had to walk in on this, but the woman was having a baby on the street and..." Val didn't get to finish her sentence. Wallace ignored her and walked towards the mother and child.

"Mr Gallymore!" Val followed him.

"You are boring me, be quiet." Wallace flicked his hand limply at Val. He knelt down next to the mother. The silence of that moment was like nothing Val had ever experienced. They all watched him, no one understanding what was happening, all fighting rising fear.

Wallace looked up. "Delta, come and get the baby."

Delta started to do as she was told.

Val couldn't believe it. It was like a really bad B-movie. "What are you doing?" Val put herself between Delta and the baby.

"What is required of me" Delta replied.

This was Val's best friend, she couldn't seriously be thinking of trying to take Eva's baby. What would she want with a baby?

Delta stepped round Val and went to Wallace's side. Eva was now crying, but was too weak to help herself. Shane moved in-between them.

"Delta, I'm not going to hurt you because I don't know why you are doing this, but you aren't taking this woman's baby," Shane said, blocking Delta's path. Delta glanced around Shane's large frame at Wallace. He rose up to stand, and then continued rising.

As the other's watched in various degrees of terror, Wallace levitated until he was on a level with Shane. Then he flicked out his hand. He didn't even make contact with Shane, but Shane felt the full force of the blow that threw him violently out of Delta's way.

"I think it's time that aunty Delta got to hold the baby, don't you?" Delta said, trying to pull the baby from a weakened Eva's arms.

"Val, do something!" Fran, screamed frantically.

Jason was making his way towards Shane when Wallace delivered a similar blow, throwing him in the opposite direction. Jason hit the counter.

Eva was crying, "He is not papa!" and trying to keep hold of the baby, but Delta had a good grip now and kicked her back to the ground. That was it! Val had had enough of this game.

"Hey Wallace, the girl says you're not the daddy. Maybe we need to take a few blood tests." Val walked forward with power in her stride. She was going to get that baby back. She had the big bad and the traitor in her sights, as Wendy had predicted, and she knew she could take Delta down. She had to trust that a little old man - even if he was floating - wouldn't be as strong as her.

"You think you can take me down don't you, Val, or should I call you V?" Wallace was laughing.

Val stopped for a second to feel in her back pocket to see if her sword was there. She wasn't going to let him distract her with things she already knew about.

"Well, I suppose it's time you saw me for who I really am." Wallace sank slowly to the ground. Once he had settled, he began to shake and vibrate violently. Val felt completely freaked out. The movement was almost faster than her eyes could see, but she saw that he was changing, not only his height but also his shape and age.

Wendy started screaming and Sam ran to place his hand over her mouth in case she suffered the same fate as Shane and Jason.

Delta was just looking on in amusement, holding the baby tightly and every so often knocking Eva back with her foot.

When Wallace eventually stopped, Val could feel her mouth was completely open. The man in front of her appeared to be in his early thirties. He was a good six-foot tall, had a thick mop of blond hair and was wearing a very strange outfit; he looked a little like Shakespeare with not quite so many ruffles. Val noticed straight away that Eva had stopped screaming. She could tell instantly from Eva's expression that this man *was* the father of that baby. However, his new appearance made no difference; she was going to sort this out once and for all.

"So you're not old. Is that supposed to impress me, Wallace?" Val asked.

"Please call me Excariot."

"There was me just getting used to calling you one stupid name and you come out with another." Val grinned at Excariot.

"Do you think you're clever V?" he hissed, walking towards her.

"Well at least I have a better dress sense than you," Val smirked.

"Do you think that this dress sense will help to keep your heart beating when I crush you?" He was now far too close for Val's liking and she could feel the full power of his presence as he circled her.

"Let's find out," Val retaliated, wondering if this was the wisest way to deal with him.

"Your blind bravery has entertained me." Excariot stopped behind her. "But you are the most stupid subject I have ever met." He lifted his hand and Val was instantly levitated several feet off the ground, her body completely rigid. Sam released Wendy and ran forward, but his fate like the others was sealed with a flick of Excariot's free hand.

"V, every person you have rescued, every pitiful life you have saved, unlocked one more piece to the jigsaw of my prison. *You* have done all for this for me." Excariot softly stroked Val's hair. "All I needed was you to change the fate of thirteen people to free me. You are the very last. You see, the ones you saved were destined to die as their forefathers have for centuries, to keep me trapped. You, the chosen one, who was destined to live, will now die." Excariot let out a slow sigh seemingly very pleased with his achievements. "Only the great V could change their futures. Moving their paths and shaking the temples of their destiny to make it possible for me to break free from a spell that has kept me prisoner for over four hundred years, thanks to your lineage." Excariot looked at Val with distaste. "These pawns have come and gone like pestilent rats and I have waited patiently for you to arrive. Now I will reap my revenge." He glanced at the others and laughed. "Your stupidity and that of your so-called friends has entertained me highly." Excariot moved across the floor towards Delta. "Although, at times, you have truly disappointed me, V. It took you so long to decipher the book I left for you. " Excariot shook his head.

"I had to come and find it for you," Delta sniggered, moving in closer to her master. "He even had to give you a stupid tattoo." Val could feel herself getting madder. She wanted to speak but he had such a tight grip it was impossible.

"Every adversary that you faced was sent to make sure you succeeded." He turned his wrist and Val was allowed one last glimpse of her friends who were spread out all over the shop floor, watching in horror.

Excariot flicked his hand back, turning Val to face him. "These disgusting people who have followed you are no better than you. They believed you were special. You all make me sick." He walked towards Eva and with one foot, kicked her to the other side of the room where Wendy managed to stop her from hitting the wall. "I sent you a pathetic grandma and you managed to attack the wrong person. My followers were weak and stupid, but each one pushed you to save the twelve from certain death. How ironic V; even this innocent baby was meant to meet its doom tonight, but thanks to you he will live a full and free life, and so will I." Excariot let out a deep and sarcastic laugh. "Ah yes, and let us not forget Wendy the Witch, the one who was sent to guide you. Trying desperately to make friends with you her whole life, but the great V was so superficial that her appearance put you off. Yet you were so easily drawn in by my friend here." He placed a finger under Delta's chin and she swooned at his touch. "Proving that you really never had a clue from the start."

Val could feel the tears starting to run down her cheeks. Delta had been her friend; they had shared summers together. She had sat at the kitchen table as one of her family. Val refused to believe it was true.

"Hard to swallow isn't it?" Excariot closed his fingers and Val felt her chest constricting until she could barely breathe.

Delta squealed in excitement. "Do it now! Finish her off. I want her powers." He stroked Delta's blonde mane with his free hand.

"Soon, very soon."

Just as Val looked as if she was going to pass out, Excariot released her weakened body to the ground. "Well, you truly are amazing. All that power and you still can't work out how to hurt me." He bent down close to Val's face and as he did, a figure leapt in the air. It was Jason making a second attempt to save Val.

Excariot waved his hand and a bright yellow lightning dome surrounded him, Val, Delta and the baby. Jason crashed into it with his whole body. The lightning engulfed him, shaking him violently until he was finally blown free. Fran ran over to him as he lay unconscious on the ground.

"Well, I would love to stay here with you and play all day but we have an appointment with some old friends and after such a long wait I would hate to disappoint the crowd that is gathering to meet me," said Excariot.

Val lay on the floor at his feet; she could see Sam helping Wendy and Eva to one side. Fran was holding desperately onto Jason's limp body. All her friends were hurt and her best friend was actually her enemy. How had this happened? As Val lifted herself onto all fours she made eye contact with Shane who was sitting with his back against the wall. He was mouthing something to her through the shield Excariot had created around them.

"You will be fine," Shane mouthed over and over again.

Val felt a strength building in her and she started to rise onto her knees. She had come such a long way and she would not allow this idiot to take it all away. And who was to say that what he was telling her was true? Val looked over at Shane and mouthed "Thank you" as she pulled herself up onto her feet.

"It's so endearing that you think you need to stand up to die. At least I won't have to bend down," Excariot mocked her.

"It isn't going to be that easy. For someone so clever, you are really boring and your little helper has very expensive tastes, so, if I were you, I would be getting rid of her as soon as possible." Val said, feeling her hands starting to vibrate. The energy in her body was beginning to fill her with power, but she wasn't sure how it would manifest itself. What she did know was that she was going for Wallace Excariot first, and then she would do some serious damage to Delta.

"Don't let her say those things about me!" Delta screamed at Excariot.

"Shut up." Excariot knocked Delta to the ground.

Val smirked at Delta. She began moving forward; the air inside the dome started to crackle. There was a massive amount of energy bouncing off the walls. Val's anger was making the dome spark and flicker. For a second, Val saw confusion in Excariot's face. That was all she needed. She pulled out her sword and flicked it into position. This man was going to hell. Val held the sword in front of her. Excariot grabbed it and began to laugh.

"Did you think you could beat me with your toy, little girl?" He pulled the sword out of Val's hand; it shrank back to size and he looked down at it. Taking advantage of his moment of distraction, she smashed him across the face with the full power of her free fist. The amazing punch rocked him in his boots.

His head recoiled violently. "Enough!" he shouted in Val's face as he felt his bloody lip. She knew that whatever happened now she had rattled him.

"Oh dear, is the poor Excariot bleeding?" Val mocked.

"Now you die!" He lunged forward. Val let out a wheeze as he lifted her off the ground. Looking down she saw the sword sticking out of her side. She began coughing, her mouth filling with a warm tinny substance, which she couldn't stop running down her chin. Glancing at the ground Val saw it was blood.

"Oh my God, I'm going to die," she thought as she felt freezing cold.

She could hear cries coming from outside the dome. Fran and Wendy were banging on it dome with their fists, even though it was electrocuting them with each stroke. Shane was still sitting looking straight into Val's eyes, his face unmoved by the whole episode. As she looked around, her thoughts moved to how much she wanted her mum right now, and she knew she would never see her again. She remembered the text she had received. As she took her last breath, Val remembered her mum and dad dancing outside the window of her bedroom on the night of her birthday. Then everything went dark.

"Stop!" Shane shouted at the girls, snapping back into the moment as Val's eyes closed.

"No, we need to get her out. She needs a doctor, Shane, What's wrong with you?" Fran screamed turning to hit Shane on the chest as he tried to restrain her.

"Stand back." Shane pulled Fran and grabbed Wendy's arm as Excariot began murmuring a strange chant while raising Val into the air. The dome started to glow. The light grew in intensity and they all had to shield their eyes against its power. Excariot suddenly dropped Val's body to the ground, like a broken doll that was no longer wanted. She landed next to Delta who was still on the floor holding the baby.

Shane pulled the girls back towards the counter. The dome, completely filled with light and disappeared, taking Val with it.

"What do we do now?" Fran screamed at Shane.

"We wait," Shane said.

"Wait for what Shane, for Eva to die as well? For heaven's sake, Jason needs medical attention," Sam said.

"I will explain everything, but first you need to look at this."

Val gasped and the breath reached deep into her chest. As she opened her eyes, her first sight was of sunlight dappling onto her through the leaves. "Wow, heaven looks like a forest," she thought to herself, "but the ground is very cold. I hope the rest of the afterlife is warmer." Reaching down she was relieved to find that the sword was gone. Val looked down at her body to see what she was wearing: her favourite black sack dress. Great!

Suddenly out of nowhere, a cloaked figure was leaning over her. "I see you are awake, my love." Before Val had time to speak, she was wrapped in a tender kiss.

"OK, I could get used to this," Val thought. Then the stranger leaned back and pulled off his hood. Val froze as he moved in for another kiss. She jumped backwards placing her hand against his chest.

"Sam? What are you doing here?" Val asked, concerned that he too was in heaven with her, although the kissing thing wasn't a bad side effect of being dead.

"I have come to collect you to go to meet with your mother. You know you cannot be late." Sam smiled and grabbed Val's hand, pulling her to her feet. Val wobbled, unsure whether she would be able to take a step forward.

"Is my mum dead too?" Val asked, tears welling in her eyes.

"Do not jest, V," Sam said as he started to lead her away.

Val started to feel uncomfortable. Sam had just called her V. That was her name in the past. Was she dreaming? She wasn't sure. It felt real and the fact that she had no shoes on and the pain in her feet was excruciating, led her to believe she was awake.

"So, where is my mum?" Val asked following Sam.

"Back at your dwelling." He looked at her with a confused expression. They moved through a clearing and Val saw in front of her something she had seen several times before: the village. Her village. As she walked past the pond, shivers went up and down her spine. Sam looked the same as the Sam she knew and he even answered to Sam, but he wasn't the real Sam. How could that be?

At the house closest to the pond, Sam pushed the wooden door open and the sweet smell of scent rushed out into their faces.

"Wyetta. V is here," he called out. Val looked at him, he'd said Wyetta, and that certainly wasn't Val's mum's name. Val was relieved on one hand that this possibly wasn't heaven yet; on the other hand, she was freaked out that she was about to meet her mother.

A small door on the other side of the room opened and out walked a woman. She was slightly taller than Val and had a long mane of brown hair just like Val's. Val recognised the woman from the pictures she had been given by Sam. This was the woman with the tattoo, the woman who had looked so much like Val. Being so close to her, Val knew that this woman was somehow, in some strange way, her mother. She didn't know how but she was going to find out.

"Samuel, leave us please. We will meet with you and the others by the pond soon." Wyetta smiled warmly at Sam, and he did as he was told, squeezing Val's hand before he released her.

Val was just about to open her mouth when Wyetta placed her finger on her lips. "If you let me speak you will learn more quickly," she said. Val tried one more time to speak, but Wyetta turned her around, marched her to a makeshift chair and sat her down.

"I know you have come here from the future, so please believe me when I say I am your mother. It was I who sent you to the future to keep you safe. The tattoo you have on your arm," Wyetta pointed to Val's arm, which was now exposed and had only the strange backwards y with the dot on it, "was the only way I could make sure that if Excariot got to you I could get you home safely."

Now Val understood why they both had the same one in the centre but the zodiac book hadn't.

"Excariot will believe you are now dead and this gives us an advantage, my daughter."

"If I'm to believe you're my mother, then where is my father?" Val looked at her for an answer.

Wyetta took Val's hands in hers and inspected them. "You haven't grown since I sent you away; it's like time has stopped for us both." She took a deep breath. "Val, your father is dead, I'm so sorry." Her face softened and Val knew that whoever he was, this woman had loved him.

"Your father was very special. He was not of this world." She released Val and started to walk around the room. "He came to our village one night and he told us of a man he was searching for, a prisoner. I remember seeing him across the room and falling in love, knowing instantly that he was going to be my partner for life. The man he was looking for was called Excariot. Your father's name was Gabrielle," she said with a softness that moved Val's emotions, bringing her dangerously close to tears. "Your father and I both felt the same way, V, and what happened next was out of our control." Wyetta blushed and Val assumed that love at first sight was a little out of the commonplace four hundred years ago.

"OK, I get the idea," Val said.

"Gabrielle and I knew I was with child within days, and things moved very quickly, more so than is normal."

Val knew she was about to hear things that were going to be strange. "Val you were born in only thirteen days. You grew at a rate no one had ever seen. You grew faster than any child in the village. Gabrielle spent his nights following Excariot's tracks and his days with us. Then, one night, when he returned from his exploration he seemed worried. He said that he would have to leave by the next full moon and you would have to stay with me. I cried until I thought there were no more tears in my body. Then the women of the village met to decide our fate. They agreed that as soon as you came of age you would join the coven, that being a witch was your birthright from me. It didn't matter to me how fast you grew or who your father was, I just loved you."

Wyetta moved towards a small pot in the corner of the room and poured two cups of steaming fluid. She handed one to Val. Val thanked her, lifting it to her lips to take a sip. As the warm fluid slipped down Val's throat she realised that this wasn't a cup of tea or coffee, it was sewage. Val choked hard and could see Wyetta's concerned face looking back at her.

"It's fine, it just went down the wrong hole," Val said. She realised from Wyetta's confused expression that she possibly didn't know there were two holes.

"One night, while we were playing with you, a messenger came from one of the nearby villages to warn Gabrielle that the witch hunter was close. Excariot had heard about your birth and was looking for you. Gabrielle told me he had to go and promised he would be back by the morning." She looked at the floor, which was covered in mud, taking a moment to compose herself. "He never came back to us. There were stories of a large battle, that he had met with the witch finder. His life was lost trying to save some of our sister and brother witches." Val could see this was still raw for her.

"So what did you do?" Val asked.

"I got strong V. I made a decision that if Gabrielle wasn't going to be with his daughter then Excariot wasn't going to get you either." Her face was now determined. "It took you one moon cycle to grow to your age of initiation and the villagers hid you. Excariot seemed to disappear after Gabrielle's death. Everyone relaxed a little, but not for long, and then it started." Wyetta's face filled with anger.

"About a week before your initiation there were witches being hung and tortured all over the area. So many innocents died, V, but no-one would betray the star child. We knew you would bring peace. We readied for your initiation and the night came when you were to be made a full witch. That night is tonight." Wyetta placed her cup down on a small wooden table. "You never made it to your initiation. Excariot had received news of our place of worship and he was waiting, though he wasn't prepared for the power we had. Your father gave me some gifts that he knew would come in handy if I ever met Excariot, and I was ready. We fought and I managed to send you to safety." She looked proud of herself and Val realised this must have been an intense battle.

"So what happened to you and all the others?" Val asked.

"We all died, V." Wyetta's expression wasn't one of fear; it was pride. "You must realise one thing ,V, you cannot kill a witch. If you take her body, her soul will return to be born again. You were the only survivor and as long as the family blood lines of the witches who died on that night continued to live their true lives, then you would be safe. But Excariot must have worked out how to change the destiny of the other twelve, or he wouldn't be here and neither would you." She started to walk around, closing wooden shutters and readying herself to leave. "But no one knew I had protected you with the symbol."

Val wanted to tell Wyetta that it was all her fault, but what was the point? Now all she could do was follow her mother and try to make it all right. "So, if you died, are we in heaven?" Val asked.

"No."

"So how do you know all this and yet you are still alive?" Val felt confused.

"I know all this because someone from your time came to tell me my fate. They told me to be ready. That the day would come when the witches would live again and today is that day. They said you would come back in time and that the future would be changed, and here you are."

"Who?" Val asked.

"I cannot say, but all that matters is that you are ready and it's time." Reaching into the pocket of her cloak, Wyetta pulled out what looked like a silver bracelet. "V, your father left this for you. He wanted you to wear it for him." Val took the bracelet. It was shaped like a V and when she pushed it over her wrist it tightened around her skin to fit snugly.

"So what now?" Val stood up.

"Now we go to the others. They are waiting." Val followed Wyetta as they made their way to the pond. The air was crisp and the night had moved in. The group of men and women looked nervous but when Wyetta met them, they all greeted her with enthusiasm.

"Is she ready?" a man asked.

"Yes brother, don't worry." Wyetta had a powerful presence and these people obviously respected her.

"Then let us go and ready for V," a woman called. They all started to leave. Val joined the back of the group, but a hand grabbed her arm.

"Not you." Val recognised the voice before she saw the face. It was Sam again.

"But I need to protect them." Val pulled free.

"No V. You will join them soon." Seeing Wyetta waving goodbye, Val could only assume that what Sam was telling was the truth.

"When do we go?" Val asked.

"You go when the moon reaches the tops of the trees." Sam smiled.

"What about you?"

"I'm just your guardian. I am not one of them," Sam responded looking confused by Val's line of questioning.

"Do I have any more guardians?" Val was intrigued.

"Yes, one more, a local girl who is gifted with the sight." Sam was moving in close. Val obviously had a relationship with this Sam and she liked it, but it just wasn't the right time for messing around.

"Moon looks almost at the top." Val turned towards the trees cutting Sam off.

"OK, if you are in a real hurry, then go," he said harshly, obviously feeling rejected, but Val knew it was for the best.

"Right, I'll get off then." Val looked at the entrance to the woods, moved far enough away from Sam to be out of range of his grip, and turned to say goodbye. He smiles as she started walking towards the forest that spread out in front of her for miles. "I'll call you tomorrow," she promised, making phone signs with her hand. Sam looked at her as if she was crazy. It dawned on Val what she was doing and she turned away feeling awkward and confused. She was out of Sam's sight within seconds, swallowed by the density of the trees and undergrowth. Val knew she needed to move quickly and that she would be expected to arrive on time. The deeper she got into the wood, the more she felt at home. She started to run, jumping over leaves and branches. Then she saw it: sticking out of the ground was the tree root from her dreams. Val smiled. This time it wasn't going to catch her out.

When she arrived at the clearing, the others were in a circle, chanting. She couldn't make out what they were saying, but she knew that this was it. She had made it, no lights, no screaming and no being thrown into the air.

Val walked towards them with a sense of belonging, a feeling of finding her path. She was comfortable with what was happening and just wanted to get on with it. Making her way out of the foliage and into the clearing, she heard a noise. She stopped, frozen to the spot listening. It sounded familiar. She turned her head trying to pick out the noise between the chants of the witches. It was a baby crying. He was here. She knew that was Excariot's baby.

"Stop! He's here!" Val screamed, running towards the others. The witches had stopped chanting and turned to look at Val who was now on top of them.

"Run!" she waved her arms, but it was too late. Excariot knocked her to the ground with a flick of his wrist. Striding forward, he created an electrical dome over the others.

Val lifted herself up and ran at the dome. Making contact with it created shocks that ran through her body and she fell to the ground. She knew there was no way in.

"Well V, I'm pleased to see you again, and alive. What a surprise! I'm even happier that you will get to see your true mother killed before I go back to the future and kill your adoptive parents." Excariot walked around the dome knocking down the witches that tried to attack him.

Val yelled and bashed on the dome in anger, sparks flying with each stroke and intense shocks rushing up her arms.

"I promise I will kill you!" she shouted, unable to contain her anger.

"Not today." He walked through the last few witches flicking them away to left and right, as if they were ants, until he reached Wyetta. "You! You are the cause of all this trouble. You and your dirty child have stopped me for four hundred years." He struck Wyetta across the face and yet she stood firm. "Why Gabrielle mixed with a dirty thing like you is beyond me." He struck her again.

"I'm going to get in there and you will wish you had really killed me the first time." Val was sobbing in anger.

"It's time for my revenge, V. It's time to fulfil my destiny, so let us have a little quiet please." He moved in close to Wyetta and peered at her face. "Not so pretty now, are we?" Excariot curled up the corner of his mouth.

Wyetta spat a mass of blood from her bleeding mouth into his face. This threw him into a rage. The dome crackled in response to his anger. His powers were awesome. Val watched, not knowing how she could help the others.

With slight movements of his hands, Excariot was moving each witch into position against the circumference of the dome. When he had finished, the witches were trapped, in positions imitating the twelve points of the clock. Excariot was in the centre. He began chanting and Val sensed that something really bad was going to happen.

His arms began to rise, and as they did, Val noticed he was wearing a bracelet that matched the one Wyetta had given her. Did this have power?

A small ball of sparks formed above his head and he looked pleased with his handy work.

"OK Gabrielle, if you want to help me, now is the time," Val said looking down at her bracelet. "I wonder?" Val focused her mind and slowly began to push her hand with the bracelet through the dome. It passed through! Val had her hand in the dome. She started to follow with the rest of her body.

Meanwhile, Excariot's small ball of sparks was now a large ball. Luckily, he was concentrating so hard that he didn't notice Val entering the dome. When the ball was the size and shape of a doorway, it changed, Beams of light shot from it, piercing each witch in turn. Out of their chests came a return beam of light that hit the sparking doorway. Val threw herself onto the ground in fear.

"At last," Excariot called out. "Come to me, Lailah. Be free my love. Come now."

He stepped back and fell silent.

Val looked up and saw wispy figures coming through the door of sparks: one, then another and another. Val knew this was very bad. She couldn't make out what they were, but they were coming through quicker and quicker, and they were filling the dome.

She had to do something. She looked at her hands; they had always been the source of her powers. She could hold fire, move the earth, and create air. Val knew that anything she touched she could transform, and now she needed to transform the most powerful thing she had ever seen: the dome.

Val crawled back to the side and placed her hand on the dome's wall. She concentrated on feeling its power, rather than fearing it. She wasn't going to let this animal get away with hurting anyone else. The stream of spirits wasn't slowing down and Val realised that time was now of the essence.

Cautiously rising to her feet, she felt her whole body come alive with the dome's energy. Carefully she moved in behind Excariot.

"Come quickly," he murmured, basking in the glory of his victory.

"Shut up!" Val shouted slamming her free hand onto Excariot's back. The dome's immense power started to flow through her. As she pulled more from it, the more she pumped through Excariot's body. He was unable to stop her and his loss of concentration was causing the doorway to close. The spirits stopped coming, and Val was draining the dome of its power, causing it to disintegrate around them. Suddenly the witches were free and collapsing to the floor in exhaustion. Val was weakening, but she knew she had done enough to stop them dying.

She was struggling to keep a hold of Excariot who was beginning to fight back, and the dome didn't have enough energy to help her anymore. Excariot broke loose from her grip and swung around, knocking her to the ground.

"You stupid child." He was shaken and still dangerous.

Val felt she had given it her all. Looking up, she could still see spirits floating around Excariot's head.

"You can't stop me." He raised his hands again.

He was right. Val had no more power to give.

When she thought it had all been in vain, a beam of light came from the trees and hit Excariot. Val turned and saw Sam. He was wielding a type of stick and out of it came beams of light that hit Excariot over and over again. Sam walked forward confidently; the closer he got to Excariot, the further Excariot backed off, desperately trying to deflect the beams with his bracelet. Sam reached down and pulled Val to her feet.

"So, you want some help?" Sam smiled.

"Well, that would have been good a while ago," Val responded.

"Sorry, I couldn't attack until the dome was down." Sam fired again. The spirits surrounding Excariot become agitated, visibly whipping backwards and forwards.

"Well V, you have been a greater adversary than I would have hoped for. You take after your father," Excariot said.

Sam stopped firing.

Excariot pulled his arm up grasping his wrist band and aimed it at the sky. "See you in the future if you make it back. I will say hello to your parents for you." Excariot laughed as he began to disappear.

Sam ran at him firing repeatedly, but it was too late, he had gone; the spirits had all followed.

"He's going to kill my parents! I need to get back to my time," Val was spinning in circles looking for Wyetta.

"V, stand still." Sam grabbed her.

"You don't get it! My parents, he is going to kill my parents!" Val spotted Wyetta. "Help me, please help me get home," Val started sobbing. Wyetta seemed incredibly calm. "Don't worry, V, we will help you, but first we must initiate you." Val couldn't believe what she was hearing; her parents were going to die and Val was going to have a party.

"No, this is really bad timing," Val said.

"V, you need what we have to give. Why do you think Excariot wanted us dead? He knew we could make you stronger than him." Wyetta called all the others together. "He will not have time to hurt your future parents and we will help you return to your time." She held Val's hand and a man grabbed her other one as they started to chant. Sam moved away from the circle.

"Do you promise?" she called out and Wyetta nodded. Val could see she had no choice but to go along with them. Without them she had no way of getting home.

Wyetta and the man released Val into the centre of the circle. She wasn't sure if she was supposed to do anything, so she just stood still.

Wyetta pulled a knife from her waistband and moved forward as the others continued circling. She called the air to her, the fire, water and earth. She blessed those inside the circle and then blessed Val. As the ceremony continued, Val started to relax and feel the energy that these people were raising. After all they had been through, they still wanted to make her one of them.

Suddenly, and without warning, they stopped. Wyetta moved forward and placed a kiss on Val's forehead. "V, you are now an apprentice witch." The others broke into applause. Val smiled, that wasn't so bad.

Everyone came to Val and kissed her. Some she remembered from her dreams and others were new. Each blessed her. Val was honoured but she needed to go home.

"Val, we can do one more thing for you, but you need to agree," Wyetta said.

"What's that?"

"We can make Excariot forget your parents."

"Do it! What are we waiting for?" Val was hopping from one foot to the other enthusiastically.

"There are consequences to all magic, V."

"Well they can't be worse than my parents' death." Val looked at the others for support.

"If we make a spell strong enough for Excariot to forget them, then they will have to forget you as well. Everyone will forget you. Excariot will watch your every move and if you see them, he will know." Wyetta's face became sad

"No, I can't live without my parents; they are everything to me." Val started to cry, turning to look at the other witches.

"Then you will have to be with them all the time, because he will never let them live."

Val walked away from the coven. She couldn't let her parents forget her; they were her life. From the age of five Val had promised her mum she would never leave home. Who would she turn to? She had lost her best friend and now she was going to lose her parents. Wyetta found her sitting on the ground with her face in her hands.

"V, I gave you up to your future mother to keep you safe and it hurt as much as you're hurting now. Your father died to protect you and many have died to keep your secret." She held Val's hand. "Sometimes we have to give up things we love to keep them safe."

Val nodded, she knew deep down that Wyetta was right. "OK," she said. "Let's do it." Val stood up. The others joined hands with her. Wyetta began to chant and the others followed. As they moved around the circle, Val felt something happening to her. She was rising off the ground, her hands were glowing with light and, as the group followed Wyetta, the chant became louder and louder. Val was losing the power to control herself and as the chant seemed to reach fever pitch, Val's whole body was glowing like a bulb. Then they stopped and a powerful beam of light shot from Val's head, piercing the clouds. It stopped as quickly as it started and she fell to the ground.

"It is done. All who knew you will forget you," Wyetta said.

"Everyone?" Val asked quietly as she sat up with a little help from the friendly old man who had been chanting next to her.

"Your friends in the bookshop are safe." Wyetta smiled. "You did want them to remember you, didn't you?" Wyetta asked.

"How did you know?" Val smiled.

"I told you, a friend came to see me." She patted Val. "It's time for you to go back, V." Her eyes were glistening in the moonlight.

"You are a great mum." Val hugged Wyetta. Val felt Wyetta's body shaking as she sobbed into Val's shoulder.

"I know that what I give up is for the good of all people." She pulled herself up straight.

"And I know that I will do everything not to disappoint you." Val stepped back and turned to look at the others. "I may not be able to bring back your loved ones who have gone, but I promise I will protect your loved ones in the future." Everyone cheered.

"V, I will miss you." Sam moved forward.

"That stick thing was really cool. Where did you get it from?" Val asked.

"Your father gave it to me and told me that one day I would need it." Sam offered it to Val.

"No, you keep it. I have a few tricks of my own." Val told him.

"So how do I get home?" Val turned to Wyetta.

"You need to let us go. When you have fulfilled a spell as a witch you must never look back, because you should be sure you did the best you could." Val realised then that when she had been saving the people in the future, she had assumed that she was allowed to return because she had finished the task. But it had been because she believed she had done the best she could. Things began to make sense.

"OK, then I must go." Val turned to walk away. She had only gone a few steps when she felt a hand grab hers. She turned to find Sam looking into her eyes.

"V, I will love you for as long as the sun rises and the trees grow." Val felt her knees buckling as he bent down and kissed her. She was going to miss this part.

"I will miss you as well, my brave Sam." Blinking back tears, Val turned and resumed walking. She could sense Wyetta watching her and, although she wanted to stay with the mother who *could* remember her, she knew that everyone would be in danger if she did that. She had no choice. She had to go.

Val was almost at the edge of the forest when she heard a familiar voice.

"Val."

Val turned around to see Delta holding the baby.

"What the hell do you want?" Val asked angrily.

"Please help me. Excariot's left me here. He wasn't interested in the baby or me; he just wanted to get to you. Please forgive me." Delta looked uncomfortable holding the baby and its whining was quite grating.

"I just died, Delta while you laughed. I have had to give up my mum and dad and I'm not sure if my friends will still be alive when I get back, so please forgive me if I don't give a damn about what happens to you." Val felt nothing but hatred towards Delta.

"If you leave us here, we'll die," Delta said whimpering.

"There is a village about a mile in that direction and they will really love you." Val placed her hands together, closed her eyes and felt herself slip into a jump. The last noises she heard from the past were the cries of Delta and Excariot's baby.

CHAPTER 13

The Beginning

Val opened her eyes and found herself staring at blank white walls. This wasn't the shop and where were her friends? She got to her feet and was wondering if she had arrived at the local asylum when a door opened.

"Hello, please follow me." A young man dressed in a black sweater and trousers moved to one side so Val could leave the room. He didn't seem hostile, but she still felt deep trepidation. However, she didn't seem to have much choice, so she followed him.

"Can you tell me where I am please?" Val asked quietly.

The man didn't answer, but he just walked on in front of her. Val looked for possible escape routes, but there was nothing; no way out. They made their way down an immense corridor. On the walls, which seemed to reach into oblivion, were imbedded endless small boxes; each one contained what looked like a wisp of smoke. They eventually arrived at another white door, only distinguishable from the endless wall by its handle. The man stopped, "Wait here. He will call for you when he's ready." The man walked off, disappearing into the distance and leaving her alone in this strange place. Val felt as if she was heading for detention. She looked around nervously. She didn't know where she was, didn't know where her friends were, didn't know what was going to happen to her. How could they, whoever *they* were, expect her to hang around here, waiting patiently? Val jumped and turned round quickly as a door behind her opened. A large, white-haired man, with a well-groomed beard was smiling at her. She was now convinced she had been kidnapped by Father Christmas.

"Welcome to Alchany," he said, starting to walk down the hall. Val followed, unsure what was happening but determined that she wasn't going to stay alone.

"Where is Alchany?" Val asked.

"Somewhere you will never find on your maps. We are a prison planet on the edge of the Bannaly galaxy," he said.

"Prison?" Val responded nervously. "Galaxy?" Val put out a hand onto the white wall for support.

"Don't worry, you aren't in trouble; you are one of us." The man patted Val kindly on the shoulder.

"What do you mean I'm one of you?" Val was still supporting herself against the wall when the man turned to face her.

"You are one of us. You belong here, in this place." He smiled then took Val's hand and pulled her back into motion. "Please let me explain. Your father, Gabrielle, was one of us, although your mother wasn't. So I suppose you could say you do and don't belong here."

"Galaxy?" Val stuttered, "I don't even like flying."

"Stop gibbering. Do you want to know the whole story?" He stopped and pushed open a door that hadn't seemed to be there a second earlier.

"Yes please," Val responded.

"OK, welcome to the prison." As they walked through the door, Val could see the true extent of the place. The corridors appeared never-ending; there were hundreds, possibly thousands, of men dressed in black making their way up and down each one. Val followed her guide out onto a balcony, which allowed them to see the immensity of the expanse in front of them.

"You are the first female guard ever to be born. These men you see are unique. We breed only the finest guards and your father was by far my greatest creation." The man looked at Val and she could sense the same sadness as Wyetta in his words.

"When you say 'breed' what exactly do you mean?" Val asked.

"Each guard comes from a perfect strand of what you call DNA. They are mixed with a female match and so another perfect guard is brought into existence, *always male*." The man pointed over to the far side, to an open doorway. "The Ransowars live there, they are the chosen females who are used in producing all new guards." Val looked over but they were too far away to see the females.

"So what am I?" Val was now intrigued.

"You are a mistake, but if you were male you would be twenty-three thirteen, although I believe you call yourself Val. Your father, Gabrielle, was twenty-three eleven. The twenty-three is your DNA job description and your other number shows when you were produced."

"So, who is number twenty-three twelve then?" Val asked.

"That would be Excariot." The man looked both sad and ashamed.

"I'm sorry, did you just say Excariot?" Val could feel her blood instantly boiling.

"Come with me. You need to understand the whole story." He turned and headed back into the door. "Your father was due to breed with a Ransowar called Lailah."

"That was the name Excariot was calling out!" Val exclaimed, and the man nodded.

"What we hadn't realised was that Lailah and Excariot had fallen in love and hatched a plan for her to escape." They carried on walking. "Excariot managed to run away with Lailah to the planet Gingua where he must have hoped they could live out their lives, but I sent Gabrielle to bring them back. Your father succeeded, as always, catching Lailah and Excariot and returning them here to go on trial. They were found guilty and sentenced. However, Excariot managed to escape before we could carry out the extraction."

"Extraction? That sounds painful," Val said.

"We are a prison for thousands of planets. As you can see, we collect and hold prisoners from all over the galaxy so we have to do it in a way that minimises risk. Each box you see contains one essence." The man patted a box on the wall and Val felt a shiver going down her spine.

"So, you are telling me you make people into wispy smoke?"

"Nearly. In a very technical procedure, we extract the essence of that person, which is indeed the wispy thing, and keep it here until they have fulfilled their time."

"Then what? Do they get their bodies back?"

He seemed amused and shook his head. "No, of course not."

"If you have dumped their bodies, what do you do with them when they've finished their sentences?"

The man didn't answer. Instead, he opened another door and Val instantly heard the screams. She grabbed the man's arm.

"Do not forget that these people are the most dangerous criminals in the Universe. They are returned to cloned bodies. Each body is engineered so that if the person attempts to cause pain or harm to another, or create or manifest what you call magic, their clone will shut down."

"You stick them in a cloned body! That is just terrible. Do they all look the same?"

"Look."

Val followed the man to another balcony from where she could see a spirit form being injected into the arm of what looked like a young man.

"The clones take on one of several forms: male, female, young and old. We also have a special form for the prisoners who have caused the worst devastation."

"What if they are have been unfairly condemned?" Val knew this might be a sensitive question, but it had to be asked.

"We never make mistakes," the man said sternly as he walked back towards the door.

"So why did Excariot choose to come to my home?"

"Your planet is the first one we have found on which our spirits can move freely into body forms."

"So all those spirits Excariot let out and took to the future are hardened criminals with magical powers, who can take on human form, is that correct?" Val asked with her hands firmly placed on her hips.

"Yes. He was trying to get Lailah, but you stopped him before he could achieve his ultimate goal."

"Don't you think it would be a lot easier to just give him Lailah and be done with it?" Val asked in an agitated tone. "So now you have a load of weirdoes to deal with."

"Not exactly, Twenty-three Thirteen. *You* have a load of what you call weirdoes to deal with."

"No! You messed up. Let him have the girl. He killed my biological father and he may even try and kill my mum and dad, and you want me to go and sort out your problems?" Val could feel her temper rising and she was struggling to keep it under control. "And call me Val."

"Sorry Val, I understand that you are upset, but we can't let people like Excariot have what they want. What would be next? These people are produced to do a job, nothing more. It got messy when it became emotional. And I can't say that the judges are pleased that I have requested you not be terminated." He opened a door. "Terminate me!" she bellowed, raising enough energy to push the door shut hard with the little air there was in this place. "You don't get to terminate me." Val walking up to the man, but he was ready for her. With a flick of his finger she was sitting on the floor wondering what had happened.

"Your courage is endearing, but it will get you killed. You were a mistake; you were unwanted, but now at last, you can serve a purpose. You are our link on earth. We have more than enough to do here without chasing people on your planet." The man grabbed Val's hand and pulled her back onto her feet.

"So what do I do now?" Val asked brushing herself down indignantly.

"You go home. You wait for him to start creating his group of followers. Excariot has to regroup and find another twelve people who are as powerful as your mother's coven to create a portal to try again to extract Lailah."

"So why doesn't he just go back to my mum?" Val asked.

"Because doing that used a great deal of energy, and he needed you to create it. You played into his hands and that is partly our fault. We should have moved in sooner."

"Gosh, so you do make mistakes." Val turned her lip up.

"Val, our portal to your planet is in the bookshop. Excariot closed it down when he found it and only you had the power to get to us, but we couldn't get to you. That will all change on your return."

"Great, so I get to pop back whenever I want," Val said sarcastically.

"No, only when you have a prisoner to bring back."

Val was lost for words as she realised she had been given a job by family default. Apparently, she was now working for a Father Christmas look-alike in some weird prison, which was not exactly how she had imagined her life. "So, where do we go from here?" Val asked.

"You need to go home, back to the shop. It will be your place of work and rest. Excariot won't come for you there because he will fear being trapped. Do you have your father's bracelet?"

"Yes." Val pulled up her sleeve to show the pointed bracelet that had moulded its self to her wrist.

"Good, it is the only way you can communicate with us and it will enhance your natural abilities which, I have to admit, are quite impressive."

"How will I know who to catch or where they are?" Val felt overwhelmed.

"You will know where as you did with your other charges. You have been preparing yourself all the way through this experience and now you are ready to get the job done. Be conscious that we will be watching you, and I will be sending you a partner soon."

"A partner? Who?" Val whined. She had enough people to deal with and she didn't need some weird bloke from a different world hanging around.

"Val, our time is coming to a close. You must return to your place. You will do well to keep your eyes open and maybe read a few of the books that you spend so much time cleaning."

"Can I at least ask your name?" Val said.

"I'm the warden." He smiled at Val and that was it, she was off again.

As Val travelled, she wondered where she would find herself this time, but screams of joy told her, before she had even opened her eyes, that she was back at the bookshop. She felt the cold smooth wooden floor below her hand and slowly opened her eyes. Her friends were all in front of her, clearly pleased to have her back.

"Well, I bet you didn't expect me to come back," Val said smiling as she started to rise to her feet. Fran was the first to grab her and embrace her. Wendy followed and Jason, with a few bandages on, patted her on the back.

"We knew you were coming back because of Shane's letter," Fran sang in Val's ear. Val looked over at Shane who was still leaning on the counter smiling.

"What letter?" Val asked confused.

"This one." Shane held up what looked like an antique parchment. Val peeled the others off her and headed towards him.

"Let me see." Val took the parchment out of his hand. It was very old and written in something that had faded. Val read in amazement.

Hello Shane,

Today will be an extraordinary day. Today you will see loved ones die and many things that make you believe all is lost. Do not despair my friend. All is well. I will die and disappear in front of your eyes in the bookshop and you must not worry because I'm going to return. Do not interfere; just keep the others safe. Give no clues, to me or the others, that you have seen this letter. Love from Val

Val held the parchment in amazement. When had she written it? "Where did this thing come from?" Val handed it back to Shane.

"You don't know? You wrote it," Shane said with a puzzled expression. He had expected Val to know exactly where it had come from and give him clarity.

"No, I've never seen it before and I'm sure I haven't written it, although it is my handwriting. Where did you get it from?"

Shane pulled another envelope out of his jacket pocket and placed it on the counter.

"This came this morning by courier from a solicitor's office. I signed for it and the rest is history." Val glanced at the other envelope, on which was written 'for Val's eyes only'. Val carefully opened the envelope. Inside were several folded pieces of paper. As she peeled them open, it became apparent that they were the deeds of a property. Shane, who was looking over Val's shoulder, read out the address for all to hear.

"It says that Val is the owner of the bookshop," he announced.

Val looked at it in silence for several moments. How could this be happening? She didn't remember writing to Shane and she definitely didn't remember purchasing the shop. Val had to admit that the writing on Shane's letter was irrefutably hers.

Suddenly Val realised that not everyone was there. "Where's Sam?" Val looked around.

"He took that woman who got knocked out by Excariot to the hospital. She was in a really bad way." Shane told her.

"Now, back to you, Val. We knew you would be OK, but you need to tell us what you have been doing and where you've been."

"Can I get a drink first, and a chair?" Val smiled at them all.

Wendy rushed over with a cup of water and Fran supplied a stool. As Val sat and slowly sipped her drink, she felt herself slowly relaxing.

"I have so much to tell you, but the first thing you need to know is that Delta won't be coming back." Val's voice stayed steady. She hadn't had time to truly feel the pain that Delta had inflicted.

"Who?" Wendy asked looking puzzled.

"Delta."

Her friends were looking at her as if she was talking in a foreign language. Did they really not remember her? Her mother had warned her about this so Val would need to tread carefully, she really didn't have a clue what changes had been created by the spell in her absence.

"Not to worry." Val shook her head. "I went back to sixteen forty-five where I met my real mother and found out about my father." Val smiled fondly taking a sip of her water.

"Oh, that's so lovely. I suppose that makes being an orphan a little less harsh," Fran said enthusiastically.

"Orphan?" Val nearly choked on her water. And then it really hit her: she had given up her parents. The pain was overwhelming, but she couldn't give anything away, couldn't do anything that might lead the others to question her. Her parents' role in this must never be revealed; to expose them would put them in terrible danger. She couldn't risk it. At that point she was just grateful to have friends that remembered her.

"Excariot was there." Val looked at their expressions and realised they definitely still remembered him. "We had a massive battle and I defeated him, but not before he managed to release a large number of criminals from a prison on a planet called Alchany."

The others were looking on in awe, yet not disbelief.

"So where are they now, on a death star?" Jason asked in a Darth Vader voice.

Val poked Jason's arm. "No, they are here somewhere. They can take over anyone's body, and I imagine they won't be choosing anyone good." Val stood up and went for another cup of water. "We have to prepare, and now I have a business to run as well so if you are on board it will mean giving me all you have. Excariot tricked us once and I'm not going to let that happen again." Val filled her glass, her back to the others, waiting in silence.

When no one spoke, Val turned and asked quietly, "So who is with me?" As she spoke the bookshop door opened.

"I am." A dark figure responded, coming into the shop. Val's heart skipped a beat when she realised it was

Sam. The memory of his kiss brought red heat to her face, and yet here he was only just getting to know her.

"Thank you, Sam," she said.

Then the others gathered around her chorusing their support.

"If Excariot wants a war he is going to get one," Wendy declared, waving her arms in the air. Val laughed as Sam made his way over to her.

"Did you have fun wherever you went?" Sam grabbed Val's hand.

"Well, I have had better times." Val looked up into Sam's eyes.

"I'm just pleased you are back. It was a very good idea to leave the letter so at least we could all relax a little." Sam took Val's other hand. "Are you OK? I found it hard very watching you dying, especially at the end of my sword."

"Oh, what has happened to my sword?" Val looked around.

"It's here." Jason handed it to her.

"Thanks. I'm very pleased to get it back." Val squeezed Sam's hand.

"So what do you want us to do now?" Sam stood back allowing the others to join them.

"You all need to go home and I need to sleep," Val laughed, opening the bookshop door.

"But you don't want to be on your own, not with that madman on the loose," Wendy said.

"He won't come here. This shop is a doorway to the prison and I'm hoping it can also be my home, so I need to get used to the idea of being here alone." Val started to pull Jason who was closest to her towards the door. "Out, before I use my statutory right to evict you from my premises," she joked.

"Can we come back tomorrow?" Wendy asked.

"Are you kidding? You're going to run the shop." Val smiled at Wendy who was almost swooning. "On the condition that you go home. Now." Wendy was already out of the door. The others followed suit until Shane was the only one left.

"Val, you don't have to cope with all of this on your own. You can come to our house for tonight," Shane said.

"Shane, you are one of the most amazing people I have ever met. I can only pray that you stay with me forever, but tonight I need to be alone." Val placed a kiss on Shane's cheek the same way she would on her dad's, then pushed him gently towards the door.

"Goodnight." Shane joined the others and walked away, waving.

"What time do I start tomorrow?" Wendy shouted.

"Late, I need to sleep," Val called back as she closed the door behind her.

Val walked back into the shop. A place she had spent so little time in had now become not only her business, but her home as well. She crossed over to the counter and found her handbag in its usual place on the shelf. Inside was her large bunch of keys. She flicked through them, removing the ones that she knew belonged to the shop. When she had finished she tried the ones that were left, one by one, in the door marked 'private'. "It's time you let up your secrets," said Val to the door.

She quickly found the key and the door opened with ease. To Val's amazement, it revealed a staircase. Hanging on the wall at the bottom of the staircase were several of Wallace's tweed jackets. There was also a telephone on a stand. "Now I know where you are." Val patted the phone and, touching one of the jackets, decided she would send all his stuff to the local charity shop.

Not surprisingly, the stairs were made of the same wood that seemed to consume the shop and the area was very dark, and slightly threatening. She found the light switch and, with a tentative hand, quickly flicked it. A light came on and Val began breathing again.

She cautiously made her way up the stairs. Pulling the sword out of her pocket, she extended it. This place was a portal to another dimension and she wasn't going to get caught out. At the top of the stairs, she emerged into a very musty, open plan flat. She could see the kitchen over to the right and on the far left a large double bed. Val was surprised to realise that it was a very nice (although dated) apartment. She switched on another light switch and the whole place lit up. There were many signs of Wallace, but nothing of Excariot.

Val was most shocked when she looked in the fridge. She had expected a sacrificial lamb's freshly beating heart. Instead, she found sliced ham, cheese, a few eggs and a bottle of milk.

This was stuff she would also dispose of; he could have left it on the chance that he might be able to poison her. Near the kitchen she found another door. Val pushed it open with her sword and entered a small bathroom. "All the usual," Val giggled. It didn't matter what side of the galaxy you were on, you still needed a toilet.

Val left the bathroom and went for the last door. She had seen everything else so maybe this was a guest bedroom or a closet for his very fashionable tweed attire. It opened easily and Val felt her breath catch in her throat as she stood gazing into what looked like a huge mirror. But she wasn't looking at herself, she was looking at

Alchany. She took a step back, worried that she might be drawn through the portal. Her wrist was hurting. When she pulled her sweater sleeve up she saw that her bracelet was glowing almost lava red. What now, she wondered.

This was clearly the way back to Alchany, but how did it work? She stepped forward again, and placed her hand on the image. Immediately a warning sound resounded through the flat.

"Warning! Warning! Prisoner in transit." Val jumped back and slammed the door shut. As soon as the door closed, her bracelet stopped glowing. "Ah, so that's how I send the prisoners back then," Val said to herself.

She moved to the bed area and, sitting down for a moment, took in her new surroundings, trying to comprehend what was happening. She felt it would be better to simply accept what was going on without question. To think too much about any of it would surely drive her insane. She was going to need a very long time to come to terms with everything that had happened to her.

The silence was broken by insistent knocking. Val froze, realising instantly that it was coming from the door to Alchany. When it didn't stop, she stood up and walked cautiously to the door. What if this was one of Excariot's friends popping in for a visit? She pulled out her sword, then slowly opened the door.

"Don't point that thing at me, girl!" A very small woman pushed Val's sword to one side, completely unaffected by the sparks flashing from it.

"Sorry," Val said as she walked backwards into the room.

"Twenty-three Thirteen you made a pick-up call. I'm the collector." The woman pulled out a sheet of paper.

"Well, I did it by mistake. I'm sorry." Val sat back down on the bed.

The woman became very agitated.

"Let's get something straight, Twenty-three Thirteen, crossing dimensions is easy, filling in the paperwork takes all my life force. I will have to tell them why you called me out under false pretences and then fill in a fifty-seven thirty. Do you have any idea how long that takes?" She poked Val in the chest.

"I'm sorry," Val shrugged and thought how much the woman's little finger had hurt her.

"You guards are always sorry. So much for perfect DNA."

"You can call me Val if you like. That's my name." Val smiled trying to help the woman warm to her.

"So Val, are you ever going to make a call again when you don't have a prisoner for me?" the woman said in a highly patronising voice.

"No." Val put her head down.

"Listen, I know you are new to this and the only female guard that has ever existed, so you are going to get it hard. I know your story and I do feel for you, but you have to start getting things right. The warden will be on your back if you don't." The little woman's face had softened and Val appreciated her words.

"If it helps, I really am sorry," Val said.

"Not unless sorry fills in the forms for an unauthorised call out, no," the woman responded, "it doesn't help."

"Why didn't anyone come through the door before now and catch Excariot?" Val asked.

"Excariot had the door shut. We can only cross through dimensions when doors are open. We can knock, but if no one answers then we can't help you." The woman turned and started to walk towards the door.

"Will I see you again?" Val needed as many familiar faces as possible right now.

"Yes, I'm your designated collector. If anyone else comes though without prior warning from the warden, then you need to exterminate them on sight." The woman walked through the door and closed it behind her.

Val was tempted to open the door so she could see the woman again, but she thought she'd better not get into any more trouble that day.

After a few minutes alone, Val realised that she had one more thing she needed to do. She stood up, making her way to the apartment stairs and switched off the light. She made her way out locking the door behind her and left the bookshop.

The sun was rising and the air felt cold and fresh. She made her way past Shane's shop and crossed the road to the bus stop. As she sat at the stop, the familiarity felt good. The bus arrived in good time, there was hardly any traffic, just the commuters who had to be some-where at crazy o'clock to please a boss who probably didn't appreciate them. At least their boss couldn't re-move their souls from their bodies Val thought.

She walked briskly and in a few minutes she was standing outside her house. The lights were on down-stairs. Val knew her dad would be getting ready for work and her mum would be cooking him some huge breakfast. She ran across the road to get a better look. Crouching down under the lounge window, she peeked in. Her dad was sitting at the table with a book in his hand. Then her mum appeared and Val felt a stinging behind her eyes that was almost too painful to bear.

"Hello," a voice came from behind her. Val's heart nearly stopped beating. She slowly turned, expecting to see a police officer or something similar, but it was just the lad who dropped off the newspaper.

"Hi," Val responded, trying not to look too much like a stalker.

"You know the Saunders?" he asked.

"Why?" Val was cautious; this boy could be an alien for all she knew.

"Because you are looking in their window at six in the morning," the lad responded, throwing the paper onto the front step. He turned and rode away. Val slipped to the door and picked up the paper. The Independent. It was her dad's favourite and her mum said that at least it burned well. Val was holding it as the front door opened and there stood Susan.

"Hello there, do we have a new newspaper girl?" Susan smiled at Val.

"Yes, here you go." Val handed her mother the paper.

"Thank you, you know The Independent is the best one to burn." Susan smiled tapping the paper on her hand, then turned away and shut the door. Val stood breathing in her mother's scent for as long as it lasted. Her mum hadn't even recognised her. Val felt sure that they were safe, but was heartbroken that she would never see them again. She couldn't take any risks because she didn't know who was going to be watching her and when. She didn't know how long it would take for her to find the criminals, or if she would survive in one piece, but at least she could be sure that her parents were not going to be Excariot's bargaining chips.

Val made her way solemnly back to the shop. As she arrived she noticed something different about the place. Above the door the plaque no longer had Wallace's name on it. It now said 'Established by Valerie Saunders'. She placed her finger on the surname and stroked it.

This was it; it was time to grow up. Val knew that Excariot was coming. He was going to do anything in his power to finish her and get Lailah back. Val was going to fight him every step of the way, but now she needed to sleep.

She opened the door to the shop and noticed that the alarm wasn't counting down. Val made her way over to the box on the wall where the words "New Code" were flashing at her.

Val knew exactly what she was going to put in and she spoke the numbers as she pressed. "Twenty-three, Thirteen, enter."

The End

Acknowledgment

Special acknowledgment goes to: Michelle & Katie Potter for all their help and support. The Albion Tea Room in Market Rasen for endless hot chocolates to keep me going. Rand Farm Park, near Wragby for free hands to work while children play. North Kesteven Fencing Club, for all their help and advice. And finally to all my family and friends past and present, who have made me who I am today, Thanks.

Lightning Source UK Ltd.
Milton Keynes UK
06 October 2010

160817UK00001B/2/P

9 781907 211133